THE DYING DOLLS

A HENRY & SPARROW NOVEL

A D FOX

SPARTILLUS

THE DYING DOLLS

Published worldwide by Spartillus.
This edition published in 2021.

1

www.adfoxfiction.com

All rights enquiries to United Agents,
12-26 Lexington Street, London W1F 0LE
+44 20 3214 0800 info@unitedagents.co.uk

Cover design © Meg Jolly

PROLOGUE

She ran like an animal. Lean flanks taut and flexing; feet striking the ground beneath a steady and economic gait, shoulders relaxed and straight, chest high and firm, core steady and engaged.

Like an animal.

Through the winding asphalt lanes, walled high on either side with whispering beech just beginning to blush copper, her feet making little noise with each strike, cushioned in well-worn running shoes.

You didn't need to see her face to know its expression; not when you'd been watching for a fortnight. It was far, far away, the face of a dreamer. Sometimes she smiled to herself at some inner amusement but mostly her features were smooth, neutral; in meditation for the hour it took to circle the village and the wooded hill beyond in a wide, looping figure of eight.

Occasionally the wildlife might break into her reverie – the call of a woodpecker or the sudden rudder-tail-turn of a red kite above the trees, rising in the early morning thermals. Then she would blink and grin and maybe jog on the spot to catch a better view of the kite or the long since vanished woodpecker, hand shading her eyes against the sun, dark ponytail drifting in the breeze.

But those engagements were rare. For ninety per cent of these runs she just ran, operating on pure instinct.

Like an animal.

Her watcher, today, was operating at a slightly higher level.

Like a trapper.

And it was easy because the prey was an animal of habit. Her route never varied more than a few feet and her running times were always the same. 7am to 8am every morning except Sunday and Wednesday.

As she approached the gravelly turn-off to the copse her trapper smiled. Three minutes in, the path would look exactly as it had when she'd run across it on Tuesday. But today, only 48 hours later, it was changed. An old fallen tree had put a kink in her route. She would need to divert by two metres to pass it.

The diversion would be the death of her.

She wouldn't have time to scream.

1

The bitch ran fast. Impressively fast – but there was no doubt she would be caught. The dark-haired woman screamed, grabbed, beat an arm out feebly as the attacker plunged forward, claws swiping through the air.

'Shit!' Kate sprinted up the path, abandoning all the *happy thoughts* she'd been trying to corral through her mind for the past twenty minutes. 'Shit! Shit! Shit! REGGIE!'

The woman was screaming louder now. She had dragged her beloved up into her arms in horror.

'I'm sorry – it's OK – I'm coming!' yelled Kate. 'It's OK!'

'It's NOT!' screamed the woman. 'It's really NOT OK! Stop him!'

'He won't hurt you, I promise!' bawled Kate, wishing that Reggie wouldn't always pick on women to terrorise. They were like catnip to him.

'REGGIE!' she bellowed. 'Come here NOW!'

Reggie, of course, paid her no attention whatsoever.

'Come and GET him OFF!' squawked the woman, her

face beetroot and her eyes livid as the attacker clawed at her denim clad thighs. 'He should have a bloody MUZZLE!'

'Oh god – did he? Did he bite you?' groaned Kate as she skidded to her knees and wrestled the Staffy-Labrador cross to the ground. 'Show me!'

The woman bristled at her. 'He didn't *actually* bite us – but he had a bloody good try! I should get the police out after you! What if he HAD got his teeth in? What if he'd ripped Ruby's throat out?' Ruby, a small terrier breed, cowering in her mistress's arms, glanced up reproachfully and whimpered on cue. 'What if he'd attacked a CHILD?'

'Seriously,' panted Kate, finally getting the metal clip of the lead onto Reggie's collar and hefting him away. 'I'm sorry – but he was just being boisterous. He really was only playing! He just loves the ladies, you see. Canine and human.'

'Well if that's playing, I'd hate to see him when he's angry!' shouted the woman, getting more boisterous herself now that Reggie was leashed. 'People like you shouldn't be allowed to keep dogs if you can't train them to be safe!'

'All right, all right, let's not get personal,' said Kate, raising one hand in an instinct borne of much practice. 'Nobody was actually hurt. I've apologised for the scare he gave you and I'll take him home now, on the leash, OK?'

'*Scare?!* Look at her!' demanded the woman, hoisting the trembling terrier up against her chest. 'She's traumatised!'

'She's panicking because *you* are,' Kate pointed out. 'If you'd calm down a bit, so would she.'

'How dare you?!' breathed the woman. 'You let your bloody dog out, traumatising other dogs and their owners and-'

'Look love, if it's trauma you want, just come along with me!' Kate felt herself snapping. She knew she shouldn't.

Didn't change a thing. 'You want to see what a throat ripped out of a loved one *really* looks like? I can show you some pictures! I just spent the last six hours on shift in the company of a guy who was killed by a couple of pit bull terriers in a gang fight over drugs money.'

The woman and her dog fell silent, while Reggie snuffled around Kate's feet obliviously.

'So let's just get a bit of perspective, shall we?' added Kate. 'Enjoy the rest of your walk.'

There was silence as she led Reggie away across the park. It was satisfying for about ten seconds. Then the regret hit. Christ! She was a professional. What the hell was she thinking?

'It wouldn't be so bad, Reggie,' she muttered, breaking into a run and hauling the trouble-maker along with her. 'If you were even *my* dog!' Reggie's tail thwacked exuberantly and he tugged hard against her. Then he switched direction and ran across her path, nearly sending her sprawling. 'Will you just run in a STRAIGHT LINE?' she yelled. 'You'll break somebody's neck one day!'

What Reggie obviously heard was: 'Will you just JUMP IN MY FACE?' because that's precisely what he did, pogoing joyfully up and down, trying to lick her eyeballs.

'SIT!' she yelled and at last he did, hopeful of a treat. Kate used her deepest growl as she crouched down next to him. 'WALK with me and BEHAVE yourself, or I will *bite* you! I bloody *will.*'

Reggie's tale thumped excitedly. As soon as she stood up, he leapt into her face again. She grabbed his collar and bit his ear. Not hard. Just a quick nip on the thin furry skin between her left upper and lower canines. Reggie yelped like she'd just stapled him to a tree. But then he fell into a trot beside her and behaved for a good thirty paces. Just until she muttered: 'Good boy - that's better.' And then he tried to trip her up again.

Kate was ready to give up. It was impossible to run comfortably with him on the lead, and impossible to run peacefully with him off it, in case he jumped on some other poor woman. He wasn't trying to be menacing, she knew. He was just a dog who loved too much. She sighed heavily and dropped back to a walk. 'You're a bloody nuisance. First you cripple Sally and now you mess up my precious headspace time. I mean, really – what are you *for,* you hairy bag of farts?!'

He grinned up at her and let one go. Sheesh! What did Sally *feed* him? Brussel sprouts and kidney beans?

Her neighbour was mortified by the fellow dog walker incident. For about thirty seconds. 'Oh, Kate – I'm sorry. He does get a bit overexcited at times,' she said, massaging Reggie's ears and dropping kisses on the fur between them. 'He just wants to snog the ladies. What can you do?'

'Have you ever thought of doing some obedience classes with him?' Kate ventured. 'Or, you know, having his dangly bits lopped off..?'

Sally cackled. 'What – deprive him of his earthly pleasures?! What do you think I am? A Nazi? Ow... mind my bloody ankle, Reggie! And you *could* try looking at least a *little* bit guilty. It's *your* fault.'

Kate peered at the thick bandaging around Sally's foot, while pulling her own foot up to nudge her left buttock, pressing the knee groundward for the stretch. The routine was instinctive although her paltry twenty minutes of running barely warranted the effort. 'How long? Before it's all mended and you can go out again?'

Sally prodded at the evidence of her misadventure with Reggie on the tight bend of the stairs. 'Two weeks, hopefully.

Doc says it's a complicated fracture. Sorry, love – I know it's a pain, taking him out. But my sister said she'll do some walks too – I won't be asking you every day.'

'Well – I will when I can...' said Kate. And she knew it would look, to Sally, as if she could most days. Even in the thick of a murder investigation she did her best to get an early morning run in, and to non runners it would seem perfectly straightforward to take a dog along. It wasn't. Dogs and runners did not mix. Not unless you'd trained one from a puppy to jog neatly alongside you rather than weave in and out of your path, messing with your pace. And nobody had trained Reggie at all. He was charming and affable but a total wilful nightmare on four legs, on the lead or off.

She was knackered. After last night's early hours shift she didn't need to be back in work until the afternoon but her rhythms were all out and she'd barely slept two hours before giving up and getting out for her usual 6.30am run. She had hoped the run would help clear her mind of the grim images of Jonno Mayhew, left like a half-eaten meal on the urine soaked flagstones of a Salisbury estate side alley. *Shit.* Don't do drugs, kids. They should put *that* on a poster. Comatose teenage girls with oxygen tubes in couldn't begin to get the message home like a 21-year-old with barely any face left.

It wasn't as if she didn't have enough to do with the RG case. She shouldn't even have been on that night shift, but for some extreme staffing issues. It was a massive favour to DS Boden whose wife had just gone into labour. She was glad she'd spared him that crime scene, though, on his baby son's birthday. She'd handed over to another DS in the early hours and left the follow ups with him; arrests had already been made and with plenty of witnesses and some security camera footage it looked like a pretty straightforward case.

The RG case - or *Marathon*, to use its official name - was a total bitch in comparison. Professionally it was a peach; the kind of thing any ambitious young copper would want on their CV... the stuff of TV dramas. Until you realised you were getting nowhere. And on a personal level this one was just... disturbing.

'You look done in, Kate. Want a cup of tea?' asked Sally, all auburn hair and plump kindness. She was a couple of decades older than Kate and had adopted a slightly maternal role in their neighbourly friendship.

'No – no thanks,' said Kate. 'I think I need a shower and maybe a snooze in front of the telly before I go in to work.'

'Tough one last night?' Sally arched an eyebrow. She knew better than to ask for details; Kate had recently been promoted to detective sergeant and Sally knew she hadn't earned that rank by cautioning teenage shoplifters.

'Yeah,' said Kate, extending a leg over the low brick wall between their front paths.

'Wool shop day?' added Sally, knowingly.

'Oh yeah. Wool shop.' Kate reached her path and went into the house, thinking of walls with little square mahogany shelves. From floor to ceiling. Each square shelf was filled with balls of wool; every colour and ply under the sun. The floor had a wool carpet and the till was an old mechanical one with no electricity feed. It was cash only in this shop. Or perhaps a hand written cheque from a regular. There was no phone. No internet connection. No Wi-Fi. Not even a radio. Just a couple of armchairs and the sound of needles gently clicking in between occasional sales.

It was after nights like last night that Kate would imagine running the wool shop. Clickety-click, drop one, pearl one. Ka-ching. Good day to you...

The shower helped a bit, soothing the stress out of her

shoulders as the hot water cascaded over her face and body. But her mobile shrilling as she rinsed conditioner out undid much of the good work.

'Yup,' she said, grabbing the towel from the hook and mopping her face.

'It's Michaels,' said her DC. 'Sorry to disturb you after last night but, well, there's another misper report come in... another runner.'

'Shit,' said Kate, stepping onto the wooden grooves of the bathroom floor and wrapping the towel around her shoulders. 'Where?'

'Out Amesbury way. Reported missing by her boyfriend yesterday. Briefing's in half an hour. '

'I'll be there,' said Kate.

THERE WAS a depressing familiarity about Melissa Hounsome; athletic, lean, twenty-something. In the photo she was leaning against another female runner – shorter and less blessed in the looks department. Both were grinning, pink and sweaty, holding out New Forest half marathon medals beside a gritty pathway through the trees. Many other entrants were milling about in the background with numbers pinned to their chests, looking exhausted.

'The boyfriend says this was taken about a year ago,' said Chief Superintendent Kapoor, glancing at the image on the screen.

'He thought it was a good shot to use,' said Detective Constable Ben Michaels, scanning notes. 'Because she wore similar running gear when she went out yesterday. She ran a lot of marathons, apparently.'

The way the past tense was already creeping into the

detective constable's speech patterns was not lost on Kate, or the Super, who shot him a dark glance which he failed to notice. She would have to have a word with him – although she hoped he'd never be that careless in front of the girl's loved ones.

Aside from Michaels and Kapoor there were eight other officers in the incident room and the tension was as tight as piano wire as the briefing went on. Nobody had said it aloud but they were all thinking it. Three missing female runners, by anyone's reckoning, had to mean a serial predator. Three women now vanished since mid-June. All of a type – fit, lean, athletic runners in their twenties. Hair and skin colour didn't seem to be a factor. The first had been fair-haired, white, the second was Afro-Caribbean and the latest was... what? Dark-haired and olive-skinned – of Mediterranean descent, Kate guessed, glancing at the shot of Melissa Hounsome. The running was the obvious link but whether this was because their killer was fixated on runners as a type or because, out alone, often off road in remote areas, female runners were a soft target, she didn't know.

Kapoor was running through the details. 'Melissa Hounsome, 25, lives in a rented flat with boyfriend Isaac Buchanan, 27, in Melksham Way, Frenley Marsh – small village about two miles north of Amesbury. She's a graphic designer, working from home; he's a sales and marketing guy for the Archway Magazine group. Yesterday morning she heads out for her usual 7am run, partly on road, partly cross-country, and fails to return. Boyfriend goes out looking for her around 9am and spends a couple of hours getting nowhere. She doesn't take her phone when she runs so he can't ring her. Then he calls it in and Amesbury logs it but doesn't get too excited until Buchanan calls in again at

7pm to confirm she's still not back. This morning they heard there was still no sign of her.'

'And nobody thought to call us sooner?' asked Kate.

Kapoor raised dark eyebrows. 'They regarded it as an ordinary misper. And as far as we know right now, they might even be right.'

'Yeah,' said Michaels. 'She could have had a row with him. She might have stopped over with a mate.'

'OK – so have we ruled out Buchanan for any reason?' Kate rubbed her eyes and wished she felt more awake. She might have to give in to one of the godawful coffees in the vending machine at this rate.

'He's prime suspect at the moment – although he seems pretty genuine according to the PS at Amesbury,' said Kapoor, nodding back to Michaels.

'No reports of domestics. Neighbours seem to think they were a normal, happy couple,' said Michaels.

'*Are* a normal, happy couple,' snapped Kate. 'Don't kill her off just yet, eh, Ben?'

'Sorry,' he shrugged. 'But – we've all seen the pictures. And we all know the MO. It doesn't look good, does it?'

The pictures. Thinking of the pictures made her belly contract. 'I need caffeine,' she muttered.

'No time,' said Kapoor. 'I want you and Michaels to get down there and speak to the boyfriend; get Amesbury onto a search of the house; check to see if anything personal is missing. Everyone else - check her social media, track who's been in touch with her, see what we can dig up...'

The list went on as they left the room, Ben bouncing along close behind her like an excited puppy. She hoped, not for the first time, that it was purely professional keenness and nothing else, but she suspected otherwise. A good looking blonde in any office got attention, like it or not. A good looking high achieving blonde with renown for her martial arts prowess and sharp comebacks encouraged very specific types of attention. She winced when she allowed herself to acknowledge her DC's occasional surreptitious glances. She wished more well-trained, fighting fit, intelligent gay men would get recruited. God, she'd love one of those in the car with her. Not so much a GBF as a GPC. A Gay Professional Colleague... All the useful attributes of a strong bloke but none of the hidden extras. *And* he'd tell her when there was a bit of lippy on her teeth.

But no... Michaels was sadly not gay, and seemed to have a thing for her. Despite her regulation pony-tail, barely a scrap of make up and literally no wiggle in her walk, this kind of thing just happened. She shouldn't get tetchy. It wasn't like she'd never been warned. From the moment she'd decided, on graduating, to join the police, people had tried to dissuade her.

'Look at you – you're five foot six of cute. Nobody will ever take you seriously.' That was the advice from her brother, Francis; three years younger and still a know-all. 'Girls like you work in – I don't know – PR or something. Or modelling. Be a model! More crack addicts to the square foot in that line of work than in Wiltshire's mean streets for a year!'

'I'm too short to be a model,' she'd snapped back. 'And I've got a bloody brain. I'd quite like to use it.'

'You'll get all kinds of sexist shit,' he'd warned her. 'You know that.'

'I'll get all kinds of sexist shit whatever I do with my life,' she countered. 'I could at least be doing something meaningful while some wanker is eyeing up my tits.'

And he'd paused; blown out a breath. Looked at her the

way her mother might have. 'Meaningful. Yup. OK. If you have to, you have to.'

A family vigil – the missing woman's parents and older brother sitting with her boyfriend - was already rolling by the time they reached the small brick and shale house, on a tree lined road in the quiet village. They'd knocked on the door around 9.45am, in company with PC Colin Hooper from the Amesbury station, who'd rung the case through to Salisbury earlier that day after *finally* making the connection with the all-stations memo she'd put out back in July when the second missing runner file had been opened.

Two runners going missing - a month apart - could still have been coincidence. Until the first pictures arrived.

The day after the second woman - Tessa McManus - had vanished, a hardback envelope landed at the Salisbury station. In it were prints of Caroline Reece; the first missing runner. Further prints arrived a week later, and then a week after that. In the first prints the victim was probably still alive. Possibly in the next set too; it was hard to tell. By the third set, though, it was pretty clear she was dead.

There was no certainty that Tessa had been abducted by the same person, but when the third hard-backed envelope of Caroline's pictures had arrived it also contained a printed note. Just three ominous letters: *TBC.*

Even without knowing the detail in the images - nobody outside the investigation team was privy to this - the press had begun to rumble about a serial killer as soon as the second runner went missing.

'The Runner Grabber' was the name which had been worked up after Tessa vanished from a woodland trail near Dinton. It wasn't a sub-editor's best work. But there was nothing alliterative or catchy which fitted the headline planning dimensions of your average tabloid as neatly. Trainer

Tracker, Jogger Hunter, Nike Man (out to *Just Do It*)... none of these worked. Kate knew this list of rejects because of her friendship with a journalist - once of the *Salisbury Journal* and now a national reporter on *The Stand*, his scoops currently delighting readers who could only just about lay claim to a central nervous system.

He'd run through the troublesome monikers for their predator with her over a coffee, following a press briefing in the second month of the case. 'We need to call him something,' Archie had explained. 'It's not just being trivial – although it *is* that too, of course; we're tabloid scum after all – it's about getting a brand. Someone the public can focus their fear, dread and hate on. And you know that's what gets them tuning in to *Crimewatch* and racking their little brains for helpful sightings or clues to phone in, so don't get all sniffy about it, Katy.'

She understood. Even the police needed shortforms. *The Runner Grabber* had swiftly been shortened to RG during their internal briefings and the investigation had then got *Marathon* as its witty operation name. It was a bit too on the nose for her liking; now in its third month and about to hit the wall.

As they sat down with Melissa Hounsome's wretched, shaking family, Kate hoped fervently that none of them were tabloid readers or internet lurkers and that they knew nothing of the Runner Grabber.

'Have you found her?' were the first four words from the white lips of Mrs Susan Hounsome.

'Not yet,' said Kate, her voice carefully marshalled to be kind and steady, evoking neither hope nor fear. 'We're here to help with the investigation. We need to ask some more questions. Um – maybe over a cup of tea?'

Tea. As familiar as a nervous tic. The boyfriend went to make it.

———

'So – boyfriend good for it?' asked Michaels on the way back.

'No,' she said, testily. They'd left the Family Liaison Officer conducting further, sensitive interviews with the boyfriend and the parents, while another two officers searched the flat. Melissa's loved ones were all a convincing picture of distraught innocence.

'Can't be sure though,' said Michaels, running fingers through his neat crop of dark brown hair. She could smell the salon wax on it. 'It's the boyfriend nine times out of ten. He doesn't look like a serial killer, mind you, I'll give you that.'

'We don't *know* she's dead,' said Kate, changing gear jerkily to get rid of the ripple of irritation running through her nerves. 'Or that it's RG. We don't even know if Tessa McManus was RG yet. Not for sure.'

'Nope. Not until her pictures show up,' he said, chirpily, as if he was looking forward to the next *Star Wars* movie. 'If it was RG, and if he's a man of habit, the next pictures should start to show up...' he checked his phone for the date '...sometime this week.'

'It takes a month,' she mused, grimly, 'to get the desired effect.'

The pictures. Another thing she was very glad to have kept from Archie and his unholy brethren. It had been agreed from the highest echelons that the details of the pictures and how they were achieved must remain sacrosanct. Copycats of the digital editing kind would turn this investigation into a living hell if those details got out. Even Michaels, with his bollock-kicking lack of subtlety, knew better than to talk about it beyond their close-knit team. The relatives of the first victim did not yet know the full details of her final days. And the only upside to this dead on its feet investigation was that the longer she failed to get anywhere the longer those families remained in blissful ignorance.

Everything they'd done; the door to door groundwork, the College of Policing analysts, the endless sifting through CCTV and cell mast data, the ever widening web of friends and family interviews, the combing through the victim's social media, the intel on sex offenders, newly released or out on licence, who might fit the MO... none of it had moved them along. RG might as well be an alien, abducting with the help of a tractor beam or an inter-dimensional portal (and in Wiltshire – crop circle capital of the world - there were many who'd accept that theory as logical thinking).

And now there was a third one. Kate pulled into the Salisbury police station car park and dropped her forehead onto the steering wheel, wishing that Melissa Hounsome might be found in a ditch somewhere, victim of a common or garden hit and run. Alive, preferably.

'You need sleep,' said Kapoor after they'd caught him up on their findings so far.

She nodded, fatigue sweeping through her. 'I know, but-'

'Sleep,' he repeated. 'You're not the only officer I've got you know.'

She smiled and nodded. She liked Rav Kapoor enormously; he was a decent guy and she knew he valued her in all the right ways.

'So,' he went on. 'Michaels can write up the family interview. You get home and get some kip and report back at six for the team debrief.'

'OK, thanks,' she said. 'That'll be good.'

She drove home on autopilot, trying to disregard the twisting sensation inside her chest. It was stupid and she had to ignore it.

She parked out front of the house and killed the engine. Five minutes later she was still in the driver seat. She needed to do something. Sleep would never come while she was thinking this way.

She needed...

...someone she'd been trying not to think about for the last two months. *Not* trying so hard that she hadn't used her position to track him down, mind you.

Sleep. Surely sleep first.

But the address was burned into her brain. Even the satnav was primed. RoadBitch, as Francis liked to call satnav woman (and it had kind of stuck), had been gagging to guide Kate there with her dulcet BBC vowels for weeks. Despite putting her up to it, Kate had been resisting steadily until today.

She pulled the Honda into a lay-by and punched a name into the device.

Lucas Henry. It was such a bad idea. She had promised herself she wouldn't.

'Where possible,' said RoadBitch, 'do a U-turn.'

'Fucking right,' sighed Kate and pulled back into the traffic.

2

Scarlet on white. The red droplets spattered in a wide arc, holding their position for half a second before dripping in *Hammer Horror* style runnels down the paper.

He stood back to examine his work. This shade of red was almost painful to look at, it was so vivid. Even on black, given the right light, it seemed to pulsate. To *communicate.* He'd known a musician once, who claimed to have synaesthesia and would describe firework displays of colour whenever he heard music. To be honest the guy was a twat and after his fifth or sixth enraptured interpretation of something on the BBC proms, sounded more like a salesman for Dulux than someone in the grip of a rare and fascinating condition. There came a night in the flat-share when he realised it would take just one more 'rivulets of gold, tumbling among the violins' assertion and the guy would get a 'cacophony of blue and green, fading to yellow' across his face for the next week. Lucas had moved out the following day.

He stood back and took in the full canvas. It occupied

the entire back wall of his studio. He had tried to make his art a little less grand in scale but it didn't work for him. He needed space in which to fling his paint. Daubing it, close up, with a brush lacked the same energy and the results always looked too dainty and contrived.

Not that he didn't *do* contrived. Over the last decade he'd painted enough portraits to fill the National Gallery. It was a living. Not a very good one, but it had seen him through many years of drifting around Europe. Sooner or later, though, the pent up frustration in his arms and hands, ribcage and pelvis had to be released. Letting his talent flow through a Series 7 Kolinsky sable brush into the shape of some winsome child of tourists in Toulouse or Florence was as satisfying as an angry outburst through a drinking straw. In his own time he was compelled to let it out on a much bigger scale. With velocity. Exhaust himself. Fling his emotions out in cadmium red, bismuth yellow, perylene maroon, cerulean blue and chromium oxide green. More than once it had occurred to him that his life was measured out in the Winsor & Newton acrylics colour chart.

He sat on the floor, cross-legged, resting the big Galeria brush on the tin and wiping a streak of red through his ill-kempt hair. The painting was achingly naive and clean at this point. Scarlet arcs above a boiling sea of golden raw umber light and brooding Payne's grey. It was tempting to leave it as it was. But sooner or later another wildly pigmented compulsion would have its way, he knew. Maybe black.

His left hand reached reflexively across the bare floor-boards for cigarettes but found only a Twix. Lucas groaned, remembering he'd given up. He unwrapped the confectionery and wedged one of the thumb-thick bars between his JPS fingers, blankly drawing upon it for a few seconds before the chocolate began to melt and he was forced to give up his joke and eat it instead. If he didn't cut down this Twix habit he'd soon be experiencing a podgy belly for the first time in his life. It might help his nicotine withdrawal if he could mainline some coffee instead, but with no electricity in the bungalow, that wasn't an option. He'd actually tried it cold, but the Nescafé granules just floated about in the water refusing to dissolve properly. Tea bags behaved in a similar way. Stubborn infusion refusal was just one of the many small privations adding up in his life since he'd come back to Wiltshire.

He should get Cokes. Diet Cokes, probably. Or a camping stove.

'Not exactly in the grip of the muse today, are we?' he told himself. But he finished the Twix, got up and reached for the brush anyway. Then froze as a strident jingling rang through from the hallway. He went to the window, lifting the tracing paper away at one corner and peering through chaotic straggles of rapidly browning buddleia. Someone was striding across the paddock. A woman, he thought, although it was hard to tell at this distance. He rubbed his chin, adding another scarlet streak to his beard, and narrowed his eyes. Company he did not need.

Still, it was good to know the early warning system was working. The blind cord and springs he'd set up around the perimeter had neatly triggered the old bell back in the house when the paddock gate had been pushed open, giving him a chance to go into a brief hibernation until the visitor gave up and went away. He no longer needed to run around shutting off the lights or the radio or CD player. The electricity had been cut off a week ago and the last batteries in the house had died in his torch yesterday. The manky smell of cold, empty dwelling was beginning to rival the whiff of paint. He knew he should do something about it. He just couldn't make himself. Not while there was still paint to fling and canvas to fling it at.

Another gate opened. Another jingle.

'Fuck off, fuck off, fuck off,' he murmured, in a reasonable tone.

THE BUNGALOW HAD SEEN BETTER days. It was almost engulfed in overgrown buddleia bushes and brambles. The whole acre surrounding it was a thicket of nettles and thigh high weeds but she still opted to park on the verge of the B road that hemmed one side of the land and walk across it rather than attempt the deeply rutted mud sink which an optimistic estate agent might describe as a driveway. Moths and crane flies fled into the air as she waded across their haven in her black leather townie boots; the sun warm on her blue cord jacket and peaking to hot on her black denims. Autumn seemed shy this year and summer was hanging on late like a party girl with no lift home. Above the continual chorus of grasshoppers and crickets, joyfully stridulating through the heat, Kate could hear nothing.

She wasn't at all sure anyone was living here. The place looked derelict, its old red bricks blown and in dire need of re-pointing and its wooden window frames bleached almost devoid of paint. In the shade of a thicket of holly trees, the side passage door was so rotten it would probably take one jab of a damp cotton bud to gain access. She knocked it gingerly, expecting to leave knuckle dents, but it held more firmly than she expected. Mould and mildew were obviously pretty sturdy here in the sticks.

Her knock went unanswered. He probably wasn't here.

Just because the place was in his name didn't mean he lived here. There was no sign of life. No car. No open windows.

She battled through more buddleia, knocking aside toppling purple cones crisping away to brown, and startling some hangers-on of the bee and butterfly variety, until she reached the front door. Painted red about a decade ago, she'd hazard, it was a little stouter than its fragile sister around the side. She knocked vigorously and called through the letterbox, noting the pile of unopened envelopes and unheeded junk mail. Obviously the postman was still dropping by. But that was more to do with the Royal Mail's duty to Barclaycard, Plumbs Upholstery and Domino's Pizza than any obligation to the occupant of The Trees, Elm Lane, Wishstart.

She sighed. She was wasting time. Even if she found him and convinced him she'd still need to deal with the derision of every hardened sceptic back at the station. Unless she got a result, of course. She smiled for a moment, imagining their faces if Lucas Henry actually delivered. Because he *could* deliver. She knew that.

But probably not today. At least she'd seen his home though. And if he did live here, as the electoral roll stated, he couldn't be doing too well. That was worth knowing.

She turned on the step and felt something crackle under her boot. Glancing down she saw it was a gleaming wrapper. She picked it up, thoughtfully, noting the crumbs of chocolate still fresh and unsullied inside its ripped foil. This Twix had been consumed very recently. The postman might have been having a snack, of course, but she doubted one of the Royal Mail's faithful would drop a wrapper. She stood very still, listening for three or four minutes, her senses prickling. Then, smiling, she took herself back around the house and retraced her route across the paddock. She skirted sideways and dropped out of sight behind some hawthorn before making her way back to the car and digging some small binoculars out of the glove compartment. Then she crept back to the hawthorn, hunkered down, found a gap, and trained the bins on the house. She might be in for a long wait; she might be looking at the wrong window, but instinct told her otherwise. After four minutes crouched on the dry earth she was rewarded. A quarter of a face appeared at the tugged away edge of some paper across the window. Through the lenses she could see a tangle of dark hair across a wide, angular brow and eyes that crinkled up against the light.

Quickly she stood up, stepped out of cover and waved at him. *Gotcha!*

Back at the red front door, she yelled with a new conviction. 'Lucas! Lucas Henry! Open up! *Police!*'

There was movement inside and indistinct cursing. Nobody came to the door.

'Lucas Henry! I know you're there. Stop wasting my time,' she yelled. Her insides were crunched into a ball. She still didn't quite believe she was really doing this. Didn't even know what she was going to say once she got inside.

At last the door opened and he stood there, tall and rangy, as overgrown as the house. The dark beard was straggly and marked, slightly alarmingly, with blood red streaks, as was the thicket over his left temple. His outdoorsy tan was faded, as if he'd been cooped up inside for weeks, but his moss-coloured eyes still burned with that same intensity.

'What?' He made no move aside to admit her.

'Hi. I'm DS Kate Sparrow. Can I come in?' She smiled tightly, palms up.

'Can I stop you?' He wiped one hand down his black T-shirt, leaving a trail of yellow ochre to augment the red and dark grey already on it.

'Probably not,' she said. 'This place is about as impregnable as a cardboard box on a wet Sunday. It's always nice to be invited, though.'

'By all means – come on in!' He stood back and swept his arm theatrically. 'Have a seat. If you can find one. Have a cup of cold tea. What the hell do you want?'

'Nice place,' she said, following him down the narrow hallway. 'Well – at some point.'

'It was my late aunt's,' he said. 'She left it to me along with a depressing collection of Charles and Diana tea cups and a drawer full of horrifying foundation garments.'

'You've kind of let it go...' she observed.

'Who are you? Kirstie Allsopp?' he said, as she reached the doorway to what was probably once a sitting room. Now it was some kind of studio.

'No heating?' she asked, shivering. Despite the unseasonable September warmth, the place was dank and the scent of mildew fought valiantly with the reek of paint.

'Cut off. Don't need it.' He turned away from her, picking up a brush from one of a dozen paint pots spread across the bare boards of the floor. On the wall hung his work-in-progress – a vast canvas hosting a brooding valley floor of dark grey and earthy yellow, a monotonal rainbow of scarlet spattered and dripping above it.

'Can't see you getting any work with Cath Kidston,' she said.

'No.' He flung another crimson spray across the room and it crackled over the paper like horizontal rain. If pushed, Kate would have to admit that she quite liked it. Wouldn't offer it as a mural for the local infant school, perhaps, but...

‘So. What do you want?’ He’d turned back to her, brush hanging and dripping like a murder weapon.

‘Your help.’ She took a deep, silent breath. ‘To find someone.’

His shoulders stiffened; his grip on the brush tightened. 'Who have you lost?' he asked.

'A woman. Well... three women. For the first of them it’s too late, the second... probably too late... but for the third one, it might not be.'

'So... someone around here, then? You’re doing door-to-door enquiries? Don't you usually do those in pairs?'

'It's not around here. Well, not close. Up in a village near Amesbury,' she explained, glancing around the room as if she was curious about his art rather than trying to avoid looking at him. She shoved her hands deep into her jeans pockets to hide the tremble that threatened to break out through them.

He wrinkled his brow and rubbed his nose with the back of his free hand. 'Right. Amesbury. Look - you're going to have to help me out here. Why do you think I can help? Is it a DNA database thing? Have you come for a swab?' His expression darkened.

'No - no! You're not a suspect!'

'Well, that's always nice to know,' he said. Without amusement.

A few heavy moments passed as she tried to frame her next sentence. She swallowed, let out a long breath and then just cut to it. 'I want your help as a dowser.'

There was another long pause during which he stared at her incredulously. 'What?' he said, finally.

'I know you are a very capable dowser,' she went on, her voice sounding steadier than she felt. 'And I was wondering whether you'd be willing to help trace Melissa Hounsome. If we don't find her she's going to die. She's 25.'

'I'm not a dowser,' he said, flatly. 'I'm an artist. You've got bad information. Sorry. Go and try Uri Geller.'

'Lucas, I've read your files. You helped the police before.'

He exhaled sharply and shook his head. 'Well then. Look how that turned out.'

'You *did* find someone, didn't you?' she pressed on. 'And... even if you haven't done it for years, I bet you haven't lost that talent. And I really, *really* need it right now. So do Melissa's family. They're in hell. They need help.'

'Thousands of people go missing every day,' he said, turning away from her and stooping to dip his brush into the paint. He flung another arc of red energetically across the paper with a low grunt. 'Thousands of people die every day. I can't take responsibility for them. That's your job.' He hurled another crimson spatter. 'For which, presumably, you get paid.'

'You'd get paid,' she said, quickly. 'As a consultant.' She sniffed at the air and rubbed her arms. 'Enough to get the electricity back on in here.'

'Is that so? Do the police now have a standard consultancy rate for twig waving weirdos? My, how very 21st century.'

'There's a system,' she said. 'It's much better than it used to be. Decent recompense. Protection. Anonymity.'

'Can I have that in writing from the Chief Constable?'

'Lucas, please.' She stepped closer to him. 'We use consultants all the time; it's no big deal. Just... would you? Would you at least try?'

A long silence as he stared at his work.

'You could buy a *lot* of turpentine,' she added, grinning.

'You don't need turps for acrylics,' he muttered. 'That's oil. I don't paint in oil.'

'Well - I bet that huge canvas doesn't come cheap.'

'No,' he said. 'By which I mean... no.'

She left the building and returned to her car. In it was a black leather folder, zipped up tight. If she opened it and showed its contents to anyone beyond her team she was breaking a lot of rules.

He hadn't closed the door behind her so she went straight back in. He looked at her with an unreadable expression and then opened a Twix. He offered her half.

'I want to show you some pictures,' she said. 'You might want to have your chocolate fix afterwards.'

3

Wendy pumped the dispenser and a gelatinous dollop of alcohol based cleanser landed on her palm. She vigorously worked it around her hands, between her fingers and across the backs, singing Happy Birthday twice through. It was ridiculous. Over the top. But it was a rule and Wendy generally stuck to rules.

'Nurse! Nuuuurse!' The voice, thin and reedy, rose above the vibrations of the laundry room below. Wendy followed it to its source: a thin old lady in a pink fleecy nightie and a thick beige cardigan who sat like a broken branch in a high back, winged armchair by the window.

'What is it, Mrs Dillow?'

'Nuuuurse!'

She tapped the bony shoulder. 'I'm right here, Mrs Dillow. What can I do for you?'

The old lady turned watery pink-grey eyes up to her and put a hand out to grasp Wendy's strong fingers. 'I need my toilet visit,' she said, cool digits digging purposefully into Wendy's palm. 'I need it now.'

'Okeydoke,' said Wendy. 'Let's get you to your feet, then.'

She cheerfully guided Mrs Dillow into the en suite and helped her settle on the toilet, busying herself with a quick tidy of the bathroom while she waited for Mrs Dillow's unreliable bowels to function. After six years at East Sarum Lodge Nursing Home she was not at all repulsed by the intimacy of the service she supplied to its 23 residents. Mrs Dillow was one of the easiest. She weighed little more than a ten-year-old and was mostly lucid. And appreciative; always polite. Others, especially those with advanced dementia, were far from polite. Often hostile, rude and downright aggressive. Wendy was a large woman and very capable with the hoists and the manoeuvrings of cantankerous nonagenarians. Some of the care staff would take the yelling, the snide remarks and the outright offensiveness quite personally, but Wendy never did. Even when Ruby Merrick referred to her as a 'stinking brick shithouse' last week, she had found it only amusing. And at least two thirds accurate. She was pretty sure she didn't stink - at least not half as much as her clients - but she *was* built like a brick shithouse.

In truth, the capacity for little old ladies to suddenly burst forth with the most obscene language was one of the highlights of her job. She and three of the care workers had once spent a highly amusing week running Old Fuckers Bingo. In the staff kitchen, on the inside of the mugs cupboard door, they'd put up daily grids featuring the swear words they might encounter and then ticked off what they got, and from whom. When 93-year-old Dulcie Graham, during a sponge bath, supplied 'Go fuck your fucking fat shitface,' at 4.05pm on Thursday, Wendy shouted 'HOUSE!' Kerry, working on Maisie Johnson across the corridor, laughed so hard she tipped the basin of soapy water into the old dear's lap.

It wasn't that they were ridiculing the residents - although it would be hard to explain that to a casual observer. Kerry said you had to laugh or you'd cry and she was mostly right about that. Wendy had never felt the urge to cry but she knew you had to toughen up in this world of creeping incapacity and lurking death. If you took it all too seriously you'd never last. And many didn't. Care workers came and went rapidly and the ones who stayed were the ones who felt-tipped ***'Go fuck your fucking fat shitface' - Mrs Dulcie Graham, 93***, on a bingo chart and watched their co-workers dissolve into laughter.

Wendy had plenty of respect for the residents, even the senile and rude ones. In fact, she was fascinated by them. As she cleaned their well worn bodies she would find herself absorbed by the tree-like blue veins threading beneath papery, translucent skin; by the blurred inky art of a once vivid tattoo on an arm or a back or even a wrinkled back-side. By the hair which sprang sparsely, fibre-optic white, from pink, freckled scalps; by ears grown large and long of lobe and knuckles calcified into impossible outcrops. There was a fierce kind of beauty in this decay; like the uncompromising loveliness of felled trees, easing themselves slowly back into the earth years after the storm that cracked them in half.

She wasn't bothered by the smell, either. She'd smelled much worse. In a 24 bedroom care home where the youngest resident was 79 (and considered a baby), the smells that followed made perfect sense. If she were to walk in tomorrow and find the place smelling like a reception class in primary school, that would be wrong. Old things smelled old. Young things smelled young. Truth be told, Graeme, the fortysomething bloke who fixed things around the home and dug over the vegetable plot, probably smelt worse than any of them. She suspected he'd never met a deodorant stick in his life and the sour breath on him suggested he smoked at least 20 a day.

After she'd wiped Mrs Dillow and helped her to wash her hands, Wendy saw the old lady back to her chair and put the radio on for her. Mrs Dillow listened to the local BBC radio station and talked about all its presenters as if they were family. She didn't seem to have noticed that some of the presenters she thought she was listening to had actually been replaced by younger ones. The music mix and the phone-in topics were very much the same, whether delivered by sixty-something Sheila Bartley (long employed mid-morning treasure), thirty-something Josh Carnegy (ambitious late-night newbie) or fifty-something Dave Berry (*The Voice of Wessex* according to his jingles). The passing of the years mattered slightly less on BBC radio. Especially since all those ageism claims.

Wendy worked her way along the corridor, ticking off her duties room by room. Hoist-in baths and showers for the livelier residents; sponge baths, tucks ins, turns, water through straws and catheter checks for the deathlier. Working during a family visit was the most stressful; it interrupted the flow and the efficiency. Compelled her to smile and cluck and laugh in a way which she normally would not. Sometimes she could see a look in a resident's eye that clearly said 'So... how did it come to *this*?' She couldn't explain that to them. Wendy was good at her job but interpersonal skills were not her strong point. There were others who could do that part.

In the last room, Mrs Newton was shouting about her glasses. They had run off again, apparently. Elsie Newton's glasses were famed for their escapes. She had lost six pairs in as many months, much to the frustration of her daughter who had to keep getting replacements. Efforts to get Mrs Newton to keep each pair on a chain around her neck had failed. She found it bothersome. So glasses hunts were a regular exercise for the staff at East Sarum. Today, though, they were in luck. Wendy spotted the spectacles under Mrs Newton's chair and handed them to her quickly.

'Here you go, Mrs Newton,' she said. 'They didn't get too far this time.'

'Thank you, dear,' said the old lady, extracting a crushed rose of tissue from her cardigan sleeve and giving the lenses a pre-emptory wipe. She popped them on her nose and her pale blue eyes loomed out, clearer and larger. 'My Sally is coming today,' she said, with satisfaction.

'She *might* be coming,' Wendy reminded her. 'If she can. Remember, she told us to tell you that she'll get here if she can. But she's counting on her neighbour to bring her, remember? And if her neighbour's late back from work she might not make it.'

'I know, I know!' snapped Mrs Newton. 'But I expect she will. Yes. She will. She's bringing my Matchmakers.'

'Well, let's keep our fingers crossed, eh?' said Wendy. 'Now - do you need help with the toilet, while I'm here?'

'I don't think so,' said Mrs Newton.

But Wendy's olfactory system told her otherwise. 'Let's just take you through anyway,' she suggested.

KATE DIDN'T SHOW him all of the pictures. Just a couple. It seemed to be enough. His face didn't change much but his eyes narrowed and his jaw was a little tighter. After a few moments he said: 'Shit.'

'Yeah,' she replied.

'That's one seriously fucked up head case,' he added.

'Couldn't have put it better myself,' she said. The pictures were black and white. In each of them was the same woman. Dead or nearly dead; it was hard to tell. The body was emaciated but it stood erect, chin held high, hair brushed and spread across her naked shoulders as if styled. Her eyes were closed and her papery lips were slightly open.

'Caroline Reece, her name was,' said Kate. 'Aged 26. Hotel manager in Salisbury. She disappeared in June during a run through remote woodland. We got the first of these four weeks to the day she vanished. Posted. Not online - literally posted, black and white prints, in a hard backed envelope. The last delivery had Ordnance Survey co-ordinates on the envelope which led us to the body. It was in a shallow grave in the woods near Silbury Hill.

'How did she die?' he asked, rubbing his fingers across his chin and depositing a little more red acrylic on his beard. His eyes were still on the images.

'Starvation, according the pathologist. And dehydration. She must have suffered horribly.'

'And... other injuries?'

'None. No sign of assault - sexual or otherwise. No trauma to the skull or any bones. No rope burns, nor any signs of her fighting against restraints. Just a few pressure marks.'

'So - what did he get out of it?'

'The profilers think he's some kind of twisted collector type,' said Kate. 'There were traces of sedative found in the body, as if he wanted her nice and still. Compliant. No trace of any DNA on her, no semen or saliva. Not that she was in the best of condition when they found her.'

'Any clues to how she was taken? Or the others?'

'None at all,' sighed Kate. 'We've been working on the

theory that these women must have known him, to be spirited away so easily, with no sign of struggle. It's like he just stepped in from another dimension and plucked them through to his own parallel universe. We've gone through all the usual candidates - boyfriends, husbands, jealous exes, screwed up family members, fellow employees with a grudge, psycho clients... and come up with nothing. Nothing remotely plausible, anyway.'

'And you've traced the postmark on the envelope?'

'Yep. It was posted in a rural box miles from any CCTV. No witnesses. Hard to know even when it *was* posted because it was over a bank holiday weekend and the last collection was noon on the Saturday. That's a 67-hour window to start with.'

Lucas stepped away from her and sat back on the window sill. 'I'm still not sure how you think I can help. If you have so little to go on yourselves.'

Kate felt herself floundering slightly. 'I - well - I did wonder if you might pick up something... from these.' She flipped the pictures in her fingers. 'Knowing that he must have touched them and they must have been very meaningful to him.'

'Those? Are they the actual prints he sent?' He looked incredulous.

'No,' she assured him. 'Those are locked away in the evidence room. These are copies, of course. Although, forensically they're much the same. No traces on the pictures or the envelope. He's been thorough. But... with *you*... well, it's not about the forensics, is it? It's... vibrations and so on.'

He grinned at her and then rolled his eyes. 'If you say so.'

'I mean - I thought if you came back with me and picked

up the originals, you might... pick up something else. A clue.'

'The burial site would be better,' he said, giving her cause for optimism for the first time. '*If* I agree to help. But I haven't agreed.'

'Not yet,' she said, smiling. He would. She knew he would. She could see the spark of fascination in his eyes, even from here.

'Let me think it over,' he said. 'I'll call you tomorrow.'

'Oh no,' she said. 'That's too vague. And too elastic. I've got a desperate family waiting for any shred of hope I can give them.' She packed the pictures back into the folder and snapped it shut. 'I'll come by at nine tomorrow morning. I'll drive you to the woods where Melissa vanished. See what you can pick up. Maybe go on to the burial site afterwards.'

He stood up and shoved his hands deep in his pockets. 'I haven't said I'm going do it yet.'

'No, you haven't,' she said, taking a quick breath and giving him her best upbeat expression. 'So I'll say it for you. You're going to do it. If you have a good reason not to, you can tell me when I come back tomorrow at nine.'

He groaned. 'Nine? *Really?* I'd normally be asleep.'

'Yeah, well,' she shrugged and let a beat pass. 'Some people won't sleep at all.'

She walked back to the car with purpose pistoning through her at last, not turning to see if he was watching from the window, not allowing herself to dwell too much on whether he would still be there when she returned. He would. He *would.* For there was nothing else she could think of. Unless the team brought back some startling new evidence as a result of the door to doors, it was going to be just the same as the others. And she couldn't stand it. Lucas Henry was going to help her if it killed her.

It was only after she'd driven away down the lane that the shudders overtook her. She pulled into a lay-by and gave in to them, anchoring her hands into the wheel and resting her forehead on them, letting out juddering gasps while great waves of horror and desolation broke across her shoulders. Almost as if it was yesterday.

4

Melissa Hounsome couldn't see much but she could tell her captor was big. And strong. With a sharp acidic smell, like a fox - or maybe that was the vapour stuff he'd used to knock her out.

Her memory of what had happened was hazy; she recalled dropping, very suddenly, in the woods. The drop had been abrupt; the ground simply falling away beneath her like a sudden landslip. The landing had knocked the breath out of her. She didn't think she'd even screamed before something like cool mist fell upon her face and her world went grey.

She was dimly aware of being lifted out of the hole she'd fallen into and wondering who her rescuer was. It was someone very capable; very calm. It was only when they didn't speak through the shifting grey that was enveloping her that she began to sense this person was maybe *not* her rescuer. There was something very purposeful about the way she was being carried. She tried to say something; burbled a few incoherent words, and then there was more mist and the whole situation just went away.

Until she woke up in a room, chained to a thin bed, without her clothes. Dread had knotted her almost in half and she screamed out. Then there was more mist and she was gone again.

How long had she been here? It was impossible to tell. It smelt intense; chemical. She wondered if she'd been raped but couldn't feel any sense within herself that she had been. She felt undamaged. Cold and hungry and thirsty but otherwise OK.

The walls around her were old brick, painted white many years ago. A single bulb hung overhead, casting a dim energy-saving light. The ceiling around it was mottled with damp stains. To her right and at her head and feet was just brick wall but to her left was a long plastic curtain, stretching from the ceiling to the floor. There was more light on the other side of it and mottled colours. Some of the colours - blue - moved. Her captor was back.

She instinctively shrank into herself, crossing her legs and bringing up her knees with a rattle of chains as if that would afford her any protection at all. The figure in blue stood above her for a while, regarding her, head on one side.

'You don't need to do that. I'm not interested in you that way. That's not my thing.'

'What is your thing?' she croaked, fear in every word.

'My thing is art.'

5

Sleep finally claimed Kate around two. It was quite a feat to get there. Her trip out to Amesbury and back had concluded by 11.30am and her surprise visit (even to herself) to see Lucas Henry had taken up little more than ninety minutes of off duty time, there and back. By the time she got home she had four hours before she was due back at the station. Three of those hours could be sleep.

Besides which, if this *was* the RG then they did have some time at least, she reflected with a grimace. None of his victims had died quickly. She knew everything that could be done was being done. Stumbling about CID like a zombie really wouldn't help anyone.

She'd said a quick hello to Francis when she'd found him in the hallway, rifling through the post.

'Go to bed,' he'd said.

She'd nodded, unlocked her door and hit the mattress about thirty seconds later, slipping off her shoes and jacket and pulling the bedspread over her. She was vaguely aware of Francis stomping upstairs to his place as she drifted away.

After Mum died they had considered selling the house

and splitting the proceeds so they could get a flat each. Then Francis had come up with an easier, more practical solution; keep the house and use some of Mum's life insurance pay out to convert it into two flats. It was well positioned in the small cathedral city, in a quiet, leafy street. It had a pretty back garden which ran down to the riverbank and a tiny wooden jetty which stretched out below the fronds of a weeping willow. Given the propensity to flooding in the area, they might have struggled to sell it anyway - mortgage companies got nervous about any house near a river these days. The lower reaches of the garden *had* flooded a few years back but only by a few inches. To reach the house, built at the top of a gentle gradient and a good three metres higher, a flood would have to be pretty biblical.

It was a comforting solution too. They each got a new kitchen and bathroom fitted and had a sitting room and a bedroom. The Georgian proportions of the terrace lent themselves well to the conversion; it didn't seem cramped. They shared gardening duties... well, Francis did most of it... and occasional meals, but mostly they didn't crowd each other. It was enjoyable, redecorating in their own styles, but it wasn't a complete gut and refurb job; little pieces of the past remained, here and there. A lamp; a mirror, the mosaic of family pictures in the shared hallway. They'd never discussed it but both of them had left just enough of their mutual family memory in the place to be comforting. Any more and it could have been maudlin.

Kate was asleep within a minute. And awake again 90 minutes later. She'd forgotten to switch the ringer on her mobile off. It chirruped like a cricket right next to her ear and she smacked her hand down on it as if it might stop like an alarm clock. But it was a call, not an alarm. She groaned and stared blearily at the name on the screen, expecting it to be work. It wasn't work; it was Sally.

Damn. Now she remembered. She'd said, yesterday, before she knew what a godawful overnight shift she was going to get, that she would drive Sally up to see her mum at the care home at 4pm.

She took the call, trying to sound awake.

'Oh, love - were you asleep?' said Sally. No flies on *her.*

'No... well... yes, but it's fine,' said Kate. 'The alarm was just about to go off,' she lied. 'I haven't forgotten.'

'Shit, you sound done in. We don't have to go. I can phone mum instead,' said Sally.

'No, no, no!' Kate was upright now and sounding alert. 'You can't give your mum her Matchmakers down the phone line. She's been waiting all day for them, I bet.'

'Well, yeah, probably,' admitted Sally. 'She does look forward to my visits.'

'I'm on my way.'

Ten minutes later Sally hopped out of her house, leaving Reggie shut in the kitchen, and into Kate's car, landing on the passenger seat with a weary grunt. 'This is SO bloody annoying. I'm really sorry, Kate.'

'It's no problem,' said Kate. 'In fact it's good for me. You're always saying I need to get out more; do stuff outside of work.'

Sally rolled her eyes. 'Driving me to my mum's nursing home isn't exactly what I meant! You should be getting out more for *fun*... with *hot men!*'

'Oh!' said Kate, eyes wide. 'Are there hot men? Have you seen one?'

Sally snorted. 'How the hell would I know? I'm stuck at home with a farting dog, a banjaxed ankle and twenty-five

17th century wigs. *You're* the one with freedom of movement. Go to clubs! Join a gym! Do Grindr!'

'I think you mean Tinder,' said Kate. 'Grindr's for gay men. Working with all those theatre types, you should know that.'

'Tinder, Grindr, Blender, Plunger - whatever - just get out there!' said Sally. 'I mean, how long has it been since Reuben?'

Kate winced. 'Don't remind me.' Reuben was the particularly earnest young lawyer she'd got together with for about four months last year. He was lovely but the realisation that he didn't really have a sense of humour pretty much doomed it by week three. She should have ended it when he told her he didn't get *Father Ted*. He'd been very cut up, though, when she did eventually finish with him. She hated that. Wished she could be more of a bitch and not care.

'Your brother's just as bad,' said Sally. 'I mean, when does he *ever* leave the house?'

'He works from home,' said Kate, changing gear as they met the steep hill that led up to East Sarum Lodge, where Sally's mum lived. 'Loads of people work from home these days. He's - what do they call them? A post-pandemical. Started working from home... never went back to the office.'

'Yes, but it's not healthy for a young man. What is he - twenty-two?'

'He's twenty-three,' said Kate. 'And he's had relationships. Just... not for a while.'

Sally sighed. 'The pair of you... you're a lost cause.' Her face softened. 'I know it's been tough for you both. I guess it's hard to trust people after... what happened.'

'Here we are,' said Kate, swinging the Honda past the open wrought iron gates of the nursing home and onto the gravel drive. She parked close to the front door of the old, yellow stone building, killed the engine, opened her door and went around to help Sally out.

'I need to get used to the crutches,' said Sally, waving away Kate's support once she was upright. 'But if you could carry the bag, that'd be great.'

Kate took a hessian carrier from the footwell and locked up the car before following Sally into the old house. Her neighbour struggled a little getting her plastic-booted left foot up the brick steps, but she had managed it by the time Kate caught up with her.

Once in the reception, Sally was collected by a member of staff and borne off to see her mother in the residents' lounge. The woman - *Wendy* according to her enamel name badge - was very tall and efficient looking, with dark hair in plaits. She took the bag from Kate with a tight smile. Kate said she would wait in the car and left the reception hall with relief. It wasn't just the decor and the several really bad paintings on the walls (*a sign said the clunky oil depictions of stiffly posed squirrels and birds were by a member of staff and for sale*); the smell of these places always made her shiver. One part pea soup; three parts pee. She knew it wasn't a fair judgement - the place was obviously well-kept and Sally was very happy with her mother's care. It was just... well... who would ever *want* to be there?

Back in the Honda, she checked her phone for messages and found a few updates from Michaels; no real news. Door to door enquiries and a fingertip search of Melissa's running route hadn't shown up any clues so far. Kate wondered how long it would be before women just stopped running anywhere but in busy parks, in broad daylight. It angered her. Running alone should be everybody's right. Experiencing nature, quietly, one-to-one, on foot... it was special.

Healing. More people should do it - but with this maniac going around snatching lone runners for some kind of sick personal biology project, who would blame anyone for sticking to the treadmill instead?

The pathologist estimated it had taken Caroline Reece two or three weeks to die. She must have been given water for a while, but eventually that was withdrawn from her too.

There were pressure sores on what remained of her skin. In odd places. Behind the shoulder blades, under the armpits, the wrists, at the base of the spine. When you looked at the pictures it made sense. Caroline had not been able to rest - literally. She was propped up on some kind of stand, as if she was a living doll in a display case. And she had been posed like a doll too. Gracefully, not pornographically. Her right arm had been held aloft and her left extended in a gentle curve, while one foot protracted forward, like a ballet dancer.

Studying the black and white photos you could see, in the early ones, that the victim was alive. She must have been efficiently drugged, because there was no sign of struggle, just a vacant, slack expression. Kate really wished that the killer had ended the photography there and they could have worked out what had happened next from the pathology report. But no. The photos came every week; sent each time from a different location - Wiltshire, Hampshire and Dorset. They continued to document the merciless process, even after death. The body was slowly emaciating and then decaying and desiccating and every stage had been expertly lit and photographed. There were props, too. A stuffed bird on her outstretched hand in later pictures. Dying flowers around her feet and in her hair. An open book nearby on the floor - big and leather-bound but with no discernible title.

Kate sighed, leaning back against the head rest. She wished there was a kind of bottle brush that could be used for the mind; something to clear all the muck and clinker out of every corner, even if only temporarily. She knew these images would fade eventually; everything did. But it was the grimmest part of her job that she was required to see this stuff.

For a while she let her eyes roam the grounds of the lodge. In the soft late afternoon light she could make out the gardens that surrounded the nursing home - a good two or three acres of land. Close to the house there were rose beds, wheelchair friendly stone paths, a summer house and a pond. There was a kitchen garden too, supplying fresh fruit and veg to the lodge caterers. It was all nicely maintained. Some distance down the sloping estate were other buildings - housing for the on-site staff, perhaps, and an old barn. A wood hemmed the perimeter on the road side of the property and a meandering old stone wall gave on to fields and meadows further down. It was a lovely spot, Kate acknowledged... if you *had* to be in a nursing home, you could do a lot worse.

Sleep was trying to claim her again, so she set the timer on her watch for 5pm, manoeuvred the driver seat back into recline and allowed herself to drift. She might yet be able to string a sentence together at the briefing if she could get in even a twenty-minute power nap.

It seemed like roughly thirty seconds later when her watch started beeping and she sat up with a start. She took a drink from her water flask and rubbed her face, aware of a regular, sharp thudding noise nearby. Glancing outside she saw the gardener sending his spade into the vegetable plot on the other side of the low car park wall. A heavy-set man with receding red hair, he glanced across at her through the windscreen for a few seconds, gave a wink, and went back to his digging. Five minutes later the gardener was still digging and she was still waiting for Sally. Sally knew she had only an hour with her mum because Kate had to get back to work. An hour was usually quite enough for her, anyway.

At eight minutes past, Kate sighed and got out of the car, ignoring a furtive appraising glance from the gardener bloke. Back in reception she asked if she might go through to the lounge. The young woman on the desk led her in. Sally was on her feet, trying to edge away from her mother, who, seated in a high winged armchair, was hanging on to her hand, talking earnestly. Mrs Newton had dementia but had never yet failed to recognise her younger daughter - a blessing and a curse, according to Sally. 'If she didn't recognise me once in a while I'd get away a bit easier,' Sally had once confessed, before biting her lip guiltily.

'They're stealing my slippers,' Mrs Newton was saying.

'What would they want with your old slippers, Mum?' said Sally.

'They sell them,' said Mrs Newton. 'They sell everything.'

'Well, if there's a black market for pre-worn old lady slippers, I want in on that action!' said Sally, rolling her eyes at Kate. 'Mum, I've got to go, Kate's got to get to work.'

'The smell,' said Mrs Newton. 'I don't like it. She smells funny.'

Sally kissed her mum and extricated herself, muttering, 'People in glass houses...'

Back in the car she said: 'She's getting worse. But... that's what they do, don't they? You don't go into a nursing home at 85 and then come out again all better.' She sighed. 'Life can be shit.'

Kate smiled and patted her knee.

'God, I'm so insensitive,' muttered Sally. 'I've still got a mum when I'm 49 and there's you...'

'Stop it,' said Kate. 'It's fine.'

She dropped Sally off, helping her into the house where Reggie was ready to leap all over her and very possibly break the other ankle, and then got back into the car and headed straight for the station.

The team was funnelling into the meeting room as she arrived and there was an atmosphere of bleakness which was somehow worse than she had expected. Marathon was not a happy case to work on, but she was surprised at quite how dark everybody's faces were. Until Michaels sidled up to her. 'Didn't you get my text?' he said.

'Um... not until now,' said Kate, catching sight of the green notification on her phone for the first time.

Three words to help her fit in with the mood.

New pictures arrived.

6

It really looked like a murder scene now. After DS Sparrow had left he'd sat for maybe ten minutes, staring into space. Then he'd grabbed his brush and his acrylics and begun flinging the colours around in a frenzy, spattering the canvas with furious velocity. He'd stopped after a couple of minutes and dumped everything. Left the room. Left the house. Went out into the field and dropped into the grass.

He slept on his back, like a lizard in the sun, a forearm across his brow. His dreams weren't too restful. Zoe and Mabel came back with a vengeance. They ran down the sun-dappled lane, hand in hand, in white dresses, like something out of a Stephen King movie, even though they had never done anything like that back then. They'd been ordinary girls wearing ordinary clothes, laughing, messing around, bitching about other girls, having a smoke in the quarry, leaping from tussock to tussock across the boggy field and threatening to push each other in, poking fun at him; endlessly poking fun at him.

That summer they had claimed their own pocket of the

plain - the quarry and the wood, the heathland and the shallow unnamed river which flanked the bogs - hanging out there at all hours. Sometimes there would be other friends; maybe seven or eight of them, and they would build camp fires and get drunk on cheap cider and JD and Coke, and dare each other to climb the cheese pie. The cheese pie was a part of the quarry cliff face which jutted out in an almost impossible overhang, shaped like a wedge of pie. Late in the day it would catch the last rays of the setting sun and gleam yellow. A serious challenge to climb up onto, it was a wonder that none of them fell off and broke their neck.

That summer Lucas learned the terrain better than the back of his hand. He learned it like the bones and sinews and flesh and blood of his hand. His dowsing talent was bursting from him back then, charged and amplified by his adolescence. He *felt* the water courses and the denser rock that rippled beneath the chalk course, the roots, buried but beautiful as they mirrored the branches of the trees they anchored, the thrum and pulse of the wildlife, from the newts in the marshes to the deer flitting through the trees.

Every so often he would get Sid out and Mabel or Zoe or one of the others would hide something for him to find. One or more of them would bundle on top of him, covering his eyes and ears, singing loudly; doing everything to be certain he couldn't cheat.

Then, when the one who'd hidden their key or watch or a coin had come back, they would sit in giggly anticipation as he spun the glass stopper beneath his fingers and focused. After a minute or so he would usually have it... the pattern... the frequency. He would get up and walk and they would caper after him, excited and silly. On some occasions he got it wrong... for about thirty seconds. These would be the times when the hider had put it in one place and then changed their minds, gone back, collected it and put it somewhere else before returning. The patterns he was picking up showed him the energy frequency of the person as much as the object he was seeking, so the places they had fixed upon were little knots of brightness in his awareness, sending their fourth dimension shivers to Sid as confirmation. Standing for a few seconds by the decoy location, he would soon catch the next part of the mind map and head off to find the *actual* location and the treasure left there.

It had been a summer to remember. An escape from home. The last August of his childhood. The month you want never to end.

Now, lying in the warm grass, Lucas slipped seamlessly from memory back to dream. He was following them on his bike. Mabel turned in the lane, her long wheat-coloured hair loose across her shoulders and the ghostly white frock floating in the breeze. She was holding something out to him, something which swung on a chain. Not Sid. A broken, blood-stained chunk of skull bone, shaped like a jigsaw puzzle piece. Zoe turned too, carrying his old Parka coat for some reason and said: 'There are mice in it. You found them.' Her short dark bob was stiffly matted with blood up one side and her eyes were opaque, and lifeless. He remembered that. She was just exactly like that. With a piece of her skull missing at the back.

Mabel didn't say anything but she kept swinging the bone on the chain and now he was trying to ride his bike backwards up the hill, away from them. There was a tickly feeling across his throat as if a confession was trying to get out.

Lucas woke abruptly. A grasshopper pinged off his neck and vanished into the grass. The sun had moved across the sky. He realised he'd been asleep for a good hour. He sat up, shaking the doziness from his head along with bit of grass and moss and at least one small orb spider. *Shit.* He hadn't had a Zoe and Mabel dream for nearly two years. One visit from that bloody DS and they were back to haunt him.

How much worse was it going to get if he went along with her stupid plan and became some kind of consultant for this case of hers? Did he really need electricity that much? Or food?

He went back into the bungalow, assailed by the cold and damp of the building as soon as he stepped in. This Indian summer wouldn't last much longer and it was only going to get less pleasant in the bungalow. He *would* have to get the heating back on at some point. His paintings would start to suck in the damp. And so might he.

Lucas went into his bedroom. Inside was an ancient wrought iron double bed with a mattress which was either very, very old or had seen such an incredible amount of action from Aunty Janine and assorted lovers that it had been flattened to a third of its original depth. His sleeping bag and a small travel pillow lay on the bare mattress. A low level chest of drawers in darkly-stained wood stood to one side of the bed, with a battery-powered camping lantern resting on it. In the top and middle drawers were his underwear, socks and a few relics from his travels. In the bottom drawer lay his passport and other important stuff, like the legal documents and deeds to his late aunt's estate (he'd been left the bungalow and an acre of overgrown paddock; no money). Right at the back of it, buried in a thick, woolly walking sock, was the thing he'd never planned to use again. Ever.

Of course, if he had been genuinely set on this, why hadn't he just dumped it down a drain or thrown it in a lake?

That sock had travelled with him, buried deep in his rucksack for over a decade. He had probably taken out its contents half a dozen times in the last couple of years. He bit his lips together and let out a long, hard exhalation through his nostrils. He weighed the balled up wool in his palm, picturing the item that lay at its centre like a baby in a womb. There was a perfectly good lake within a five-minute walk of this place. Maybe now was the time. He set out into the late afternoon once more, striding across the field in a storm of disturbed insects, and out onto a dry dirt track which led down to what was barely more than a pond, known to the locals as Hex Water. Apparently it was a popular hotspot for drowning witches back in the day. Maybe it was apt that he should finally rid himself of his little unlucky charm there.

A thin copse of elder and ash shielded the lake from the casual view of passing walkers or motorists on the B-road which cut along the lower edge of Salisbury Plain. It wasn't a tourist destination; he'd only ever encountered the occasional dog walker or angler here and today there was nobody at all. He found a log close to the water's edge and settled himself on it for a moment, the balled up sock warm in his hand.

The lake was oval, with a small island in the middle; sanctuary for ducks, coots and visiting geese. The water shone almost white under the bleached out sky and the leaves on the trees around it were darkest green, some just beginning to turn to reds, golds and yellows. The rich earthy scent of new autumn gently percolated.

Lucas unballed the sock and pulled out a steel chain with fine but strong oval links. On the end of it, swinging just like the skull jigsaw piece in Mabel's hand back in his dream, was a blue piece of glass. It must once have been the lower part of a stopper for a bottle - the kind of thing to be found on the highest shelf in a 17th century apothecary shop. The inverted cone of frosted glass was battered by who knew how many years but its shape was still perfect, despite having been drilled into and connected to a spike of steel and a jump ring.

Others he'd met had used metal or crystal pendants. He'd been given this one by Aunty Janine when he was ten. She'd been given it by someone else; no relation. The way it had found him wasn't mystical. It was just happenstance.

The chain seemed to wrap itself through and around his knuckles; slick as a slow worm. The glass cone swung in an awkward spiral. Instinctively he steepled his hands, resting his elbows on his knees, and stilled himself completely. The pendulum steadied itself and continued to mark an ever decreasing, ever more perfect circle in the air. After a minute of this he said, aloud: 'Stop.'

It stopped dead, pointing to the earth, utterly still.

Lucas felt a thud in his solar plexus and didn't know whether it was joy or fear.

He stood up, suddenly, swiping the pendulum and chain into his fist and hurling his arm up like a discus thrower. Time to let it go. He flung it away from him and saw the glitter of the chain arc through the air, the bottle glass spinning high over the water and then vanishing beneath it with barely a trail. He *saw* that, but it was a mirage. The chain had caught around his paint-spattered thumb and snagged itself a reprieve from the watery grave. The pendulum swung down and hit him dead centre on his chest.

He snatched it back into his fist, his heart pounding as if he'd just rescued a baby from the edge of a cliff.

'Shit,' he grunted, and went back to the bungalow.

7

Tessa McManus wore an expression of calm distraction. Her eyes were closed and her dark skin looked as if it had been slicked in oil. Her arms were posed as if she was holding a large invisible ball, the right palm cupping downward from above and the left palm cupping upward from below; it reminded Kate of a Tai Chi move. The wires holding the woman in this position were disguised with loops of ivy.

Her body was not yet showing signs of advanced malnutrition. Her naked form was lean and athletic, like the first victim. The studio lighting revealed a gleaming flat belly beneath firm, high breasts. Her left leg was raised at the knee, the toes pointed downward, a snake wrapped around the ankle. Her right leg was straight, the foot planted on the floor; a stag beetle beside it, antlers raised. It was impossible to tell whether the snake was real or fake or stuffed. The rig and the suspending wires to keep her held upright in this position had more plants and flowers wound around them. A dragonfly sat in one of the cornrows across her scalp. A wasp rested at the top edge of her dark pubic hair.

There was a thick silence as the team stared at the picture up on the screen. Nobody was going to say that she looked beautiful... but she did. Kate felt a lump in her throat as she realised that the woman in this image was almost certainly already dead of starvation and dehydration by now.

'I'd like to you to meet a new member of this team,' said Kapoor, softly.

A man she'd not noticed before stood up to the side of the room. His light brown hair had a tousled, boyish look about it, and he was wearing a vintage brown jacket over his blue shirt and tie. He gave everyone a slightly lopsided, regretful smile, as if apologising for his presence.

'This is Conrad Temple - criminal psychologist,' said Kapoor. 'The College of Policing has lent him to us for the duration of Marathon. He's our go-to guy for serial killers.'

Conrad Temple nodded at them all, clutching a card-board folder to his chest as he perched on the edge of a table.

'I've written up notes,' he said, surprising them all with what was either a Canadian or a soft American accent, 'on the kind of guy we're probably looking for.'

Everyone glanced at each other. There had already been substantial profiling done for RG. What else was Conrad Temple bringing to them?

'I know, I know,' he said, raising one hand. 'You've had a profile to work with already and I'm not saying it's so very different to mine. We all know the standard fit; he's a loner, probably lives with his mother or another older relative, has a lowly or insular job, fascination for violent porn in his own time. Thing is... I'm not convinced this is a *sexual* predator. The victims are female and attractive, sure, but there was no evidence of sexual assault on Caroline's remains.'

'Doesn't mean he wasn't jerking off in a corner, watching his little stage set,' said Michaels.

'Fair point,' said Temple, not missing a beat. 'I've considered that too and it may be you're right. But... the images...' He glanced up at the screen where all of Caroline Reece's pictures were now on display in a grim mosaic alongside the first, but certainly not the last, pictures of Tessa McManus. 'The poses are almost... respectful.'

Kate tilted her head and narrowed her eyes. 'Well, yes, we ladies *are* suckers for the respect thing. Because even if some psycho's going to starve you to death on a stick, it's kind of sweet that he takes the trouble to put flowers in your hair. Or wasps.'

Conrad looked her way and smiled, pressing his lips tight as if holding in a laugh. 'Fair point, DS Sparrow,' he said. 'All I'm saying at this stage is that we may need to look beyond the obvious suspects; it might *not* be a sex offender.'

'So what's he getting out of it, then?' said Michaels.

'Attention,' said Temple. 'Notoriety. A feeling of massive importance and power. All the things he would never normally get in his every day life.'

'So... all we need to do is run a search for every sad, awkward loser living with his mum and failing to fulfil his dreams,' said Michaels. 'In 21st century Britain. Well, that shouldn't take long.'

There was an amused reaction which Temple didn't miss. He smiled, shrugged, and nodded ruefully. 'We shouldn't assume it's a man, either. Although it usually is. Anyway, the notes are available to you all,' he said. 'If you think of anything... run it by me. Any questions or ideas; I'm all yours.' He looked at Kate as he said this.

He caught up with her as the briefing ended, tapping her lightly on the shoulder.

'Sorry to be snippy,' she sighed. 'Sleep deprivation.'

He laughed, giving her the benefit of some nicely ordered white teeth. *American,* she decided. Nice eyes too. Brown. Crinkly at the edges, suggesting good humour. He was probably a few years older than her but he had a very youthful demeanour.

'It's OK - I can be annoying,' he said. 'But... you get what I mean?'

She nodded, falling into step with him as they hit the corridor. 'Yes, I guess. Have you ever listened to *Living Doll*? Cliff Richard?'

'Gonna lock her up in a trunk, so no big hunk...' he said.

'...can steal her away from me,' she finished. 'I always thought Cliff was a psycho.'

'OK - so yeah, I like the doll theory. Kinda.' He nodded, his eyes sliding up to the right, visualising this possibility. 'Maybe he wants to protect her from the world,' he went on. 'But... nah. I don't buy it. If she was his living doll I think he'd be feeding her; keeping her pretty. He's not into that. He's into decay.'

'Can't argue with that,' she said.

'So... you're a runner, right?'

She paused and turned to look at him. 'You've been reading my file?'

'Everybody's file. I'm a nosy Boston son of a bitch,' he said, grinning and raising a hand in admission. 'But you're a woman and you're a runner so, you must understand the habits of female runners... to some degree. Would you stop your run and hop into the van of some guy? Even if you knew him? I mean... runners aren't looking for lifts, are they? They're looking for PBs.'

'True,' she said, considering. 'Or headspace, if you go alone. I guess it would have to be someone you knew who had a problem... needed your help right there and then. Or maybe had bad news. You know... *"Come quickly, little Jimmy's in the well!"* kind of thing. But you'd have your phone with you; you'd make a call. Although... not every runner takes a phone. Melissa didn't. She wanted to get away from the matrix.'

'OK - so that makes it easier,' said Temple, pausing as they reached the stairwell and resting a hand on the black banister. '*Hey - Tessa - your guy's just broken his leg! He needs you back home; couldn't raise you on your cell.*'

'Yep, that could work,' she agreed. 'Still would have to be someone she knew, I think. And the other thing is...'

'What?' he prompted, looking at her with intense concentration.

'They're off-road,' she said. 'Very little pavement time; mostly the woods. And it would be easier to grab them in the woods without getting seen. The guy in the van... it doesn't stack up so well for me.'

'What have they found in the woods? On the trail this, er - Melissa - runs?' he asked, riffling through the notes in his folder.

'Nothing,' she said. 'Footprints here and there, which fit with hers. The dog team picked up her scent and there were various points where they reacted around her circuit but there was nothing else - no scuff marks, no hair or fibres in the trees, no sign of struggle. However he did it, he did it like a pro.'

'It's a puzzler,' said Temple, as if he was discussing a tricksy crossword clue. But she found she liked him all the same. There was something robustly good humoured about him; a rare thing among her jaded British colleagues. She wondered what nickname they would work up for him. Tip Top Temple would be her offering.

'You wanna go for a run?' he said.

She blinked. 'Really?'

'Yeah. Some time. I run too,' he said. 'I do the barefoot thing.'

'You run barefoot? Around *here?*' Kate pictured all the broken bottles and dog mess on an average pavement.

'Not *actual* bare feet,' he said. 'But barefoot running shoes - no sponginess. I run forefoot. It's the way we were meant to. So... want to come out on a run?'

'I'll give it some thought,' she said.

'Good. Do that. Gotta go. Tell me if you have any other thoughts!' he called over his shoulder, heading along the corridor as she ascended the stairs, shaking her head and smiling.

He'd made her think, though. She wanted to see Melissa's running route. First thing tomorrow. She might even run it. She could at least take her Asics and wear her sports bra under her shirt. Running helped her think. Sharpened her up. It might help her think better in a location she needed to be sharp in.

There was only one snag - an appointment she'd made first thing. Her new consultant. The one she hadn't quite got around to mentioning to Kapoor just yet.

She wondered if Lucas Henry had running gear too.

8

Her mind was foggy. She wasn't sure it was still connected to her body. She couldn't feel anything - pain or cold or even hunger any more. These feelings would return; she dimly knew this. Whatever it was she'd been injected with, it didn't last forever. At first she'd been terrified of the needle; now she welcomed it. The hunger and the pain would return like a polluted tide every few hours and only the needle in her arm could send it away again. Somewhere across the room she could make out lots of pink shapes; similar but not identical... like star fish. They got clearer as the drugs wore off but she still couldn't really make them out.

She tried to remember things in her life: her parents, her boyfriend, her brother, her home. Tried to remind herself that she *had* once been a person. She remembered running. It was the last thing she had been freely able to do; the last thing she had known any control over. Here she didn't even have bladder or bowel control. Through the numbness in which she now existed, hanging like a puppet, she was vaguely aware that she was being cleaned up from time to time; efficiently. It had horrified her at first, back when she still had the strength to be horrified; now it was routine - and happening less often. There was less and less left inside her to expel. She had only been given water, through a straw, just a few times since arriving here.

Her captor rarely spoke, even when moving around her, changing her position in small ways; putting things in her hair and around her feet, sending shafts of light this way and that. Once she had mumbled, 'Why are you doing this?'

The reply was cool. 'We're going to be famous.'

9

Mariam was just closing up as Lucas arrived at The Henge Gallery. A light rain was falling and in the glass of the door he could see his hair was curling up into the girlish ringlets he loathed. He'd tried keeping it short but as soon as it grew out it frizzed into a ball around his head.

Inside the gallery, in a side street off the Salisbury market square, Mariam grinned at him, framed by a back-drop of colour. Her current exhibition was of African inspired textiles and the artfully lit walls vibrated with colour and tactility.

'Lucas!' She dragged him inside and pulled him into a hug, her cheek cool against his. 'You actually showed up!'

'I said I would,' he replied, squeezing her shoulders and then stepping back to look at her. 'You're looking great!'

She snorted. 'Not bad for a granny, anyway.'

She'd been in her forties when he first met her during his brief dalliance with an art degree in London. She had been one of his tutors then but later, after he'd dropped out, they'd become friends. Back then she was exotically bohemian and regarded as pretty sexy by a number of his fellow undergrads, with her Egyptian colouring, long black hair and vintage clothes. He got what they meant, but her interest in *him* was definitely of the more maternal kind. They had stayed in touch and now she owned her own gallery and seemed to make a decent living from it. The hair was still black, but had streaks of silver at the temples now; it might have been natural or she might have applied it herself. It looked striking and interesting, either way.

'Come on,' she said, grabbing a turquoise silk shoulder bag and her phone. 'I need wine and cake. You need wine and cake, too - just look at you, you skinny youth.'

She led him to a bar just a street away where they ordered a bottle of Rioja and two rum babas. There was a full bar menu and she insisted on ordering Lucas a lasagne and herself a veggie pizza to follow. Mariam didn't get why a sweet dish had to wait for a savoury one. 'Rum babas as soon as humanly possible,' she said to the young waitress, with a wide ruby smile. 'My friend is fading in and out of consciousness. He needs wine and sugar and carbs.'

The waitress smiled back, giving Lucas an appreciative glance, before heading off with their order. The rum-soaked cake and the wine arrived within five minutes.

'So,' said Mariam. 'How is it coming along? You've only two weeks left, Lucas.'

'It's nearly there,' he said. 'But are you sure you want it on your walls? Do you really think the art lovers of Salisbury will fancy it?'

'Of *course* they will,' she said. 'You're the real deal. I've been promoting you for months now and there's a *lot* of interest. *The Journal* arts writer has already confirmed she's coming to the launch - with a photographer - and wants to interview you next week for a profile piece.

Lucas felt his shoulders tense and he swallowed the last of his rum baba. It had been a day or two since he'd had a proper hot meal, but the twinge in his belly wasn't just hunger. 'This reporter,' he said. 'She... she's only interested in me because of the art, yeah?'

Mariam patted his hand. 'It's OK,' she said. 'She's far too young to know you from Adam.'

'Someone else on *The Journal* might remember,' he said.

'Well, it's too late to change your name now,' said Mariam. 'Perhaps you should have done that a few years ago. But to be honest, even if it does get out, it'll be no bad thing for sales. Your stock will probably triple overnight.'

'Yeah, I can see the headline now,' he mumbled, picking up the wine glass. 'BUY A PAINTING BY A MURDER SUSPECT.'

She didn't say anything for a while, sipping her wine and eyeing him thoughtfully over the rim of the glass. 'Stop dwelling,' she said, finally. 'That was then and this is now. You're bloody lucky I'm giving you wall space. Do you know how many artists come in to see me every week, begging for an opportunity like this?'

He grinned and nodded. 'I know. I know. And I really appreciate it.' He'd only been back in the UK for a few days before he'd sought Mariam out in the early summer. He'd needed to anchor himself to someone he trusted while his aunt's estate was settled and he tried to work out what it all meant to him. He hadn't actually asked for an exhibition; Mariam had suggested it, told him she wanted at least ten pieces from him by the autumn. He was fairly sure she had rescheduled someone else's exhibition to accommodate him, although he'd never asked. Because she would have denied it.

'You wouldn't believe some of the ghastly outpourings

I'm expected to rejoice in,' said Mariam. 'Artists can be so incredibly up themselves. It's not just the endless water-colours of the cathedral and the water meadows; it's the twigs on a plank of wood with 'KARMA' sprayed across them in silver - or the crayon depictions of genitalia - or the photographs of stuffed animals in ballet poses. Dear god, that one was persistent. She sent her revolting pictures to me every month for a year. Then there was the goth who kept painting *himself* and asking to stand motionless in a corner.' She sighed. 'I told him nobody really wants art that farts. Of course, occasionally you do get lucky; Ursula Rank-ine's exhibition last year was a great success. She's up for the Tate Modern Prize this year and *I* exhibited her here first.'

'Well, there's something to aim for,' he said. He didn't add any further comment.

'What's up, love?'

The lasagne and the pizza arrived so he had time collect his thoughts and then put them neatly away before she tried again.

'Something's on your mind,' she persisted. 'You're not about to tell me you've only done one painting, are you?'

'No,' he said. 'I've only one left to finish. The others are ready, more or less.'

'So... what then? Is it your Mum? Everything OK there?'

'Mum's fine,' he said. 'Still out in Spain, still happy with Stefan as far as I know. I've not been out to see them for a while. But I call her from time to time.'

'Good boy,' she said. Mariam knew enough of his back-story to remember that Joanna Henry - long widowed - had remarried a few years back, and led an uncomplicated life in Spain these days. Uncomplicated by her son, at any rate. Lucas and his mother had never been very close and now she seemed much more at ease when he *wasn't* in her life. He couldn't blame her. She'd suffered a lot, thanks to him.

'So... this thing?' she prodded, as he shovelled in lasagne with the grateful certainty that she would not allow him to pay for it.

'What thing?'

'It's not your art and it's not your mum so I'm guessing it's England; Salisbury, the plain... everything that goes with it.'

'It was sixteen years to the day last week,' he said, quietly. 'Feels like...'

'Yesterday?' she prompted. He nodded.

'I wish I could just... cauterise my memory,' he said.

'But then you'd be cauterising part of you,' she pointed out. 'There would be a bit missing.'

'I could live with that,' he said. 'It's just that... nobody's past is ever history. It's right here isn't it? Right here even now. Messing up a nice evening.'

'There's therapy,' said Mariam. 'Techniques you can use.'

'I know,' he said. 'I saw a guy in France for about six months... did some CBT. I've used it. It's worked pretty well. Right up until today.'

'What happened today?'

'Someone came looking for me,' he said. 'They tracked me down to the bungalow; asked for my help.'

'Who?'

'This police detective; Kate Sparrow her name is. Said she'd read my files.'

'What did she want you to do?' Mariam looked baffled and worried.

'She wanted someone found,' he said, reaching into his shirt and pulling out his chain. He held it up and allowed the pointed cone of dark blue glass to dangle from it. 'With this.'

Mariam reached out and steadied the pendulum in her fingers. 'Lucas,' she said. 'Whatever it is, you don't want to be doing this.'

'That's what I told her.'

'So why are we even having this conversation?'

He sighed and steepled his hands, his elbows planted on the table and the pendulum suspended over the half-eaten lasagne. 'Can I avoid this?' he asked it. 'Circle for yes, swing for no.' The pendulum swung back and forth.

'Lucas - that's just your inner whatnot making that thing swing,' said Mariam. 'Which means some part of you *wants* to help. You have to know that.'

'You hold it, then,' he said, passing the chain and the glass pendant across to her. 'You really *don't* want me to do it, so I'm guessing you're inner whatnot is going to make it circle.'

She took it with a short sigh, pushing her pizza aside, and copied his pose, letting the pendulum dangle and then stop still between her steepled fingers, elbows steady on the table.

'Can I avoid this?' he asked it. 'Circle for yes, swing for no.' The pendulum circled for a few seconds... and then abruptly swung.

'Dammit,' she muttered. 'I'm *making* it circle! Why is it bloody swinging?'

The swinging got more intense. He shook his head and went back to his lasagne, muttering 'Stop it,' through a mouthful of pasta and sauce. The pendulum stopped dead.

Mariam handed it back to him, looking a little freaked. 'Who is she trying to find?' she said.

'That's the thing,' he said. 'She told me she was investigating this Runner Grabber case.'

'Bloody hell,' said Mariam, with a wry glance at him. 'Nice and low-key then.'

'Two women are currently missing; one almost definitely already dead, they think, but another one only just taken and likely to be alive for a while,' he said. 'So... she wants two women found.'

'And..?' prompted Mariam.

'Something else,' he said, abstractedly tapping his fork on the edge of the lasagne dish. 'She wants me to find another person too, because Sid the Stopper here...' He stopped the cutlery percussion and cupped the pendulum in his palm for a second before putting the chain back over his neck. '...is definitely counting out three. Only this Kate Sparrow woman isn't saying who yet.'

'Are you going to ask her?'

'Oh no,' he said. 'I never ask. I just wait to be told.'

10

He was watching her again. She could sense it even before she got out of the car and walked across the gravel. She could smell him.

Wendy blew out a disgusted breath. It was an unpleasant fact that if you could smell someone's cigarette smoke, you were inhaling the same air that had been in their lungs moments earlier. It was an unwanted exchange of intimate airborne fluids that bordered on assault.

Sure enough, there he was, sitting on the steps to the main entrance, but tucked just out of view beside a planter of hydrangeas so he couldn't be seen from the reception desk.

'You know you shouldn't be smoking in the grounds, Graeme,' she said, eyeing him coldly as she reached the steps.

'Who's smoking?' he said, grinning inanely and holding both hands up; a fan of nicotine and earth-stained fingers. Even in shadow the butt end of his roll-up was clearly visible, smouldering in the earth of the planter.

'Late shift for you, isn't it?' she asked, glancing at her

watch which showed just before 9pm. 'A bit dark for gardening?'

'Doing a bit of grouting,' he said.

'Out on the step?'

He got to his feet. 'In the wet rooms. Back to it now. Break's over,' he said, following her in, too close behind. 'Has anyone ever told you, Wendy, that you're a fine figure of a woman?'

She turned, narrowing her eyes at him. 'Has anyone ever told *you* that in dim light you could almost pass for a man?'

Rolling her eyes at Rowena on reception, she went to leave her things in the staff changing room. It was an area through a door behind the main reception, with hooks for coats and racks for boots and shoes, as well as a number of metal lockers for bags. One half of the anteroom was filled with folded wheelchairs, portable ramps for the minibus, blankets, absorbent seat pads, plastic ponchos, rugs and other travel accessories for the occasions when residents were taken out on a trip.

Wendy was one of the staff tasked with keeping inventories so it was instinctive to her to count. She noticed one fewer wheelchair than usual in the line up and made a mental note to deal with that. Wheelchairs should always be returned by the end of the day; she would chase that up before she finished her nightshift. She had an idea where it was. She also made a note to put in another order for absorbent pads; the pile was looking low.

After going through the handover with Karen, the other full time RGN, she made her way up to East Wing and called into Elsie Newton's room. The old lady was already in bed, watching *Who Wants To Be A Millionaire* on her small set, fingers resting on the remote. Her glasses were safely on her nose for a change.

'Stupid woman,' said Elsie.

'Who's that then?' said Wendy, checking the pot in the commode and finding a high tide of yellow urine.

'This one,' said Elsie, waving a bony hand at the screen. 'Doesn't know what year the Queen was crowned! She's phoning a friend!'

'When was it then?' asked Wendy, putting on some plastic gloves.

'Well, 1953 of course! Any idiot knows that. Stupid woman.'

'I thought it was 1952.'

'*No,*' scoffed Elsie. 'That was when her dad died. She was Queen in 1952 but she didn't get crowned until 1953. Stupid woman. Bad smell too. Like cat's piss.'

Wendy snorted. 'You can tell that, can you?'

Elsie turned to look at her with a stare. 'It's wrong,' she said. 'You know that. It's wrong.'

Through the window Wendy could see Graeme lurking by the planter again. That was wrong too. She was running out of patience with Graeme. She was tempted to have a word with Margaret, the manager, about him. Probably wouldn't, though. She wondered how he'd swung the job here and then remembered he was the nephew of one of the trustees. That would explain it, then.

'If I were you,' said Elsie. 'I'd wash it all off.'

11

The scent of woodsmoke and damp leaves filled Kate's nostrils as she and Lucas stepped out of the car at the side of the track. She took a long, deep breath, partly to enjoy the autumnal cocktail she was inhaling, but also to steady her nerves. Being in the car with him for twenty minutes had been unnerving.

She'd shown up at his bungalow bang on nine o'clock, expecting to have to hammer on his door for five minutes and then wait another twenty to extract him from the building. To her surprise, though, he'd been up, dressed, and sitting on an ancient wrought iron bench in the front garden. He'd washed off the paint spatters from yesterday and was wearing a thick-weave red and black checked shirt, slim-fitting black jeans and aged brown walking boots. He got to his feet as she rolled the Honda up to the edge of the drive, then opened the passenger door and wordlessly slid in.

'Thank you,' she'd said. 'I didn't expect you to be ready.'

'You said nine,' he replied, belting up and staring straight ahead through the windscreen.

'The original photos are in here,' said Kate, passing him a hard backed envelope inside a sealed plastic bag. 'Can you just hold the package? Is that enough? You'll need to put gloves on if you look inside.' She felt a frisson of anxiety when she thought of the contents. She had taken them without an official sign out. She planned to have them back in the evidence locker before anyone noticed. In theory they should only have left the locker after she'd inputted her request on the station's computer system, but she'd taken advantage of the evidence room being unattended and helped herself. If she got caught out she could claim she *meant* to log her actions but forgot in the rush... maybe.

'This is fine,' he'd said, resting the package on his knee, his hand on top of it. 'I'll see what seeps through.'

They hadn't spoken much on the short journey to Frenley Woods. He seemed to understand what she wanted from him and, honestly, she was too overwhelmed with the sheer idiocy of her plan to make small talk. How she was going to square this with Kapoor she had no idea. As open minded as he seemed to be, she couldn't quite picture him signing off a consultancy fee under the heading *Dowser*. Meanwhile, Lucas's very presence in the car next to her was making her skin prickle. She couldn't be sure if it was with an intense *wrong*ness or a long overdue *right*ness; the two halves of that coin seemed to have melted into one another. One second she felt a magnetic pull and the next an equal repulse. She was a breath away from calling the whole thing off before they even got there. If Lucas was aware of her extreme jangles, he didn't let on. His long-fingered hands rested on the envelope and he mostly just stared out of the window.

But here on the edge of the woodland trail where Melissa Hounsome took her last run, he seemed to sharpen up. Stepping out of the car, he took a deep lungful of air and turned in a slow circle, scanning the trees, the track, the fields of box-stacked hay and the smoke from a distant red brick cottage back up on the B-road. Then he put the envelope back onto the passenger seat and shut the door.

'Anything?' she said, finally.

'Well... it's a wood,' he said, widening his eyes. 'And a track. And there are rooks.'

She gave him a thin smile. 'I've not been able to get anything of Melissa's; not yet. I know you'll need something to go on, I was just hoping you might get - I don't know - a *feel* for something, as we go round. This is the route she runs most often. After this, I can take you to where Caroline's body was found.' She reached back through to the rear footwell and pulled out her Asics. 'I'm going to run this,' she said, slipping her boots off and pulling the running shoes on. 'If you want to walk that's fine - I'll just double back to you every couple of minutes.'

He looked at her with something like amusement. 'Is this standard procedure?' he queried, folding his arms across his chest and tilting his head.

'I don't always do standard procedure,' she said, pulling her hair up into a scrunchy. 'She's a runner; so am I. I just might go more instinctively where she did if I run.'

'Didn't they get dogs out to sniff out the trail?' he asked, as she flung her boots into the car and swapped her needlecord jacket for a lightweight zip-up runner's fleece.

'Yes - but it wasn't very conclusive,' she said, locking the car and transferring her phone and keys to the fleece's pockets. 'They picked up her trail in lots of different places, which was no surprise because she runs here nearly every day. The dogs couldn't give us any clues on where she was taken and so far nobody's found any sign of a struggle; no clothing, nothing. A few footprints in mud in several locations that might have been hers yesterday... but might also have been hers on the day before. The weather's been cool and settled - no rain and not too hot; the mud on the track is much the same across a couple of days like that.'

'So... maybe she never got here,' he said. 'She got picked up on the road.'

'Yes, it's possible,' she said. 'Although cameras around the through routes only picked up nineteen vehicles that passed through in our time frame. And they've all been checked - mostly local people and farmers. The team is working through them and forensics will go over any that could be a fit but none of them look likely. Also... there are farm tracks; loads of routes in and out that are nowhere near a camera.'

She broke into a gentle jog, not much faster than walking pace, and he lengthened his stride and easily matched it. They headed along the track into the woods, quiet but for the sound of the rooks and the wind in the trees. She wondered how he would do it... *if* he would do it. Shouldn't he have rods or hazel twigs or something? She hadn't seen anything like that tucked into his jacket or jeans pockets. Was it a pendulum..? She couldn't remember.

The track was wide and covered in a collage of leaves, acorns and outcrops of fungi. Their feet made little sound as they moved along it. Two squirrels chased each other up and down the trunk of a beech and a jay chakked angrily in the distance.

'Don't you use... you know... rods or twigs or something?' she eventually asked.

He gave a muted chuckle. 'Would you like me to? I mean, I don't carry rods but there are plenty of twigs around, if you like. I could wave some about if it makes you happy.'

She stopped dead, anger suddenly crashing through her. 'OK, right, stop.' She raised her hands, palm down. 'It's clear I've made a mistake. You've only come along to take the piss, haven't you?'

He stood, pushing his fingers deep into his jeans pockets and regarding her with an unreadable expression.

'I mean - sorry!' The jangles finally settled into *repulse, repulse, repulse.* She was suddenly quite certain she wanted to eject him from this investigation. 'I know I promised you money and it must have seemed like a pretty easy gig; some dumb copper hoping for a miracle. Obviously I've got the wrong guy.'

'Wait, hang on,' he said, crinkling his brow and wiping a lock of dark hair off it. 'Are you... doing *reverse psychology* on me now?' There was a glint of amusement in his eyes which only smacked her repulsion metre up to 11.

'Fuck it,' she said. 'Come on. We're going back to the car. I'll take you home and we'll forget this ever happened.'

'But I'm enjoying the walk,' he countered cheerily. 'We might as well see if we can get our ten thousand steps in.'

'*You* can walk,' she said, snapping back around. 'I'm going to run; do what I came here to do, with or without you; see if *I* can pick up something. If you want a lift back you can meet me at the car at ten-thirty.' And she sprinted away, fury propelling her feet, leaving him and his stupid play-acting and his smug beardy face and his nonchalant walk behind.

She'd had him out of sight in seconds. She wished she could leave her mood back there with him; she was so rattled. Where was her head at? Why on earth had she gone to him? Suppose he recognised her? Suppose he remembered? It was sixteen years ago and she'd changed a lot in that time, but he *might* remember.

Stop it. Focus. Put the stupid bastard out of your mind, her common sense commanded. *Look around you. Breathe it in. Run and think and feel.*

So this was it: Melissa's run. Probably her last run ever. The route was clearly marked as a walking track and bridle path, but there wasn't much evidence of horses along it. It was wide enough in places for two runners to travel abreast but at other points it narrowed considerably, rising and falling with the land, edging a fast running brook for two or three minutes before angling up again through a thicket of holly and beech. There were other trails criss-crossing it - deer paths and fox lanes - but a runner would normally avoid these. Bracken, nettles and brambles snagged across these snaky routes, disguising the terrain beneath. A runner wouldn't usually risk twisting an ankle on a hidden knuckle of tree root or a fallen branch. Not on her own, this far away from the road. She would stick to the broader, safer path wherever she could.

It took Melissa an hour usually, so the boyfriend had said. That included the run from the house, through the village and along the B-road to the farm track turning. Seven or eight minutes to reach the woods, then out along the woodland path in an elongated anti-clockwise loop, then back to the farm track before retracing her steps to the village. She might do it in reverse, of course, take that woodland route clockwise, but Isaac had said she didn't because she liked to push herself harder in the first part, going uphill. The last third of the woodland loop was a gentle, easy-going slope back down.

She should be feeling something. Picking something up. She wasn't given to flights of fancy but she'd always had good instincts. She had found a clue or a new line of inquiry more than once just on a hunch. Of all the times, out here, running the route of an abducted woman, *now* would be good.

But there was no great insight rising in her mind as she reached the downhill slope, twenty minutes later (it seemed she and Melissa shared a similar speed). No, the only thing accompanying her now was embarrassment. The trees thinned out a little on the final part of the run and she could glimpse the blue of the Honda parked at the edge of the track. A figure was leaning against it. He'd waited then. Damn. She'd half hoped he'd just bugger off so she could avoid the awkward journey back with him. Maybe he was staying put to insist on payment for his time.

She reached the car, her breathing hard but not overly laboured. 'No walk for you then?' she asked. 'What about your ten thousand steps?'

He shrugged, looking at his boots. At least he wasn't smirking any more.

She unzipped her fleece and felt about in the pockets for her phone and keys. The phone was there. But the keys were not. She patted the fleece down again, checking the inside pocket... nothing. She dug into her trouser pockets, even though she was certain she'd not put the keys in there. 'Shit,' she said. 'Keys.' She walked quickly around the car, scanning the ground, then hunkered down and peered beneath it.

She became aware of him crouching down next to her. 'Are you trying to test me?' he said.

'What?' She stood up abruptly. 'No! No I'm not trying to bloody *test* you. I've actually lost them.' She groaned, realising what had happened. The keys had been in her right fleece pocket. When she'd gone to unzip it just now, it was already two thirds open. The keys must have been jolted out during her run... *somewhere* in that wood.

'Shit,' she said again. 'Look - I'm sorry, Lucas. You'll have to wait a bit longer. I'm going to have to retrace my steps.'

'I'll come with you,' he said.

'I don't need your help,' she snapped.

'Oh, I think you do,' he said, falling into step with her as she ran, jogging easily alongside her in his heavy walking boots. His fingers were curled but relaxed, moving in front of him as he ran along with an easy, mid-foot gait. She noticed something shining in them; a chain with a blue pendant dangling from it.

'God, this could take another half hour,' she puffed. 'What a waste of time.'

'It won't,' he said. 'They're not that far in.'

She shot him a glance, eyes narrow. 'Oh - you know that, do you?'

'Yup,' he said.

They ran on for another five minutes and then he stopped, dead, in the middle of the path near the brook. She had been ceaselessly scanning the route, keeping an eye out for the bright green fob as they'd travelled, aware that he wasn't bothering to look at all.

'Stop,' he said. 'It's here.'

'Where?' she snapped, sweeping the ground with her eyes and seeing nothing.

'Ssh,' he said, raising his right fist and letting the thing on the chain dangle still for a moment. He locked his elbow into his side and held his forearm out at a forty-five degree angle, perfectly still. 'Go on,' he said. The blue conical thing began to circle lazily. Then it moved into a figure of eight and then a straight swing. Lucas snapped it away into his palm and strode to the edge of the path.

'Down there,' he said, pointing to the muddy bank of the brook.

She edged towards it, seeing nothing.

'Try under the bark,' he said.

She clambered down and lifted a curved chunk of bark the size of her forearm. The key, still on its fob, lay beneath. She couldn't stop herself letting out a surprised chuckle. Then she stood up and stared at him hard.

'No sleight of hand,' he said, one eyebrow up. 'It's not a trick.'

'Well,' she said. 'Thanks. I guess we can go now.'

'No, we can't,' he said.

'What?'

'There's more to find here,' he said. 'Back the way we've come and then off the track... just a little.'

There was something in his voice that made goose-bumps rise across her shoulders. There was no teasing now, no playing along. She followed him as he walked back down the slope towards a pronounced bend in the path.

'Is this Melissa?' she asked. 'Are you picking up-?'

'Shh,' he said. 'It's not that. It's not *her.* It's just... the patterns. There's something wrong in the patterns.'

'OK,' she said. 'How do you mean?'

'It's not magic,' he said. 'It's patterns... wavelengths... natural maths. I can sense the patterns; the frequencies of things. I know what the patterns should be and when they're *not...* I get that too.'

He stopped again, as suddenly as he had before. He stared down at the path, the pendulum hanging quite still by only an inch of chain from his fist, although he didn't seem to be paying it any attention. She stood still and scanned all around their feet. She could see the lightly trodden earth and leaf litter; a couple of thin roots rising through it; a few twigs and a spray of stinging nettles.

'This was wrong,' he said, like a mathematician calculating aloud. 'Less wrong now but still wrong.'

'Wrong *how?*' she asked.

'Move over,' he said and waved her back along the path as he stepped off it into a cluster of bracken beside a fallen log. '*You,*' he said, pointing at the log. 'You... *weren't there.* You were...' He suddenly knelt down and grasped the log, which was maybe as long as he was tall and topped with green lichen. He pulled it with a grunt and then called: 'A little help here!'

She ran across, wading through the bracken and into a patch of leaf litter to grasp a protruding stump which rose up from one end of the log. Together they heaved it across onto the path where it rocked heavily and settled still. It was a thick old torso of tree and rose to knee height.

'You were here,' said Lucas, rubbing a thumb across his beard and staring down at the body of wood. He moved backwards along the path, facing in, the way Kate had run through, twice now.

'Would you jump it?' he said. 'If you were running this path today?'

Kate followed him, turned around and surveyed the obstacle in the path. Around to the left the flattened earth where it had lain a minute earlier looked manageable. 'I might jump it,' she said. 'But probably not. The broken stump poking up isn't good and, honestly, you can't see what's on the other side. I'd detour around it, hop over the bracken and rejoin the path further along.'

'Do it,' he said.

And then, after she'd run three steps he flung out his left arm and said: 'STOP! Don't do it!'

'What the hell?' she huffed, but he shoved her firmly back with his forearm and stepped carefully along the newly revealed detour. He crossed the bracken and the leaf litter patch then very abruptly sank to his knees. At least, that's what it looked like to Kate. His grunt of shock and annoyance told her it hadn't been intentional and she couldn't see his feet. Settling onto his backside, he glanced over his shoulder at her, a curiously triumphant look on his face. She moved closer and realised that he hadn't knelt; his legs had sunk - up to knee level. The loose leaf litter had looked as if it continued on flat and firm, but here it was just a thin layer over a pit of what looked like sticks and paper.

'Someone made a trap,' said Lucas, very slowly bringing his legs up through the woodland pit. 'They moved the log onto the path and they dug a deep hole... a metre and a half at least... and then they covered it in a thin layer of sticks and black paper and a carpet of leaf litter.'

Kate gulped, taking in the full significance of what he was saying.

'Shit,' she said. 'Lucas, get out of there carefully. You're in a crime scene.'

'She's not down there,' he said, now up on his hands and knees and peering into the damp woodland and paper stew. 'She was, but she's not now. This isn't her grave; it's just how she was trapped.'

'Still a crime scene,' said Kate, her heart thrumming somewhere near her throat. 'I'm calling it in. You need to move away.'

But he didn't. He kept looking into the muddy stew of stick, earth, paper and mulch and she realised he was holding that little blue glass pendulum again in his left hand. Then, before she could make him stop, he thrust his right hand into the pit and pulled up a handful of matter.

'LUCAS! For god's sake, I just *said*! That's a fucking crime scene!'

He turned to her, holding out his fist and then slowly, slowly opened out his fingers. The earth and twigs and a panicked woodlouse tumbled between them but right in the centre of a soft clump of mud something glinted. She leaned over and stared at it.

It was a tiny gold star.

'Don't move,' she breathed, reaching into her trouser pockets for a plastic evidence bag. She turned it inside out and gloved her hand with it before carefully extracting the stud earring from the mud.

'That could, of course, be anyone's,' she said.

'It's not, though,' said Lucas.

12

She was all business now, sending him back to her car with the keys to get some police crime scene tape while she stood guard at the pit; obviously not trusting him to stay away from it while she went herself.

He wondered how she was going to play this. When he rejoined her, handing over the blue and white DO NOT CROSS tape, she was just finishing her call. 'Cavalry's coming,' she said.

'So... do you want me to hang around, or would it be easier for you if I made my own way home now?' he asked.

She looked up at him, calculating. 'No... no, I brought you here to help and - bloody hell - you have. I mean...' she turned to look at the abduction site. '...if the dogs didn't locate this, I can't imagine any of *us* would have. This is just too big a location to cover.'

'So... when your boss gets here, you're just going to introduce me?' he asked, watching her closely and feeling, not for the first time, an odd tickle of recognition. She and he had met before, but he had no clue where or when. With his talents it ought to be easy to find the answer but one thing he'd discovered over time is that **a.** any personal involvement muddied the water and made it harder to read the patterns and **b.** if it was relevant, it would make itself known in its own time. Chasing it never helped.

She took the scrunchy out of her hair, allowing it to fall in gold strands around her face before collecting it and recreating the ponytail more neatly. She was playing for time.

'You didn't tell them about me,' he said.

'No... not yet,' she admitted, picking up the tape and unravelling it.

'Wanted to try before you buy?' he said.

She flushed just a tiny bit. 'Look, police use people like you... it happens. We just don't advertise it. We get enough nut jobs on the phone as it is, whenever there's a serious missing persons case or a murder that gets a lot of publicity.' She flicked a look at him and then turned away to snag the tape onto the nearest branches, creating a rough quadrangle around the path and the pit. He offered to help but she just said: 'No - really - you need to stay back now. Don't want any more of your DNA sprinkled around.'

He felt a chill at this and then realised why he had to stay; why she had to explain his presence. It wasn't likely that much trace of him could be found in this setting, but it wasn't impossible, either. And all things considered, he'd rather not get arrested. Especially when his prints and DNA were already in the system.

'But, you know, coppers are a cynical bunch,' she went on, looping the tape around the trunk of a slender ash tree. 'And if any of my guys get wind that I'm using a dowser to help out I will never hear the last of it. There'll be runes on my desk this time tomorrow, a dream-catcher on the back of my chair by tea time... a ticket to the Glastonbury Goddess Convention in my pigeonhole by Friday.'

He snorted and nodded. 'I hear you.'

'So... I'll tell my superintendent but I won't be advertising it to the others. As far as they're concerned, you're a friend of mine - a fellow runner who I just asked along because I needed to bounce some ideas around.'

He looked down at his boots. 'In these?'

'We were walking the route so we had time to look around,' she explained. 'And that's true... apart from my occasional fartleks.'

He grinned at her.

'Sudden spurts of speed!' she said, rolling her eyes. 'It's Swedish.'

'Ja, jag vet vad det betyder,' he said, the words rolling easily off his tongue.

'What?' she stared up at him, eyebrows arched in surprise.

'I know what it means,' he translated.

'You speak Swedish?'

'A bit,' he said. 'I've spent a few years travelling the continent. I get by in a few languages.'

There was a shout through the trees and several figures came into view: three in uniform and two in civvies, heading fast along the path towards them. Lucas fought the instinct to melt away into the undergrowth. Dealing with Kate was one thing; actual boys in blue was another.

He felt acid rise in his throat as the full consequences of what he'd just got into began to seep through his mind. Kate's superintendent would soon be thumbing through his old files, digging out the backstory on his detective sergeant's new consultant. Would it seem a little too coincidental that the boy who'd been a chief suspect in a murder and missing person case sixteen years ago had arrived back in the country around about the time these runners started vanishing?

For the first time another thought occurred to him. He turned away from Kate to hide the shock he could feel creasing his own face as his stupidity fully dawned on him. Kate knew about his past too... and she'd just shown up out of nowhere yesterday, apparently to ask for his help.

But what if that was *not* her plan? What if her *real* plan was to bring him out here to the scene of the crime and watch him as he dowsed for it, in the full suspicion that he'd know where to find it because *he* was the kidnapping, murdering bastard she was after? That keys thing... that was an easy piece of theatre to set up, just to warm him up for the main show.

He could guess at the basic profile of this killer - someone who was revelling in the notoriety; sending pictures to the police. That was the same kind of person who would probably love to stand by and watch the investigation as a 'consultant' - hiding in plain sight.

Fuck. What an idiot he'd been.

But running was not an option, unless he was really *gagging* to be their prime suspect. He marshalled his thoughts and smoothed his face. Turning, he watched as they arrived at the scene. He stayed put, leaning against a tree, arms folded. Sid was now back inside his shirt, involuntarily dowsing the erratic heartbeat beneath his skin.

A guy in a white boiler suit showed up with lights on tripods, photographing the cordoned off area from all angles. Kate had handed over the earring to her boss on his arrival. She was exchanging information with him and a younger man with short, laboriously styled dark hair and a grey suit, who was checking her out whenever he thought nobody was looking. Eventually the boss man sent the younger man away to assist the forensics guy, who was now setting up a small tent. Then he and Kate approached.

'I'm Chief Superintendent Rav Kapoor,' said the man, nodding to him. 'I gather you've been a big help to us today.'

Lucas shrugged. 'Happy to do what I can.'

'I hear you're a friend of DS Sparrow's... a running mate from time to time?'

He glanced at Kate and saw a blank expression on her face. *Shit.* So she hadn't told him. She'd bottled it.

'She's a better runner than me,' he said.

'Well, if you can hang around to give a statement, DS Sparrow will drop you home afterwards. As you can see, we've got our hands full here now. We very much appreciate your help.' He nodded and moved away back to the tent.

Kate stood still, watching the ground. 'DC Michaels will take your statement,' she said, waving towards the young guy in the grey suit.

'You didn't tell your boss.'

'Not yet,' she said. 'I will... but not now. Too many flapping ears around. OK? Are you OK with that?' She looked up at him with something like apology in her eyes.

He shrugged again. 'Guess I'd better get down Sports Direct and get some trainers, for when they come and search the bungalow. Make our little cover story a bit more convincing.'

She glanced over her shoulder and then back at him, brow creasing. 'Nobody's searching your place! You're just a friend... and, soon, a consultant. That's all. You can relax.'

He shook his head in wonder. 'You haven't got a fucking clue, have you?'

She looked stung but he walked away from her, towards DC Michaels, offering his statement. It didn't take long; he just went with her story and the DC noted it down swiftly, barely keeping eye contact. Much more exciting stuff was going on in the tent. Someone had already sent an image of the muddy earring through to the boyfriend of the missing woman - and it had just come back as a positive ID.

'Are we done, then?' he asked.

'Yeah, sure, for now,' said the DC, shoving his notebook away. 'We'll be in touch, but you're good to go.'

Lucas didn't wait for a lift from Kate. He sidled away along the path, unnoticed, choosing to make his own way home. He couldn't guess at the going rate for police consultants but he suspected it could never possibly be enough to make up for the bad, bad situation he was slip-sliding towards with every passing minute since DS Sparrow had shown up in his life.

13

It appeared they'd found the killer's MO for capturing his victims. Teams had been despatched to the last known running routes of Tessa McManus and Caroline Reece with a brief to look for fallen logs beside the running paths. By the end of the day another pit had been found beneath a log beside the woodland trail where Caroline Reece had taken her last run. In it were the pulpy remains of black paper and sticks. Tessa's trap was uncovered just an hour later - a copy of the others. There was a palpable excitement among the team; this break had been a long, long time coming.

'We still don't know how he gets them out of the woods and back to his place, though,' said Michaels, staring at the fresh images now exhibited across the glass wall back at base. The earring, blown up many times its actual size, hung next to several shots of the excavated Frenley Woods pit. The forensics lighting picked out the precise rectangular shape of the hole. It was, as Lucas had said, about a metre and a half deep; the same again in length and a metre in width. There was another image - of the torn paper underlay for the faked woodland floor, carefully pieced back together to reveal the ragged tear the runner had made as she'd plunged through it.

'So... we're looking for someone fit enough to dig a big hole... probably in the dark or the early hours,' said Kate. 'And then able to pick up a fully grown woman, probably unconscious.'

'So he carries her out to a vehicle; probably a van,' said DC Sharon Mulligan, taking a sip of coffee as she leant against a table at the back of the room. A year younger than Kate, Sharon had joined Salisbury CID six months ago, on Kate's recommendation. Sturdy, stoic and sharp, she'd proven herself in uniform and was a natural at getting just about anyone talking. Born in Rotherham but half Jamaican, she didn't harm Wiltshire Police's equality quotient either. 'A workman of some kind?' she said. 'Fit and with a van?'

'Could be,' mused Kate. 'Someone who works fast. Filling that hole in again, right after the capture, would have to be done quickly. Covering the tracks, disguising the scene, moving the log back.'

'And what about all the earth dug out of it in the first place?' said Sharon. 'He'd have had to carry it some distance and drop it in undergrowth. It was like a military exercise.'

'But it's got to be someone with some education too,' Kate said. 'To know how to knock them out.'

'Well, anyone can slam chloroform on a rag over someone's face,' said Michaels. 'You can buy it online!'

'Yeah, but chloroform alone wouldn't work,' said Kate. 'It takes about five minutes to work... and only then if your victim agrees to lie still and inhale it. The traces they found in the pits were of chloroform *and* diazepam. That's quick but even so, according to the path lab, it's not enough to keep anyone under for long. They found needle marks on Caroline's body, so it's a fair bet she was injected with something too, once she was down.'

'It does all suggest training,' said Conrad, sitting back in his corner, to the left of the super. 'And I wouldn't rule out military; perhaps in the medical corp. Could have skills in woodland tracking too. Maybe we should be checking out the army bases; plenty of them around here.'

'And going back to the running clubs,' said Kate. 'See who's new.' She'd been around once already, checking out group after group of runners based in the county to see if anyone suspicious had joined their number; so far it hadn't turned up any good leads but that could have changed.

'Was Melissa a running club member?' asked Kapoor.

'No,' said Michaels. 'Nor were the other two. Lone runners.'

'Running clubs might be a dead end,' conceded Kate. 'But they're part of a wider network; a tribe. I'd like to get a list of subscribers to Runner's World and other magazines and sites for runners... see what Wiltshire addresses crop up in it. Take a look at the comments in the forums. Our guy might not be a runner himself but he's stalking runners, so he's on the periphery. A lot of runners post their favourite routes on these sites. It's a badge of honour to get off the beaten path and they like to boast a bit.'

'Get on it,' said Kapoor to Kate. 'And see if Caroline, Tessa or Melissa used those sites.'

'Good thinking,' said Conrad, smiling at her broadly. She smiled back thinly. It was only good thinking if anything came of it and there was no certainty of that.

'Anything back on the vehicles yet, Guv?' Michaels asked.

'Nothing helpful.' Kapoor stared up at the Marathon

collage. 'The vehicle is key but we can't nail it. There's just not enough CCTV coverage in these rural locations and if he's got no tech running and his phone's switched off, we can't track his movements that way either.'

'But,' said Conrad. 'He - or she, let's not be sexist - has slipped up once. Left an earring behind. And he's gonna notice that when he starts setting up his nasty little diorama of decay, don't you think? That might unsettle him. So... clever, organised... but not invincible. We can get him. Or her. Them.' He shook his head, wearying of the politically correct vernacular.

Kate was exhausted by the end of the briefing - not least from the extreme stress of smuggling out the RG photos and returning them to the evidence locker before the briefing, expecting at any moment to get caught out by one of her colleagues.

It appeared she'd pulled it off, but she wasn't going to be breathing out any time soon. She needed to get some food and some rest... and then start combing through the running club sites and magazine subscriptions people. She could at least drop a few emails around tonight; get the ball rolling. She could do some of it on her phone while she waited in the car for Sally to see her mum again. A text had arrived from Sally earlier that day, begging another lift this evening. Sally hated to ask but apparently her mum had got quite agitated about some mystery issue and the home was insisting her daughter call in to see her. Kate had promised she'd help. She was tempted to suggest her friend got a cab, but she knew Sally had issues about that. She was borderline agoraphobic and tended to anxiety outside her comfort zone. And her comfort zone was her house, her car, a short walking route for Reggie, when she was able, and... increasingly, Kate's car.

Kate sighed as she slipped on her jacket and grabbed her bag from her desk. Sally was going to have to deal with it sometime; a friendly neighbour wouldn't always be around to help out and Francis showed no sign of learning to drive yet, despite getting his provisional licence a year ago. He was the Uber generation, she guessed, and just didn't see the point.

She was about to descend the stairwell when Kapoor called her into his office.

'Shut the door, Kate,' he said, in a voice that made her insides clench. He didn't look angry, just tired. 'Sit down,' he said. She did.

'So... Lucas Henry,' he said and then just left it hanging, raising his greying eyebrows at her.

'Sir?' she said, at length.

'When did you plan to tell me about him?'

She knew better than to play dumb. She dumped her bag and leaned her elbows on the edge of his desk, sighing heavily. 'You've found his file,' she said.

'Indeed I have,' said Kapoor. 'Makes interesting reading.' He picked up a buff folder of print outs and old photos. Most of this detail was digitised and accessible via the data system, but fifteen years ago it was routine to print this stuff off and keep it in actual files, down in the basement. Kapoor had obviously decided to go old school, possibly because he was trying to be subtle about it and not leave a digital trail. For her sake, maybe.

'So,' he said. 'Sixteen years ago Lucas Henry is arrested in connection with the murder of Zoe Taylor. And the disappearance of Mabel Johanssen.'

He didn't miss the involuntary way she sucked her breath in.

'It appears the boy led police to a quarry where Zoe's

body lay under a pile of rocks, her head bashed in. He said he had dowsed her location. You know... using twigs or rods or...' he peered at the detail on the page... 'no - apparently a bottle top on a chain. Who knew?'

Kate said nothing. She fixed her eyes on her fingernails, still grimy with the earth at the crime scene.

'Naturally he was a prime suspect for the Zoe murder; he was a friend of both girls - possibly a boyfriend to one of them; he never said. And the last person, it would appear, to see either of them alive.'

'Whoever killed them was the last person to see them alive,' said Kate, quietly.

'You've accepted that your sister *is* dead, then?' he said, compassion in his voice.

'Years ago,' said Kate. 'Mum said we had to or we'd never have any peace.'

He nodded. 'Wise lady.'

'It didn't work for her, though,' muttered Kate. 'It just ate her up. She made a good show of it. We moved house; started using her maiden name; went to a new school where nobody knew us. Began again. But it just killed her in the end, not knowing.'

'And you?'

'Me? I'm fine,' she said. 'I was ten when it happened; young enough to blur out a lot of it.'

'I doubt that,' he said. 'And if you're fine, why the hell is Lucas Henry back in your life?'

'He didn't kill Zoe... or Mabel,' said Kate. 'There was never a real case against him. He was just young enough and stupid enough to offer his help without thinking it through. It ruined his life.'

'So... you and your mother never had any doubts about his innocence?'

'He went to school with Mabel and Zoe; we'd known him for years,' she said. 'He used to hang out at our place sometimes. His mum used to work long hours and sometimes he'd have his tea with us.'

'Often it's the people closest to the victims who do the crime,' Kapoor pointed out, needlessly.

'It's not that,' she said. 'It's... the dowsing. We *made* him do it. We begged him.'

He glanced down at the papers again. 'That's what his statement said too. You'd all begged him to find the girls. So he did. Doesn't mean he didn't kill them first. Easy to pretend to find someone, isn't it?'

'You don't understand,' said Kate, letting out a heavy sigh. 'He really *could* do it. He could find lost things. It was his party piece. His aunt taught him to do it; she was one of the old school types with rods and twigs; a bit pagan. Harmless, though. A nice lady. We would hide things around the house and the garden and he would find them. It was... phenomenal. I really mean it, Guv. You had to see it to believe it.'

An unwelcome flash of memory hit her; she and mum, frantic, calling him on the phone. Mum, so white her lips had no colour, saying: 'Lucas - you've got to help us. You need to do your dowsing thing. Please!'

'It's true he had an alibi,' Kapoor said. 'At least that's what this file says; but it wasn't the strongest. I think it was the testimony of your mother that really kept the heat off him. But the case was never closed, you do know that? He remained a person of interest and that hasn't changed, even now.'

'If you say so,' she said.

'Kate - you do know that Lucas arrived back in the country in May, don't you? For the first time in eight years.'

'His aunt died. He came back to sort out her estate; she left him her bungalow.'

'I'm not arguing the facts,' he said. 'But if you hadn't already made contact with Henry, we would have got to him in the next couple of weeks, regardless, as soon as he'd shown up as a recent arrival in the patch... with a backstory like this.' He tapped the file. 'Are you sure you weren't just jumping the gun on this one? Do you think he's involved?'

'No!' she said. 'I heard on the grapevine that he was back... and I just went to him to ask him to dowse. I know I should have run it past you first but... it was just an instinct thing. If it helps us to save Melissa...'

'And he did dowse for you,' said Kapoor. 'And he led you right to the trap pit.'

He didn't say anything else.

He didn't need to.

'I... I may have... not fully thought this through,' she said. *Damn.* She understood what Lucas had meant now, back in the woods, when he'd told her she didn't have a fucking clue. She had just planted him right in the centre of suspicion. With all her experience in cases like this, it just beggared belief that she could have been so dumb.

'Look... I am as certain as I can be that Lucas has nothing to do with this,' she said. 'He's not our Runner Grabber. He just agreed to help because he's broke and I said there could be a consultancy fee in it for him. I picked him up and drove him to the site and then he... he dowsed.'

'Right away? Straight to it?' asked Kapoor.

'No - he found my keys first,' she said. 'I ran ahead of him and doubled back and realised they'd fallen out of my pocket. He found them for me.'

'Well, I guess that would be the convincer,' said Kapoor.

'It's not a trick!' She heard the shrill edge to her voice

and tamped it down. 'He didn't pick my pocket and plant them, if that's what you're thinking.'

'You're sure about that?' said Kapoor.

She was silent. What could she say? She *wasn't* sure. She didn't *think* he'd done that but she couldn't swear to it.

'Go home, Kate,' said Kapoor. 'And do not contact Lucas Henry again.'

14

The pain tide had come in. She was becoming more aware of her surroundings... of her state of being. Confused, disorientated, viciously sore, honeycombed with intense hunger and thirst.

Several times since she'd been brought here her captor had given her water through a straw. She'd gulped it down desperately, sucking in the moisture like an arid desert floor. It eased her headache just slightly but did nothing for the other pain in her limbs and at the pressure points where the metal and wires held her. She itched too. And that was almost driving her insane.

The small pink things began to take some shape and now she was starting to think she might know what they were. It wasn't something she wanted to acknowledge to herself but she knew it. They were bodies, weren't they? Dozens of thin, pink bodies, held in poses just like her. Even at this distance - there must be many metres between them - she could make out that all of them were naked and silent. There were dark-haired and fair-haired woman among them, all in standing poses. Most were pink-skinned but two or three looked brown. They seemed to have their eyes open and some were even smiling. Maybe her face looked the same; the drugs might cause a grinning rictus the victims could do nothing about.

She could only conclude that she was one of many in some vast warehouse of captive women. Dying women. Because she knew she was dying. Whatever was going on in her captor's sick head, it wasn't a plan to release her.

She was in some kind of science fiction nightmare. The only escape from it was a deeper sleep. She knew waking up wouldn't make it go away.

15

Sleeping wouldn't make it go away. Lucas knew this as he lay on the bed. He was tired. Very tired. Dowsing always took it out of him but dowsing a fresh crime scene and planting himself right in it like a total cretin had really wiped him out.

Why the hell hadn't he just packed up and left, right after DS Sparrow's visit yesterday? He was under no obligation to help her; he didn't owe the police anything. Yes, that would have been the time to go - *before* it all kicked off. He guessed they might still have come after him once they'd worked out that he'd returned to Wiltshire just before that first woman went missing. He knew he was of interest to them even now; that the Quarry Girls case had never been closed. It was one of the reasons he'd moved abroad for so long; to escape the endless scrutiny and suspicion.

He didn't necessarily blame them for it. Boyfriends often *were* the culprits in crimes like this. It was usually a sex-related thing. He pictured a scene in a quarry: two girls get drunk and start fooling around with one boy and then one of them goes off the idea but he thinks she's just teasing and doesn't get the message. Then she starts screaming and the boy shoves her and she falls and her head hits a rock. Now she's lying bleeding, maybe dying… and then her friend gets hysterical and wants to call 999, but the boy is scared and just wants her to shut up, so he puts his hands over her mouth and then around her throat and then…

It didn't take a master storyteller to conjure up a scenario like this. It was pretty much what the police said in the interview room. Over and over again. If there'd been any DNA evidence of his presence in the quarry, he'd probably be serving time now. But there was none. He'd told the police he'd not seen the girls all weekend, not since walking home from school on Friday, but they didn't seem to buy that.

They also didn't buy the dowsing thing. He'd been tempted to demonstrate for them but the truth was, he didn't know if he could do it when he was in such a state of fear and dread. To dowse effectively he needed to be able to find a calm place in his mind; to focus. He'd made it work when Mabel's mum had called him, full of anxiety about her daughter being missing for hours, because at that time there was no reason for anyone to assume Zoe and Mabel weren't alive and well; just late.

He'd gone round to Mabel's place, taken Sid out right away and said: 'Come on then, show me where to go.'

And Sid had.

16

There was a high-pitched whine just behind her head. She tried to ignore it. Then there was breathing, hot and persistent on the back of her neck. Then he licked her skin.

'Oh for god's sake, Reggie, give it a bloody rest!' snapped Kate, turning around to glare at the dog. He panted noisily, giving her a wide grin, and then settled down again on the back seat.

There were a lot of running sites to work through. She'd signed up to six already and was working her way through lists of local running club online forums, lurking and reading comments and hoping to see something that would make her spidey senses tingle. But the only thing tingling was her irritation gland as Reggie continued to whine. Then she heard something worse. Dripping.

'Oh *shit*, Reggie!' She flung open her door and got Reggie out of the back too late. The weak glow of the courtesy light revealed a delta of canine piss spreading along the stitching of the seat and dripping into the footwell. Reggie sat down next to the car, tail thumping occasionally. She guessed she should have paid attention to the noises he was making, but she didn't speak Dog. That was Sally's job. *Bloody hell.* She grabbed some tissues from the glove box and started mopping up, cursing her neighbour and her neighbour's needy mutt. She should have stuck to her guns and made Sally leave Reggie at home, but Sally had said he really needed to get out. He was stir-crazy. He'd only had a fifteen minute run with Kate that morning, after all. Kate suspected Sally was hinting at her; hoping she'd spend the visiting time helpfully taking Reggie for a walk. There were woods around the lodge grounds.

But Kate had made it clear she was still working.

'Any breakthroughs?' Sally had asked on the drive up here, nudging her usual rule aside. 'I mean... you are working on the Runner Grabber case, aren't you?'

Kate had rolled her eyes as she drove. 'I think it's a fair guess that every copper in Wiltshire is on the Runner Grabber case,' she said. 'We're making some headway. And I've got to make more while you're in with your mum, so Reggie's just going to have to stay in the car with me.'

She put the wet tissues into a spare plastic carrier. Then she glanced around to see Reggie on the gravel, making the shape of the letter r - lower case - and pumping out a chunky brown dog egg. 'Jeeezuz,' she muttered, steeling herself to add this to her bag of wonders.

Just as she was dropping the tissue-wrapped turd in with the yellow roses Reggie let out a volley of barks and shot away into the straggly bushes at the edge of the car park.

'SHIT! Reggie! COME BACK!' she bawled, before slamming the car door shut, dumping the carrier, and taking off after him. The dog had vanished into the twilight; no sign or sound of him. It didn't help that a gusty wind had whipped up, stirring the leaves in the woods. The light was fading fast; she thumbed the torch app on her phone and shone it ahead of her while she trod through the most likely path through the bushes and towards the wood. 'REGGIE! REGGIE!' she yelled, swiping away a springy runner of bramble before it took out her eye. She thought she saw movement off to her right, down a narrow woodland path between some thickets of holly. 'REGGIE!' She took a breath and told herself to think like a dog. Would *she* want to run back to someone who was screaming like a banshee? No. 'Reggie!' she called, her voice light and sweet. 'Reggie, darling! Reggie, baby!' she went on, as welcoming as a Teletubby on Class A Tustard. 'Reh—jee, you little sack of shit. Come back to Aunty Kate and have a treat!'

Nothing. She stood still, listening. The sky she could glimpse between the branches and leaves was darkening fast as the last of the sunset evaporated. Down at ground level it was all gloom. Without her phone torch she'd struggle to get back to the car and even with it there was a serious danger of tripping or impaling her eye on a twig.

Reggie would just have to find his own way back. He was better equipped for it than she was. She turned slowly, still listening. There was a crack off to her left. Something in the undergrowth. 'Reggie?' There was no further sound; no scuffling or panting. There was *something,* though. A presence. She felt the hair rise up on the back of her neck; her primeval warning system kicking off. The silence beneath the rustling leaves suddenly seemed thick and expectant. Then there was another crack; heavy and forceful. Something weighty - man sized - had made that noise.

'Come out,' she said, readying herself. 'It's OK. I'm a police officer. Just come on out.'

Nothing. Except the hairs on her neck standing up at 90 degrees.

'Fine,' she snapped. 'Don't bother me and I won't bother you.' And she began to stride back the way she'd come, waving the torch beam ahead of her and retracing her route to the car. She couldn't hear anything else above the wind in the leaves and her own footfalls but the sense of being watched... maybe being followed... wasn't leaving her. Twice she abruptly turned back and swung the beam of light around but it picked out only the pale, witch-like arms and skinny fingers of the trees.

Back at the car she found Reggie sniffing around the tyres. 'You little furry bastard!' she cursed, grabbing his collar, opening the rear door and shoving him up on the back seat.

She slammed it shut, turned around and gave an involuntary shout of shock at the figure standing behind her, holding a spade.

'Sorry,' he said. 'Made you jump, did I?'

She raised her hands and tried to laugh convincingly. 'Just put the spade down and we're fine.'

'Oh!' he glanced at the implement and lowered its business end to the ground. 'Sorry. You waiting for someone?' She recognised him now - the gardener. He smelt of old cigarettes rather than earth and greenery. He was checking her out with all the subtlety of a twelve-year-old; eyes lurking at breast level even though they were well out of sight under her jacket.

'Yes, my friend Sally is about to come out,' she said. 'Um... were you in the woods just now?'

He frowned. 'The woods? No. I just do the garden; the hedges and that. You don't want to be wandering around in the woods when it's getting dark, you know.' He gave her an unpleasant wink.

'I was looking for the dog,' she said. 'Anyway...' She went

around to the driver's side. 'I've got him back, as you can see.'

Reggie started to growl as soon as she opened the door, but another sound took her attention. Sally was calling across the car park. 'Sorry! So sorry, Kate! I'm coming now!' Kate glanced at her watch; it had been ninety minutes - half an hour longer than promised. Now a nurse arrived, coming in from her left, rolling an empty wheelchair with some difficulty across the gravel. It felt like rush hour.

'Sorry - Mum was in a bit of state,' said Sally as she neared the car. 'I had to distract her with lots of talking. Tell her all about my day - which wasn't much to tell, let's be honest.' She paused to wave at the nurse as she passed. 'Thanks for everything you do for Mum, Wendy! Sorry she's being so nasty to you right now.'

The nurse - the tall dark one Kate vaguely recognised - smiled and nodded, saying: 'It's nothing I'm not used to.'

'She keeps saying Wendy smells,' Sally told Kate, opening the passenger door. 'It's so embarrassing when Wendy's right there in the room with us! I had to tell Mum all about the Runner Grabber just to keep her mind on something else. She does like a nice bit of crime; loves her *Midsomer Murders*.'

'Well, I'm glad it's entertaining her,' said Kate, drily, noting that the gardener had ambled away towards the house, earning himself a glare from Wendy as he caught up with her.

'It's all over *The Journal* again,' said Sally. 'Those poor women; what does he do to them?'

Kate said nothing.

'Sorry! I know you can't say,' said Sally. 'But you be careful when you go out with Reggie first thing. Although I hope he'd protect you if anyone tried to grab *you*.'

'I'm sure he'd shag their leg until they ran away,' said Kate.

'Come in to mine when we get back,' said Sally. 'There's chicken casserole in the slow cooker. Enough for two... or three if Francis wants some.'

Kate smiled, forgiving Sally as she backed the car out and drove towards the gates. Casserole would definitely hit the spot. The woods were just a blur of dark now. She was tired and hungry and, for god's sake, *nobody* had been in the woods, watching her.

17

'Somebody's watching us.' Francis found her by their shared front door, lacing up her running shoes just before 7am.

'What the hell are *you* doing up?' she asked. He worked from home; a junior project manager for a software development company. In truth, Kate hadn't a clue what he actually did for them, but she knew he spent the majority of his life in a darkened room filled with screens and keyboards. What was originally the third bedroom upstairs had now been made into his study, while the second was where he slept. The master bedroom had been remade as an open plan lounge and kitchen. He spent most of his time in the study, at work and at play. She worried about his lack of social life.

'I was getting coffee,' he said.

'At 7am? You got up to get - oh no, wait,' she took in the puffiness under his blue eyes and the scruffy dark blond hair. 'You haven't been to bed.'

'I'm into something big,' he said, loftily. 'I don't keep standard office hours.'

'So... who's watching the house?' she asked in a faux fearful voice. 'Reggie?'

'Sexier,' said Francis. He reached over and opened the door. 'Check her out!'

Stuffing her phone in one zip-up pocket and her door key in the other, she stepped outside, peering in the direction he was pointing. It was a short front garden, a little overgrown, with a grassy lawn alongside the one-car-length gravel drive, ending in a hedge of box, fuchsia and cotoneaster. The hedge was contained by a redbrick wall to the front and the side (built low enough for her usual route over the top of it when she went to Sally's). Standing by the wall, supported by the higher brick post at its corner, was a naked woman with long golden hair. She was smiling wistfully and not quite looking them in the eye. She might have got more attention from early passers-by if she hadn't been about twenty-five centimetres tall.

'Is that... a Barbie?' Kate walked down the drive to pick it up and then stopped herself dead. She stood as still as the doll. The pose. She had seen that pose.

Something cold clawed through her belly as she made the connection. The doll's right arm was held aloft and her left arm out in a gentle curve. One foot was extended forward, pointed, like a ballet dancer.

She sank to her knees, studying it with a sense of unreality.

'What's *that* about?' said Francis. 'Some kid must have dropped it, but why put it there?' He moved to pick it up but she held up her hand, sharply.

'No,' she said, getting out her phone. 'Don't touch. Francis... did you see anyone near the wall?'

'No, I only just noticed this. I haven't looked out of my front window for about a week!'

'OK,' she said, keeping her voice light. 'It's probably nothing, but it reminds me of something which might be... important. Go and have your coffee. Leave this with me.'

'Oh no. Are we being stalked by a Barbie nut?' he chortled.

'Bugger off, Francis,' she said, sounding much less freaked out than she felt. He huffed and went back inside, pulling the door shut. She took a shot of the doll and texted it to both Kapoor and Michaels, along with the message: *Could be coincidence, but check out the pose. Outside my house this morning. Should I be worried?*

Kapoor called her back a minute later. 'Stay where you are. Don't touch it. Are you alone?'

Behind her, Sally's door opened and her neighbour stepped out, wondering what was keeping Reggie's running buddy.

'No, I've got company,' she said. 'Is this... something... do you think?'

'Nobody's seen the photos outside Marathon, have they?' he said. It wasn't a question; it was a statement. She felt her face get hot. There was only one person outside Marathon who'd seen the Caroline Reece photos. Well, two, if you counted the photographer.

'I'm coming out,' he said. 'Stay put.'

'What's up?' Sally called across the wall.

'Sally... I'm not going to be taking Reggie out,' said Kate. 'Something's come up at work.'

'That's OK, love,' said Sally. 'I'll give my sister a call; see if she can take him out today.'

Kate sank onto the damp grass, cross-legged, and stared at the doll. Could this be just a bizarre coincidence? Or did it mean something? They would need to find out if a doll had been found near Melissa's place... or Caroline's or

Tessa's. If it had, the families of the victims would not have made a connection... because none of them had seen the photos. Naked Barbie dolls littered the charity shops, tips and jumble sales of the western world; it wasn't uncommon to see one. It wasn't even unusual to see one left somewhere in a pose. People found dropped dolls, action figures and teddies in the street and then they often put them somewhere visible, in case the child in question - or its mum or dad - came back looking for it.

Maybe that's what had happened here; maybe someone had stood her there because they thought a little girl who'd dropped her lived here, in the house. Maybe that pose was just coincidental. If it had been the Tai Chi pose of Tessa McManus it might be more definite... more scary.

Even so, she wished it *had* been posed like Tessa. Because Lucas Henry had not seen Tessa's photos. He had no idea of the pose in those shots. He'd only seen Caroline's deathly ballet pose.

Hadn't he?

18

Lucas came up out of the cellar to get more blankets. It was cold down there but seemed dry enough for storage. His art didn't do well in direct light or in damp. Soon it would be time to move his body of work and it would need blankets. Aunty Janine had left him a full linen cupboard with many very useful old candlewick bedspreads, perfect for wrapping and protecting.

He'd finished the last canvas in the early hours of the morning, unable to sleep and determined not to dwell on Kate Sparrow and the insistent call of Sid, now back in his sock and buried in the bottom of the rucksack where he belonged.

Number 12 was blue and magenta and sand. Actual sand, picked up from Bournemouth beach earlier in the summer. It was as close to a recognisable seascape as his original work would ever get. He had booked a rental van to get the collection to Mariam's gallery next week. Since returning to the UK he'd been weighing up getting a car, but couldn't summon the enthusiasm - or the budget. In the bungalow's standalone brick garage he had found his late aunt's elderly Triumph

Bonneville, a reminder of her wild child biker days in the 1970s, covered in old sacks and pretty well preserved. He'd worked on it a little over the summer and it was rideable. For now it would do him just fine, but van hire was the only option for the collection. He didn't like to think of hiring it a second time, in October, when his slot at the gallery concluded. The hope was that his work would be sold to assorted collectors; not that he'd carry it all back to the bungalow again once the great and the good of the art world had deemed it undesirable.

He needed to think of a name for the exhibition, and for each picture, but he was struggling with it. Words weren't really his thing; pictures and patterns were.

He counted another six bedspreads and some flannelette sheets in the linen cupboard, stacked neatly above the cold boiler. Then he decided to leave them there while he went to the kitchen. There were fresh, ripe blackberries in a cardboard punnet in his fridge (only acting as a cool box at present, without electricity). He'd got some oats, too, so he made some porridge with UHT milk, boiling it up on the camping stove he'd borrowed off a neighbour yesterday. He tipped the porridge into a tin bowl and sprinkled the berries on top, thanking the bountiful brambles that bordered the acre of land out back.

A name. Mariam had been hounding him for a collection name for weeks, for her posters, leaflets and online platforms as well as the press releases. He'd come up with nothing so she had simply titled it: LUCAS HENRY: WAITING.

But she'd said that could change at any time if wanted to edit it. Truth was, WAITING was probably an excellent name. He had been waiting for half a lifetime, for something which would probably never arrive. Absolution. He could offer that up for a title... but it was probably a little on the nose for the Wiltshire Constabulary, which was undoubtedly planning another visit in the next few days. Not Kate though. She had texted to say that a consultancy fee would be sent to him on BACS as soon as he let her have his account details. There was no sign off; no actual *thanks and goodbye* but he knew she wasn't planning to see him again. He could guess why. She had acted on impulse, getting him involved in the Marathon case, and now she was paying the price. Her superiors would have discovered who he was by now. She should have passed this up the chain of command before coming to visit him.

He still wasn't sure why she *had* come to visit him. How she had happened to find him. But people talked and maybe she'd heard something from someone who knew Aunt Janine. Salisbury was a small place, barely more than a market town; only named a city because of its cathedral. People knew people.

And she had that other one, didn't she? Someone else she wanted to ask about. Sid didn't lie.

Still, he'd probably never know now. She wasn't likely to be back; one of her colleagues would be knocking on the door next, asking for alibis. He hoped he could supply them, but he wasn't sure he could.

He felt a small pang at the thought of not seeing her again. It wasn't disappointment, exactly... she'd actually messed up his life quite a lot, whether she knew it or not. He had been on a simple, relatively contented mission to get his art on show and to start making some money. Maybe live in the bungalow, maybe sell it. He hadn't decided. Now he was without doubt going to get called in for questioning, it was throwing his momentum out.

Mind you, it would also be great publicity. Mariam would probably love that.

BUY A PAINTING FROM A SUSPECTED MURDERER!

Lucas Henry... suspicious then, suspicious now!

Of course, he had seen Kate again after he'd left the crime scene yesterday. It's just that she hadn't known it. She'd be pretty surprised... and probably creeped out... if she knew where he'd been yesterday evening. After walking back to his place (it was about an hour, cross country, from Frenley Woods) he'd tried to shake off the disquiet of their morning's work. But Sid was having none of it. It was as if the adventure in the woods had woken up a sleeping dog; the dowsing pendulum just wouldn't settle down again. He could feel its vibrations through his chest. Sid wanted him to go somewhere.

He'd ignored it for several hours, but in the end, as the afternoon sank into evening, the buzzy little bastard had worn him down. Lucas had given in. Standing out in the paddock with Sid for five minutes, he'd let the old stopper drop and swing where it would over an old map of Salisbury and its outskirts until the path it wanted him to follow was marked in his mind. It was a bit of a journey. Lucas got the Triumph out and rode most of the way until he reached the bottom of a hill and another wood; happily nowhere near the scene of the runner trap. This wood meandered up to a large manor house of some kind on the brow on the hill.

He'd parked the bike by a dry stone wall, chained his helmet to the back wheel, and then hopped over the wall into the quiet gloom beneath the branches. Sid seemed satisfied that he was following the path, so Lucas began to trudge up through the wood. It wasn't a large expanse of trees; he could make out the glow of setting sun on the western horizon at the far side of it. It gave way to the downslope of a meadow and a shallow valley where a stream ran. He couldn't see the stream but he didn't need to. Water was the easiest thing to sense, above or below ground. He always knew where water was.

It was only a ten minute walk to the top of the hill and the house - and it seemed likely that this was where he was meant to go - but then he heard a dog barking and running through the trees towards him. He felt a frisson of fear - what if it was a guard dog? But no. He wasn't sensing that; it was definitely coming to check him out but it wasn't the kind that would attack. Twenty seconds later the creature arrived at his feet, jumping up and clawing at his jeans excitedly. Lucas crouched down and rubbed the dog - some kind of Staffy cross by the look of it - behind its ears. 'Shhh,' he said, and the dog did. Lucas had always connected well with animals; it seemed to be a subset of his dowsing talent.

'You need to go home now,' he said, and the dog backed away, tail wagging, and then turned and disappeared into the undergrowth.

Lucas carried on up the hill, feeling an almost physical pulse from Sid and a sensation of pressure, somewhere around his solar plexus, as if a cord was attached there and some invisible entity was gently but firmly pulling him. This was always the way when he was on a strong line of inquiry. Of course, it helped if you knew what you were dowsing *for*. And he had no clue... except that it had to do with what had happened today. He really hoped he wasn't about to find a body... but the patterns in his head did not suggest something dead.

Then he heard a shout and all his senses shot into high alert. That voice! He knew that voice. It was *Kate.*

'Ooooh, right,' he groaned. 'So that's what you're up to,

you sneaky little bastard!' He stopped dead, overwhelmed by the suspicion that Sid had sent him on some wild goose chase of the heart, like a kindly mate, setting up a date with a friend of a friend. There *was* a connection between him and DS Sparrow; he knew it; had felt it the moment they met. But that didn't mean he wanted to act on it. He stopped dead, cursing quietly, aware that his new detective buddy was making her way through the trees towards him. *Damn it, Sid! If I wanted to see her again I could have called and made a date for coffee! Do you really think stalking her through a darkened wood is the way to go?!*

Sid chose not to comment. Lucas slipped deep into a thicket of holly and stilled himself utterly as a figure emerged through the trees.

'Reggie!' The familiar darkened outline of Kate stood in the gloom, turning this way and that, listening for the dog. And then she seemed to grow very still. The air felt thick between them, like jelly. He knew if he so much as breathed, the vibrations would reach her and she would see him in the shadows.

'Come out,' she said, in a calm, cold voice. 'It's OK. I'm a police officer. Just come on out.'

He didn't even breathe. She was staring right at him... but no, she couldn't make him out in his hiding place. 'Fine,' she said, suddenly turning away. 'Don't bother me and I won't bother you.'

Then she marched off, back the way she'd come. She'd no need to chase after the dog anyway; it was heading back to her at a tangent, from further west in the wood. Lucas got ready to turn around and get away from here but then he picked up something else... some other life force was also heading for Kate. And he didn't like the feel of it. Not at all.

So he followed her, treading lightly and holding his

breath. It nearly backfired; she turned around, shining her torch, twice. But the beam of light just missed him. Then she was in the car park and he could hear voices and see lights and the sense of danger seemed to fade. He let out a long-held exhalation and turned back. He was on the bike and away home a few minutes later, cursing Sid for his matchmaking tendencies.

The stopper and chain were back in the sock and the rucksack as soon as he got home.

All morning he'd tried not to think about it. He'd helped out, finding the pit and giving them some useful intel for their investigation but that was as far as it was going. He'd done as Kate had asked and that was that. He was an artist and he had a project to continue. He guessed he should get the canvases to Mariam as soon as he could; because he had a bad feeling that his plans were about to be disrupted.

He went back to the basement door. It was time to see if his last work was ready to be moved.

Then his phone buzzed. He looked at it and noted the withheld number above the message. He sighed, leaning against the door frame and briefly closing his eyes. He could ignore it, but what would be the point? They'd just show up on the doorstep. He picked up. 'Hello?'

'Lucas Henry?' The tone was familiar, if not the voice. 'Chief Superintendent Kapoor here; we met yesterday.'

'Oh. Hello. What a surprise.'

'I wonder if I could ask you a few questions..?'

19

DS Kate Sparrow had seen a lot of disturbing things during her career. Bodies with slit throats, gouged eyes and unrecognisable faces; small children left starving and naked in their own mess; a suicide bomber's remains spread across a railway station, looking like so much smashed pink watermelon... and teeth.

But nothing had got to her quite like this. The Barbie in her nude pose was now among the photographs up on the Marathon display; right alongside the real life doll in exactly the same position. Photographed at eye level, it was clearer still that the arms and legs - even the slight leftward angle of the chin - were precisely the same as the shape that poor, dying Caroline had been moulded into.

DC Michaels put down the phone and turned to look at Kate, as she slumped, chin in her palms, elbows on her desk, waiting. His end of the conversation hadn't given much away but now, as he turned to look at her, she knew what was coming.

'Yes,' he said, somehow looking both excited and aghast. 'John Reece just went out to the front of the house. He found it lying in a pile of leaves just inside the gate. He hasn't touched it and he knows not to until we get there. But he reckons it must have been there for a long time. Spider webs all over it.'

Kate gulped, picturing Barbie beaming vacantly through an orb web's handiwork. She wondered if that doll had been posed just so, too. Had the killer already set up the picture in his head before taking her? At this stage it would probably be too late to tell.

'And nobody noticed it before?' she asked.

Michaels shrugged. 'He says not, but there's been a lot on his mind, hasn't there?'

John Reece had been through hell over the past few weeks. As the husband of the first runner to go missing he'd been the prime suspect until some pretty watertight alibis had taken that title away from him. Now he was just a grieving widower, navigating a baffling new world of hurt, rage and despair. His torment had been given a fresh boost in the last 24 hours with a family liaison officer update about the runner traps discovered in the woods - and now there was another sick twist to wreck his world. He still wouldn't get the full significance of the doll; he was aware that photos had been sent but had not been privy to their contents. With the case still very much ongoing, there was just cause in not sharing the full details. Kate wished there might be ways and means to *never* let him see the horror show his wife had become, alive and dead.

'OK,' she said, 'You call Tessa's partner - I'll call Melissa's.'

'Let me get you a coffee first,' said Michaels. 'You look like shit.'

'Thanks,' she said, and meant it.

She *was* shaken. It was annoying to admit it, but it was

true. Because she didn't really know the significance of the Barbie. Until they could work out *when* the Barbies had been left (assuming there were others staking out the addresses of Tessa and Melissa) she couldn't be certain of the message. If they'd been left *before* the kidnaps and murders, it was a clear statement of intent - a sinister marking out of the victim for the pleasure of the killer. If they'd been left afterwards it might suggest some kind of sick tribute.

Either way, the message had to be for *her.* She was the only female runner at her address. It might, of course, be entirely random; the killer might not have any idea who she was. She could be - entirely coincidentally - the next on his list. She fitted the bill; she was slim, athletic and in her 20s. She was considered attractive. She had a regular running route, albeit a bit thrown out since having to take Reggie out. Normally she ran further and deeper into the woodlands that bordered the outlying streets of her home, taking a route along the river and then deeper into the trees, following the fox and deer trails where few other runners or dog walkers went. She needed the headspace; to get away from people. If she was being watched it wouldn't take long for the killer to work out her route was a remote one.

Alternatively, it might have got out that she was working on the case. The only police name mentioned in *The Journal* and other online coverage had been Chief Superintendent Kapoor; he was the public face of Marathon and he always took care to keep his officer's names out of the press as much as he could. Once a case came to trial there was no anonymity, but by then it was usually no longer a security issue.

Nothing was watertight, though. People talked. Innocently, too. Even Sally might have talked; she was certainly having a great time entertaining her old mum with her detective friend's notorious case. Who knew who else she'd told? Her sister? Her other neighbours? Sally was lovely, but she did like to talk.

If it *had* got out, it might just be that the killer had somehow got wind of who she was and decided to mess with her mind. It was pretty obvious that he liked an audience for his work and enjoyed goading the police. Conrad Temple, their friendly crim psyche, was going to flip his lid over this development. He was on his way into the station now to be briefed.

Michaels came back with coffee; white, one sugar. 'Thanks.' She took it gratefully, had a few steamy sips, and then picked up her mobile. 'Let's phone,' she said.

Isaac Buchanan snatched up the call on the second ring and she had to immediately tell him there was no positive news... yet. The hope was the worst. She felt like a murderer herself, every time she killed it. 'Isaac, listen, something else has cropped up,' she said. 'It might not be relevant, but it could be. Can you take a look around the front of the house? In the garden and on the road outside? See if you find anything unusual?'

'Unusual how?' He gulped.

'Like... a doll... a toy... something like that,' she said. 'PLEASE - if you do see something, you absolutely *mustn't* touch it. Do you understand? In fact, don't touch anything, anywhere in the garden or just outside. Just walk out there carefully and look. Stay on the phone with me while you go.'

He got up and left the house, taking the mobile with him. She could hear his nervous breathing buffeting the inbuilt mic as he stepped outside. She knew there wasn't much garden for him to check; if she remembered rightly there was a wooden fence, just six or seven steps out, and a few straggly bushes; no driveway.

'Can you see anything?' she asked, after thirty seconds of his ragged breathing.

'No,' he said. 'I can't see anything. What's all this about?'

'Isaac, keep looking. Try the street. Anywhere outside which faces towards the house.'

He sighed and she heard him walk out onto the narrow lane. 'Look, unless there's someone hiding in the post box, I can't find anything,' he snapped. Then she heard him mutter, quietly. "What the *fuck?*'

'What? What is it?'

'Something's in the hedge,' he said. 'Something pink.'

'Isaac - don't touch it!'

'Wait,' he said and then the phone beeped and she realised he'd gone into live-stream video mode. She accepted the feed and saw the shaky view of a thick dark hedge to one side of a red post box; the kind of small rectangular box found in the country. Buried in the hedge was a face; a face she was getting to know uncomfortably well.

She became aware of Michaels at her side, abandoning his call and staring at the scene on her mobile. Even through a satellite transmission and a grainy screen image it was possible to make out the pose of the Barbie's limbs, held firmly in the twigs and leaves. One hand up, palm down; one hand down, palm up, one knee raised. Naked Barbie Tai Chi. Kate felt her flesh crawl.

'We're on our way, Isaac,' she said. 'Whatever you do, don't touch it. Please, get back on your doorstep and keep an eye on it to make sure nobody else touches it either, but don't touch it and don't talk to anyone about it. Do you understand?'

'Yes,' he said. 'Just get here, please. And tell me what the fuck is going on.'

They checked in with Kapoor, updating him fast. 'I can't reach Tessa's family.' Michaels said.

'Pass that call on to Mulligan,' said Kapoor. 'Get out to Isaac Buchanan and gather the evidence.'

'We're on it,' said Michaels.

Kapoor cast an appraising look at Kate. 'I'm not sure you should be going.'

'Why not?'

'Isn't it obvious?' he said. 'If naked Barbie is the calling card, I think we all know who he's lining up next.'

'He is *not* going to stop me doing my job,' she said. 'And he's hardly going to catch me while I'm in a car with another copper, is he? If he really wanted to get me, he wouldn't have warned me like this!'

'You're assuming he knows who you are; that he's aware you're on the Marathon case,' said Kapoor. 'If he doesn't know - if it's just a wild coincidence - then that's not a warning. It's just part of his sick little game, purely for his own satisfaction. A little theatre he's getting off on.'

'Either way, I *am* warned,' she said. And then she paused while both men idled, watching her. Michaels was looking clueless, but she realised that Kapoor must be thinking what she was thinking.

'If he *doesn't* know...' she mused. 'Then...'

'Oh no,' said Kapoor. 'You are not going to be a honey trap for a serial killer.'

She stared at him and then raised both palms. 'You can't ignore it. It's a massive opportunity.'

Michaels was looking from one to the other like a spectator at Wimbledon. 'What?' he said, slowly cottoning on.

'You mean she should go running and hope he digs a hole for her?'

'I'm not at all comfortable with that,' said Kapoor. Which didn't mean he wouldn't do it.

'So... if you find you *do* get comfortable with it,' said Kate, 'there's still a lot of time between now and my next run tomorrow. Time for us to get back to Frenley Woods. And maybe out to Tessa's place on the way back.'

'Agreed,' said Kapoor. 'Go. Stay in touch.' His desk phone buzzed and he picked up, waving them away. Kate heard him say: 'Right. Take him to three. No. I'm doing this one.'

She didn't make the connection until she and Michaels reached the stairwell and met Lucas Henry walking up it with Sharon Mulligan .

He didn't say anything to her. He just gave her a thin, weary smile. A smile that said: *Oh look. It's happening again.*

20

'Where were you between 4pm yesterday and 7am this morning?'

Lucas shivered uncontrollably. He was still in shock. It didn't seem real. None of it seemed real. He kept thinking he could wind back time and reset everything; untangle all this mess and make it work properly; the way it should be. Nobody dead. Nobody missing. No dull staring eyes gazing lifelessly up at him through a broken tomb of stone.

He should never have agreed to help. He should never have led them to the body. What had he been thinking?

'Lucas,' said DCI Gary Phillips, sounding world weary. 'It's not a trick question. We need to tick your name off the list of suspects. If you can tell us where you were and what you were doing, that's going to help us a lot.'

'I was at home,' he mumbled. 'With Mum.'

'And your mum can vouch for you, can she?' asked the other one; the one called Sarah who smiled at him sympathetically.

Lucas closed his eyes. Could she? She probably *would*

but the truth was she had been out for the count from mid-evening onwards. Mum did battle on the daily basis with the demons that whispered *'Drink!'* in her head. She tended to lose the battle round about teatime. She was usually asleep on the sofa by 8pm. Occasionally she reached her bed before she lost consciousness but more often than not he would fetch her quilt and put it over the deeply drowsing form on the sofa, propping the cushions around her to keep her on her side so she wouldn't choke if she was sick. Usually, sometime in the early hours, she would wake and stagger up to bed, taking the quilt with her, so that when the morning started it seemed like anyone else's morning. She was a functioning alcoholic and often up at breakfast.

Anyone popping into the Henry household in the morning would see nothing much out of the ordinary. Joanna Henry would be getting ready for work and Lucas would be pouring cereal into a bowl and getting his school stuff together. If he looked quiet and withdrawn, well that wasn't unusual for a 15-year-old. Of course, anyone with a good sense of smell might notice the sour scent of two bottles of Chablis still on his mother's breath and maybe spot the shakes as she poured her first coffee of the day. But if anyone ever did, they didn't let on.

So, no. Mum couldn't vouch for him. And the truth was, he often did go out at night, meeting up with Zoe and Mabel or Eddie, sometimes Zac. In the summer they'd all hang out in the parks, misusing the little kids' play area, or go off down the quarry, trying to slingshot the rats - which were as big as rabbits - or dare each other to climb its precarious cliffs. Sometimes he just hung out around his friends' houses. He wished he'd done that last night. But Eddie and Zac had gone to the Odeon and he hadn't joined them - he was broke - so there was no one to vouch for him but Mum.

'Yeah, she can vouch for me,' he said. He assumed she would. Mums lied for their kids, didn't they? And she wouldn't want to admit she was too drunk to stay conscious for best part of the night.

The coppers exchanged glances.

'How did you know where to find Zoe?' asked the one called Sarah.

He shrugged. 'I dowsed for her. It's a thing I do.'

'How do you mean... dowsed?' The man sat back in his seat and folded his arms, waiting to be enlightened. He was heavy set, in his forties or fifties, Lucas would guess, and did not have the kind of face that might readily wear an expression of wonder.

Lucas got out the old bottle stopper on a chain that his aunt had given him when he was ten. He didn't tell them he'd named it Sid. Why make his life harder?

'Some people use rods or twigs,' he said, letting the chain slip a little through his fingers and allowing Sid to swing back and forth. 'I can use them too if I want to, but I prefer the pendulum. It's easy to keep in your pocket.'

'So...' DCI Philips raised an eyebrow. 'You swung that about a bit and it magically told you where to find the body of Zoe Taylor?'

'It's not magic,' said Lucas. 'It's just a skill. Anyone can do it, really.'

Phillips glanced across to his colleague. 'Flippineck. We missed this bit in training college. This must be where we've been going wrong all these years.'

She smiled tightly at him and then focused back on the teenage boy opposite her. 'So, you used this... to tell you where Zoe was.'

'I was looking for Zoe and for Mabel,' he replied.

'Mabel's mum asked me to. She knows I dowse for stuff. I've done it for years.'

'So how does it work?' she asked.

'I don't know, really,' he muttered, keeping his eyes on Sid. 'I just feel... patterns. I can sense the shape of things. The frequencies. The way they vibrate.'

DCI Phillips leaned across the gouged veneer of the interview room table. 'So how am *I* vibrating right now, Lucas?' he asked.

'On a low frequency,' said Lucas. He eyed the man stonily. 'Like a cow.'

Philips smacked his fist down on the table. 'Why did you kill her, Lucas? Turned you down, did she? Did you try it on with Mabel too? Did you bury her somewhere else?'

Lucas closed his eyes. He gathered Sid and the chain into his fist, pressed the fist to his forehead, and tried to breathe steadily. Perhaps he'd always known it would come to this.

'WHERE WERE you between the time you left Frenley Woods yesterday and 7am this morning?' asked Chief Superintendent Kapoor.

Lucas felt a shiver pass through him. A shiver from sixteen years ago. 'I walked home, cross country,' he said. 'Then I carried on working on my art collection.'

'Art collection?' The super raised his dark eyebrows. Beside him a female detective who'd introduced herself as DC Sharon Mulligan, also raised her brows.

'Yes,' he said, trying not to sound testy. 'I have an exhibition in Salisbury in just over a week. I've been creating a series of canvases.'

'Was anyone else with you, while you were at home, working on your collection?' asked Kapoor. 'Can anyone verify what you're telling me?'

'This,' said Lucas, 'is the reason why the police don't get more help from dowsers. If we help out we just incriminate ourselves.'

'I'll take that as a no, then,' said Kapoor. 'And is that it - you were just at home throughout? Until this morning?'

'No,' he said. AMPR may well have picked up his journey, so there was little point in hiding it. 'I went out on my bike - my motorbike - early in the evening.'

'Around what time?' asked Kapoor.

'Shortly after six, I'd say,' he replied. 'And I was home again by around eight.'

'Where did you go?'

'Just for a ride. Around the B-roads mostly. I enjoy it. It's a good de-stresser.'

'And that's all? No actual destination?'

'Ah - no. Actually, I stopped at the Co-op on the way back, picked up some dinner.' This was true. It was all true. He didn't, though, mention stopping the bike by the dry stone wall, climbing into the woods and mildly freaking out their colleague in the dark.

'So... if we ask at this Co-op, they're going to have some security footage of you wandering in for your dinner, yes?' said DC Mulligan.

'I hope so,' he said. 'Because I didn't get the receipt. It was one of those self checkout tills.'

There was a moment of silence and then he just lifted his palms and came out with it. 'Look - you know and I know that I've been here before. Let's just cut to it. You think I look good for this serial killer thing. But we also all know that you don't have any real evidence to pin this on me, apart from the fact that I *very stupidly* agreed to help Kate Sparrow.'

Kapoor exchanged a wordless glance with his colleague. Lucas had to hand it to the guy; he was much cooler than old DCI Phillips back in the day.

He sighed. 'Take some swabs - do what you have to do. And then, I'd like to go home please. Unless you have a reason to charge me, I believe I'm entitled to do that. I've got a lot to do to get ready for my exhibition.'

Kapoor looked at DC Mulligan and said: 'Well, if he's offering...'

'I'll get the kit,' she said.

21

Melissa Hounsome was nil by mouth now. It was time to withdraw fluids. Already there was a graceful concave arc below her ribs; no food for three days could have quite a surprising physical effect.

Her belly was taut and flat between her hips, which were also more pronounced now, like the fins of an old iron radiator. It had been necessary to drug her more heavily because she had thrown out the pose a little with some struggling. It was irksome because the heavier drug load had made her drool for a while. But now, with no further fluids, that would soon stop.

The moaning had been annoying too. It had been worth a little drool to stop the moaning.

But this moment - as she hung there in silence, back in position, starvation beginning to sculpt her form into something more beautiful and dehydration just about to begin its finer work - was a moment to savour.

The work was nearly complete. A tryptic had always been the plan. But now a fourth part was on its way. This was the curse of the creative; just when you thought you had your work done something random would come along and hijack you; push you further on. The muse could come at any time.

DS Kate Sparrow had suddenly presented herself when the collection was nearly complete, her very existence proving that it was not. DS Sparrow had opened up a whole new ending. It was a delicious way to end it too. Incredibly apt. This whole exhibition had become a love letter to the police, after all.

And how sweet it would be to conclude this work with a dying doll which would understand, as it was dying, what it was dying *for*.

For art.

22

The eyes staring through the plastic sent a chill through Kate. She tucked the bagged up doll into the evidence satchel and dropped the satchel in the footwell.

'Straight to the McManus place, yeah?' said Michaels.

She nodded, still seeing poor Isaac's baffled, haunted face. He'd been desperate for information but she'd been able to tell him very little. 'It's just that another one of these was found near another missing woman's house,' she'd explained, as Michaels took an assortment of photos of the doll in situ. 'It may be coincidence... but...'

'Some sick bastard is leaving dolls around?' Isaac had muttered, eyes burning and jaw rigid. 'As a warning? Or what?'

'We don't know, and as I say, it might be-'

'You're not telling me that's coincidence!' He pointed a shaking finger at the Barbie, which Michaels, in sterile gloves, was now extricating carefully from the hedge.

'No,' she said. 'No, I'm not telling you that.' She touched his arm. 'Isaac - we're getting there. We're making more progress than we have with the other two. There is still hope - you've got to hang on to that.'

She couldn't tell him how she knew. She couldn't say, 'It's OK - it usually takes them two weeks to starve and dehydrate to death.'

There weren't more than a dozen neighbours in the road. She and Michaels had quickly visited all the addresses to ask if anyone had seen anything, anyone, anytime, leaving something in the hedge by the post box. Only three of the neighbours were in. None of them had anything helpful; just time wasting concern. Nobody had posted a letter that week and if you weren't looking for it, the Barbie would be easy to miss. There would have to be a check with the Royal Mail to find out who had emptied the box in case he or she had seen the doll; maybe help to create a time frame around when they first noticed it.

She felt a sinking sensation below her ribs as she watched the hedgerow blur past the car window. This was all just chair stacking. The dolls wouldn't have any DNA or prints; she was certain of it. But they *would* have been touched and held by the RG, through plastic gloves. She was certain of that. And that should be enough. If she could just take this one directly to Lucas, he might-

'Are you freaked out?' Michaels asked, glancing across from the driver's side. 'I would be. I would be MIGHTY freaked out.'

'Yeah. Thanks for that insight,' said Kate.

'But... at least you've got the warning,' he said. 'And maybe this creep is on CCTV along your road. They're on that, back at base. And uniformed are working along your street, asking.'

She nodded. Yes. There were quite a few security cameras on houses along her street. Security lighting too.

None outside the front of *her* house, obviously. Like a doctor who smokes, the policewoman had neglected to think about her own safety when it came to home security. She had a feeling nothing useful would show up, though, whatever quantity of CCTV they waded through. It was impossible to know when the doll had been left. When she'd arrived home last night it had already been quite dark and she hadn't glanced back at the hedge as she'd got out of the car and gone indoors; it could have been there then. She was sure she *would* have noticed the doll when she set out yesterday morning - and she hadn't. So the Barbie had to have been left there after that. This seemed to offer up a 24-hour window. Great.

Of course, in the dark was more likely. It would be easy enough to walk along her road in relative shadow and then duck behind a parked car or van and crawl or crouch-run to her front wall. Kneeling down below the range of any nearby security light sensors, it would have taken only a few seconds to position the doll.

It really didn't take a genius to work out how to do it. And not get seen.

'Did you have one when you were a little girl?' Michaels asked.

'What - a Barbie? Not really,' she said.

'Not really? I thought every girl wanted a Barbie. My sisters were nuts about them. I used to draw beards on them with felt tips; drove them wild. My sisters; not the Barbies.'

Kate sighed. 'My sister had one when she was little and I sort of inherited it for a while but I didn't like it. It was an old version, I guess - all pneumatic boobs and tippy-toes and those stupid vapid eyes and rosebud lips. Me and my little brother used to take turns chucking it out of the bedroom window, to see what shape it made when it landed in the garden.'

'Sick,' said Michaels, and she didn't think he meant cool. More... well, sick.

'Yeah,' she said. 'It broke in the end. Wires came out of its arms and legs.'

'Health and safety alert!' tutted Michaels.

'Like I said, it was an old one. You could do serious damage with one of those spikes. They don't make 'em like that anymore...' She gave a dry chuckle.

They both glanced towards the bag in the footwell and lapsed back into silence.

Tessa McManus had lived in a cottage on the edge of Dinton, a village about twenty minutes drive to the north west of Salisbury. They'd had a message from DC Mulligan that Tessa's partner was away. Paul Cartwright had gone to stay with his parents in Kent, trying to come to terms with what was almost certainly the murder of his girlfriend of three years.

The cottage was on the end of a terrace, on a quiet side street just off the main road of the village. A quick scout around the front garden showed no sign of a Barbie or any other doll. There was a high hedge and some ash trees on the far side of the road; the perimeter of some fields. Plenty of backdrop for a Barbie diorama. But it had been nearly a month now since Tessa had vanished and whatever might have been left, there was no sign of it now.

They worked their way through the neighbours again and once more got nothing helpful.

'I'm starving,' said Michaels. 'I need a sausage roll. Let's try the village shop.'

They walked around to the main road and found the shop; well-stocked with food, sweets, household stuff, stationery, an incongruously massive LOTTO and scratchcards display and a dispirited young man slouched at the till, staring at his phone.

They bought sausage rolls and orange juice and, once they'd paid, Kate took out her badge. 'We're investigating the disappearance of Tessa McManus.'

He brightened up immediately and put the phone down. 'Any news?' he asked. 'My mum won't shut up about it.'

'We're not here to give out news,' said Kate, smiling. 'But we were wondering if anyone's seen a Barbie doll, lying around in the street. Any time in the past four weeks. Probably naked.' She shrugged and unscrewed the top of the orange juice.

The young man stared at her. Yep. That was about all she'd got from anyone today. Including Barbie.

Then he leaned back on his stool and yelled: 'Jasmine! Jaaaaaz!'

Kate exchanged a surprised glance with Michaels.

A small dark haired girl, around eight or nine, emerged through the beaded curtain behind the till, sucking an ice pop. 'What?' she asked.

'You found that doll, right?' said the young man, who Kate was now sizing up as the girl's brother.

The girl shrugged, gnawing on the chilly blue stick.

'Hi,' said Kate, giving her a wave. 'No school today?'

'Teacher training day,' said the young man, looking weary.

'We're looking for a doll,' said Kate, smiling at the girl. 'It might have been left in the streets around here. What kind did you find?

'A Barbie,' she said.

'OK,' said Kate. 'Whereabouts did you find it, sweetheart?'

She shrugged again. The boy suddenly broke into an angry torrent of what Kate took to be Punjabi. The girl rolled her eyes and disappeared.

'She is getting it for you,' he explained. 'And she will show you where she found it.'

Jasmine returned with a bedraggled-looking Barbie in an orange dress.

'Did it have the dress on when you found it?' asked Kate.

Jasmine, who had lost the ice pop but had much blue evidence of it on her lips, shook her head. 'She had no clothes on,' she said.

Another sibling was found to mind the till and the boy, who introduced himself as Mo, took them to the spot where Jasmine thought she'd found the doll, his little sister trotting along beside him. Kate and Michaels said nothing as they were led back to the high hedgerow directly opposite Tessa's front door.

Their helpers didn't protest as the doll was bagged. They looked pleased to be of service. Jasmine thought she'd found it there about three weeks ago, leaning against the hedge, but she wasn't sure. Summer holidays didn't help kids to pin down exact timings, Kate remembered; they floated on for a vast stretch of six weeks - and then ended abruptly one cool September morning.

'Thank you,' said Kate.

'Will you give it back?' asked Jasmine.

'Um...' said Kate.

'To the little girl who lost it?' Jasmine went on, swinging on her brother's arm, wide-eyed. The brother looked less buoyant. He glanced across at Tessa's cottage and clearly made the connection.

'Maybe,' said Kate. 'Would you like to have the dress back?'

'No,' giggled Jasmine. 'She shouldn't be going around with no clothes on!'

The sausage roll didn't do it for Michaels. He was still hungry as they drove back to base.

'Mind if I pull in here and get a sub?' he asked, breaking through her dark reverie as they drove along a line of shops about five minutes from the station. There was a Post Office, a newsagent's, a Greggs, a hair salon and a charity shop, and a dozen parking spaces against the kerb.

'No, go ahead,' she said, and he pulled in.

'You want something?' he said as he got out. 'You didn't eat the sausage roll. I can get you a sub or a pizza slice.'

She wasn't hungry but she registered that she really should eat something. 'Pizza would be nice. And some water.'

He nodded and shut the door, leaving the keys in the ignition. She leaned over and took them out. She'd seen too many movies where the bad guy leaps into the driver's seat and makes off. Her eyes roamed the suburban strip of shops. In the window of the charity shop, amid a tangle of bric-a-brac and toys, a small pink face smiled out at her, chilling her bones. Another bloody Barbie. She just couldn't get away from them.

Suddenly she undid her seat belt, grabbed the evidence satchel and exited the car, locking it behind her. Her feet carried her to the shop window and she stared down at the doll. It was wearing a grubby lace wedding dress but aside from that detail it could be the exact same Barbie as the one in her satchel. Same scruffy blonde hair; same expression; same body shape, without any doubt.

Kate gulped. She looked up and down the row of shops. The Greggs had been pretty busy; she'd noticed four or five people queuing in it before Michaels had headed in. She checked her watch. It was just past two. He'd be another five minutes at least.

Once she had decided, she moved fast. She stepped inside the shop and bought the Barbie for a quid, getting out again fast, mumbling something about how her niece would love it.

Then she turned left and ran to the Post Office. Inside she bought a Jiffy bag. Leaning closely into the customer parcel wrapping area beside the greetings cards, she extricated the plastic evidence bag and hooked the Barbie out of it. The sin of touching it without gloves reverberated through her policewoman bones, but she pressed on; it was immaterial now. The doll she'd just bought had been put into a paper bag by the charity shop assistant; Kate hadn't touched it at all. As soon as she'd pulled the orange dress off the Dinton Barbie she shoved the doll into the Jiffy bag and then tore a lined page from her police issue notebook and used the pen on a chain to scribble: *This was held by the RG. Do your thing, Lucas. K*

She stuffed the note inside with the doll, her heart thumping. Then she sealed the padded envelope, addressed it and took it to the counter. Mercifully the clerk was free and took the envelope at once. 'What's in it?' he asked.

'A doll,' said Kate. 'Next day delivery please.'

The clerk nodded in that aimless way they always did (was he about to rip open the parcel and check?) and stickered it up before slinging it into the sack behind him. Kate paid and then, as the clerk's attention was taken by a new customer, paused back at the parcel wrapping area. She surreptitiously pulled on her plastic gloves and extracted the charity shop Barbie from its paper bag. Ripping the wedding dress off it, Kate re-dressed the doll in the orange frock, shoved it into the plastic evidence bag and then back into the satchel. She threw the wedding dress into the waste paper bin beneath the parcel wrapping shelf. If any of the four people in the post office noticed her behaviour, they didn't give any signs of it. Nobody was looking her way. She couldn't see a security camera anywhere near her, either.

She let out a steadying breath, made for the door and walked back to the car. To her enormous relief, Michaels wasn't sitting there, wondering where she'd gone. She could just see him heading out of Greggs now. So she walked on towards him. 'Did they need to nip over to Italy for the pizza dough?' she quipped.

He laughed and handed her a paper bag and a bottle of water. 'Guy in front wanted to pay in coppers!' He rolled his eyes.

Back in the car they took a five-minute lunch break before resuming their journey. It was with a will of iron that Kate poked down the pizza. Guilt was clamping her throat shut. She had just broken the law in a massive way. She had not only tampered with evidence... she had actually *disposed* of it. She had sent it to someone who was now a *suspect*!

Was she *insane*? This was career-ending stuff.

But no, she reasoned, she wasn't insane. It had been a logical decision. She was as certain as she could be that the Dinton Barbie would have shown up no more helpful DNA or any other clue than the others. It didn't matter whether it reached the police or not. There was nothing more to learn from it. Even if it *had* been sprinkled with traces of their killer back when it was left, three weeks of play by Jasmine would almost certainly have wiped that away. The charity shop decoy would, genuinely, be just as useful.

But the Dinton Barbie, now on its way to Lucas, would still have its connection to the killer. Lucas, unlike anyone at Wiltshire Police's forensics team, *would* be able to pick something up from it. And it might just be enough for him to locate the killer… or Melissa.

Would she ever have been able to convince Kapoor to let her do that?

Never.

So… she'd had no choice. She'd made the right decision. It might be illegal but it was the only thing she could do.

'Bad call?' asked Michaels, peering at her closely.

She started, a cold sweat blooming across her shoulders in an instant. 'What?'

He nodded at the doughy slice of pizza which she'd managed only two bites of.

She focused on it and then put it back in its bag. 'Yeah,' she said. 'It's just really hard to swallow.'

23

'There is no way I'm sending you out on a run, on your own,' said Kapoor.

Kate shook her head. 'I wouldn't be on my own. Not if we stake the place out. And I'll have a tracker on me.'

He looked extremely put out. Because he knew she was right. This was an opportunity they could not pass up.

'It probably wouldn't happen *tomorrow* anyway,' she said. 'I think he'd need to be watching me for a while. Working out my route. The route I've run with Reggie the last couple of times isn't off-road enough; nobody would try to pull off a kidnap in the park and along the river walk; there are too many people about. No... what I need to do is go back to my old route. If he's watching me, that's the kind of regular route he'll be hoping for.'

'We don't need to wait 'til morning,' said Temple, who was leaning up against the windowsill, clutching his ever present folder. 'Our guy is a prepper. He finds the girl, then finds her route and then he gets out and lays his trap, the night before. If we know her route we can watch it for late night activity. We could get him then. No need for bait in running shoes.'

Kapoor nodded. 'That I like better,' he said.

'So... we need to know your route before you go out in the morning,' said Temple. He put up his hand like a keen boy scout. 'I'm up for a run; I need to work on my PB. We can go out today if you want. Early evening..?'

'I can run too,' said Michaels, looking aggrieved.

'Um... I think running with two bodyguards might actually turn our guy off the whole idea,' pointed out Kate. 'I should go on my own.'

'No,' said Kapoor.

'OK, so how about Kate goes on her own this evening but I go running too and we happen to meet up along the route... just before it gets too off-road?' said Temple.

'I could do that,' said Michaels. 'I'm her partner.' He gave Temple a condescending look.

Temple laughed. 'Sure... her policing partner in the woods! That wouldn't raise any questions in a serial killer's mind, would it?'

'How would he know that I'm her partner?' said Michaels.

'You're right,' said Temple, grinning. 'He probably doesn't. It's probably just a random coincidence that he's Barbied up our Kate here and he has no idea what he's up against.' He tapped his fingers percussively on his folder and added: 'But if he *does* know Kate's a detective on his very own case, it's a very different game he's started playing. He may well have watched you both working together. I'm new here. I haven't been to any of the crime scenes. He won't know me. So I'll run along this evening and we can work out some good surveillance points. What do you say?'

'I say,' said Kapoor, 'that you're a crim psych, not an officer, and you have no business taking your duties outside this station.'

There was a pause. Temple looked at his nicely polished brown shoes. Kapoor chewed on something invisible.

'I also say it's not a bad idea to make use of you. Assuming you can keep up with her.'

Temple shrugged and made a cartoonishly modest expression. 'Sub four hours in the New York marathon last year. I think I can keep up.'

Michaels looked extremely pissed off.

'Then we're on,' said Kate. 'I'll head out from mine around six-thirty this evening. If you're running past the kids play area around six forty-five, you'll see me there. We can head off on the same path after that point. Act like casual running acquaintances... exchange a few words here and there... but don't run side by side. Just in case I *am* being watched - although I don't think he'll be on the clock until the morning, if he is at all. We can fit one of my running shoes with a tracker. I'll get one from tech before I head home today. '

She looked at them all, registering Michaels' disappointment, Temple's enthusiasm and Kapoor's reluctant acceptance.

'If he *is* watching me... great. Let's reel him in.'

'Just remember,' said Kapoor. 'He's not a trout. He's a pike.'

24

Wendy was unpleasantly surprised to encounter Graeme in the corridor outside Mrs Newton's room. He was wearing blue overalls and carrying a bucket of wet grout. He winked at her. She ignored the wink and angled her shoulder away from him so she could get past him in the narrow passage. She was a bulky woman, though, and he wasn't making it easy, deliberately angling himself so that he brushed against her.

'Graeme, move over,' she hissed, aware that the door to Mrs Newton's room was ajar, and Mrs Newton's daughter was in there with her, talking.

'Oh Wendy,' he groaned. 'You know what I want from you.'

'If you don't shut up you'll be eating that grout,' she warned, glaring at him.

'It's been too long,' he muttered. 'I'm running out of happy here...'

She turned to face him fully and spoke in a low, calm voice. 'Get on with your work and leave me alone. I do *not* expect to be accosted by you in my workplace. If you keep this up I will complain.'

'Will you?' he said, smirking. 'I don't think you will. Because if you tell on me... I'll tell on you.'

'Your word against mine?' she countered. 'A respected, long-serving RGN versus a creepy handyman with personal hygiene issues..?'

'You've been quite happy with our little arrangement, though, haven't you?' he said. He poked a yellow finger into the grout, leaving a sucking hole in it as he pulled out again. 'It's suited you pretty well. I bet you want more, don't you? It's never quite enough is it? You think you can stop... but you can't. There's always another-'

She stamped on his foot; her stout black clogs flattening his worn old trainers and he sucked in his shout, also aware of the old lady and her daughter just a few steps on the other side of a half-open door. His eyes bulged though and he went pink in the face.

She stared him down and he finally limped away, calling her all the worst names he could summon up. She cursed herself too, though. She should never - *ever* - have embarked on her little secret life with Graeme. If she hadn't needed the money so much, she would never have done it. At first it was just a few times; and purely - she thought - for his own gratification. After a while, though, it had become a regular thing and he wasn't the only one who wanted what she could supply.

An assortment of drugs. Drugs to get you high; drugs to calm you down; drugs to improve your sexual performance; drugs to send you to sleep. In her position it wasn't difficult to get them; it was often down to her professional opinion whether a resident needed a higher dose of their medication. She would request more and the doctor would supply extra on the subsequent prescription. Then she simply continued to give the lower dose, pocketing the extra tablets or phials. It was also easy to skim a little off from her old ladies and gents; a missed dose here and there. It did no harm. There was no way she was compromising the health or safety of the residents. The carer's weren't qualified to guess at what she was doing so nobody had a clue.

Once she'd set up her supply chain back in the spring it had become almost routine to factor in her extra needs. The packages were left in the kitchen garden, under an upturned bucket behind the compost heap. The rolls of cash were left in her locker; she'd given Graeme a copy of the key. She needed to stop, though. Soon. This couldn't go on. And recently she'd been getting the impression that Graeme wasn't just messing with her when he did the sexual predator thing. She was experienced in anatomy - female *and* male - and there had definitely been a hard on in evidence in the corridor.

She shivered. Took a breath. Stepped into Mrs Newton's room.

'Oh, hello Wendy,' said the daughter - Sally, her name was.

'Hello,' said Wendy, ratcheting a smile up her face and going to check the bathroom. 'How are we doing, Mrs Newton?'

'She wants to get a cat, she does,' Mrs Newton says. 'Dogs is just a pain in the arse.'

'*Mum!*' said her daughter, reprovingly.

'It's always the same. You have to get back for the bloody dog,' said Mrs Newton. 'The same bloody dog as broke your leg!'

'It's just a minor fracture, Mum,' Sally replied. 'And it hasn't stopped me from coming to see you, thanks to Kate giving me a lift, bless her. *And* she takes him out on her runs in the morning.'

'What kind of dog is Reggie?' Wendy called out as she mopped the wee off the toilet seat. These small tasks were well below her pay grade but she often did them anyway. Also, it helped to be doing something. Her appraisals always said she should try harder with her small talk. It was easier when she didn't have to do eye contact too.

'He's a Staffy-Labrador cross,' said Sally. 'He's good for my health; you know, he gets me out walking him every day.'

'Not so good for your health now, is he?' her mother pointed out, gleefully.

'I'm getting better,' said Sally. 'In fact, I might even see if I can take him out in the morning because I can't keep relying on Kate. It's not fair. She wants to get out for her proper run tomorrow, round the woods. She can't do that with Reggie in tow. He'd run off and get lost - or jump up at some lady. She can only go round the park with him. I told her to take a day off from looking after my mutt and just do her usual run. She needs the headspace. She's the police-woman, Mum, remember?'

'Oh,' said Wendy, coming back into the room and checking the drug chart stuck to the wall. Mrs Newton seemed to be up to date.

'She's dealing with that Runner Grabber case,' said Sally. Then she put her hand over her mouth and stretched her eyes comically. 'I shouldn't say!'

'It's OK,' said Wendy. 'Your mum's told me all about it!'

'Well, it's not like Kate actually *tells* me anything,' said Sally. 'She doesn't. But you know, it's a shocker, isn't it? I keep telling her to be careful.'

'Have you had your tea, Mrs Newton?' Wendy asked.

'No,' said the old lady, looking baleful. 'You smell bad.'

'Mum!'

Wendy nodded. 'I'll nip down to the kitchen and see what the hold up's about.'

Passing through reception she saw the policewoman in question, leaning on the wooden counter. 'Can you call through to Mrs Newton's room?' she was asking. 'I'm taking Sally home and I really have to go now.'

By the time she'd come back through from the kitchen the reception was empty and, glancing through the front door she could see, in the deepening twilight, the gleam of the policewoman's blonde hair as she waited out there in her car. She could also see Graeme, leaning at the side of the porch, sneaking another fag and staring at the policewoman too.

She went to the door and stood, silently, until he looked her way, dropping the roll-up into the planter in a reflex of guilt before he realised it was her.

He grinned and held up a grout flecked flat blade. 'Work, work, work,' he said, getting up and ambling back inside.

She wanted to tell him he should be on some kind of register. But then she remembered the truth. Since the spring of this year... so should she.

'Busy, busy, busy,' he muttered. 'Grouting today, clearing out the barn tomorrow.'

Wendy was hit with the certainty that it had to stop. She just needed to work out how.

25

The insoles came as a pair but only one held the GPS tracker. Kate dug her ordinary insoles out of her running shoes and poked the new ones into place. They weren't a good fit; buckling slightly over the instep, so she tried an old pair of Nikes that she hadn't yet managed to bin (she always found it hard to give up her old shoes). Fortunately there was still a fair bit of wear in the Nikes - and they were a bit roomier, so the tracker insoles fitted inside more easily. She tried them on and they felt OK.

She checked the clock; she needed to get going if her rendezvous with Temple was going to happen. She wished she'd been a bit firmer with Sally about getting a cab to the nursing home. Arriving home around four-thirty, the plan had been to have an early meal and then get changed into her running gear in plenty of time to get out at six-thirty. After the stresses of the day, she could have used a little downtime.

But she'd found Sally on her doorstep just as she was finishing her microwaved curry. 'I'm SO sorry,' Sally said. 'Could you possibly run me up to the home? Mum's kicking off about something again. I don't know what's got into her lately. I think maybe her medication's being changed. I can get a cab back... I think.' Sally had looked so woebegone at that moment, Kate had rolled her eyes and said: 'It's fine. I can do it both ways, as long as we're back by six - six-fifteen at the latest.'

And so she'd spent another visiting session in her car, checking e-mails and messages and thinking. Thinking a lot. She shivered every time she recalled her mad moment in the Post Office, sending the Barbie to Lucas. What was she *thinking* of?! What on earth did she expect him to do with it? Use its little tippy-toed legs for dowsing sticks and follow a magical path to the killer's lair?

But he did it before, didn't he?

OK... so he found the keys...

No. Before then. Sixteen years before then.

Yes. He'd found Zoe's body. But not everybody believed he'd found her with dowsing. A lot of people believed he'd found her because *he* put her there, buried in that quarry. Mum had never believed that, though. Had she..?

As usual, Kate had needed to go into the reception area and get someone to call Sally down, or she would have been late. They'd only got back with five minutes to spare. Now, as she laced up her trainers, she knew she'd need to sprint to reach the kids' play area on time. There was only about an hour of light left now, as summer gave way to autumn. Enough to follow her usual route and allow Conrad Temple to tail her and make a note of good surveillance points. She could have done it alone, really. Her phone app supplied a neat, shareable map of her route and she was perfectly capable of advising on surveillance spots herself. But she understood everyone's concern. She would have been taken aback if they hadn't shown it.

Anyway, assuming she wasn't kidnapped right away the next morning - and she wouldn't be because the killer would surely need some plotting time if he *was* tracking her - some surveillance could be put in place tomorrow evening in case the RG dropped by overnight to dig a pit.

It wasn't very likely, was it? She just felt it. It was way too straightforward. Their guy was sharp; it couldn't be that easy. Unless he *wanted* to be caught.

'Does he want to be caught?' she asked Temple, fifteen minutes later, once they'd gone off-road and she was fairly sure nobody was following.

'Maybe,' said Temple. 'Sometimes they do. But I don't think our guy really wants that so much as the notoriety. And it's early days. I mean, three women... it's nothing, is it? Not when you compare it to Fred and Rose West or Ted Bundy. I think RG's got a lot more pictures to send.'

'Why is he sending them to us, though?' she went on, running a few paces ahead of him and not turning back; if anyone was watching from a distance it wouldn't be obvious they were talking. 'Why not get them online? Send them to the papers? Print out fliers and drop them around the city?'

'Well, for one thing, all those options are quite easy to trace back to the offender,' Temple said, barely puffing at all despite her quick pace. He clearly wasn't bluffing about his marathon prowess. 'And for another... I think he's getting off on the evidence board.'

'What? *Our* evidence board?'

'Uh-huh. That's his gallery, isn't it? He's seen all the cop shows; he knows there's a big evidence board. He knows his work is being scrutinised more keenly than any fresh installation at the Tate Modern. Every detail of his composition, lighting, any little props that might be clues. To him... it's an exhibition.'

'Sick bastard,' Kate couldn't help but mutter.

'It's perfect,' said Temple. 'A guaranteed audience; breathlessly awaiting the latest release; emotionally charged and engaged at every level. Total attention.'

'You sound impressed,' said Kate, risking a glance back.

He was smiling as he ran. 'Oh yeah - I'm impressed,' he said, cheerfully. 'I'm gonna bang a left... see you round the bend.'

She nodded, understanding. They were not meant to be buddy runners and, just in case someone *was* watching, he needed to be taking another path for a while.

When they met up again, Temple a few paces ahead of her this time, she said: 'Do all crim psychs secretly want to *be* a criminal, do you think? You know... plan and execute the perfect crime and get away with it?'

He gave a shout of laughter. 'How do you know we're not? I could have pulled off half a dozen perfect crimes and gotten away with them by now! The point being that you wouldn't know.'

She felt the slightest prickle of unease. 'What made you want to be a crim psych, then?'

'I'm just fascinated by the human mind,' he said, heading towards the pale light at the edge of the woods and the last few minutes of her route. 'What makes people tick.'

'What makes *sickos* tick,' she pointed out. 'Admit it - you've got a thing for psychopaths.'

'You're right,' he said. 'But don't misrepresent psychopaths. They're not all killers. Most of them just lack empathy. In fact, it's a useful characteristic if you want to get on in life. Did you know that most world leaders are psychopaths? One in five CEOs displays psychopathic traits. These guys - they don't worry about your finer feelings while they're planning their career. They don't waste time with self-recrimination or guilt. They don't care what makes *you* tick - unless it helps them in their plan for success. And the statistics suggest they've got it right.'

'So... RG is a psychopath, yeah? So why isn't he just running the country? What makes him kill women instead?'

'I think he's an attention seeker,' said Temple. 'But that's pretty standard; it's always more nuanced than that. I'm guessing he's taken a shot at getting attention in a more conventional way and maybe had a lot of knockbacks. So... he probably thinks he's very clever and very talented and can't understand why the rest of the world doesn't agree.'

'And is he? Clever and talented, I mean?'

'He's pretty smart to have got this far, I guess. He knows how to cover his tracks. And there's art in what he's doing, I guess. If you like that kind of thing. You know... some people are into decay and suffering. They think it's kinda beautiful. You know about the hunger artists, right?'

'The what?' said Kate, watching his broad shoulders brush through springy limbs of holly and holding herself back a few beats to avoid getting thwacked in the face.

'Hunger artists. They were a thing from the 18th right up the early 20th century. People would pay to watch these guys starve themselves. Kafka wrote about it. Hunger artists would present themselves - slowly emaciating - as an art form.'

'That's a hell of a way to earn a living,' said Kate.

'Sure was. These guys - they normally were guys - would put themselves in a cage and get guards in to watch them to be sure they weren't cheating. Water only... usually for forty days. I think your good people showed great appreciation for David Blaine when he did something similar, suspended over the Thames a few years back.'

'Oh god, yes,' Kate laughed, remembering. 'In his Plexiglass coffin! They chucked kebabs at him, I think. That's how Londoners show their love of culture. But I don't see RG starving *himself*. Can you make someone *else* a hunger artist?'

'Sure looks like it,' said Temple. 'OK - I think we got you all mapped out now. I'm going to head down this way and you go on and get home. See you in the morning. Well... you shouldn't see me.'

'OK,' she said. 'Wait... you mean first thing?'

'Yup. Kapoor's got me in harness now. That's what happens when you volunteer. He doesn't want to take any chances. But don't worry - I'll be out of sight. Just keeping tabs from a distance. Just in case.'

Kate shook her head. 'Nothing will happen tomorrow. It's too soon. If he sticks with his MO I'm guessing it's going to be another week or two before he makes his move. He waits for the current victim to die before he goes after the next one.'

'Don't set too much store by the MO,' said Temple as he headed away. 'People aren't dependable. Not even psychopaths.'

26

Sometimes the joy of establishing a pattern was breaking it. There were some things which couldn't be changed; some habits that no artist would break, but that was usually in the realm of execution, not preparation.

Tessa's second set of photos were sent - but Melissa wasn't yet dead. It wouldn't be long; she didn't seem to be hanging on as tenaciously as Caroline or Tessa. True, the withdrawal of water had happened rather sooner with her - but that was down to a sense of urgency which had a beautiful rhythm all of its own. Even before Kate Sparrow had presented herself as the fourth part of the work there had been this sense of speeding up; an almost mathematical, exponential velocity that could not be slowed. When the muse took you, *owned* you... you had to go with it.

There was also a sweetness about the overlap. To have the next dying doll in place and able to witness her predecessor breathing her last had become an integral part of the whole installation. If this project wasn't about stills it would be very tempting to film it on Hi8 - to capture that moment when Sparrow understood her part in the work. But for this her face would need to be mobile and the drugs didn't really allow for that. It was fascinating to ponder how much the dolls understood; how aware they were of what part they were playing. There had been conversations - attempts to explain, but it was impossible to guess at what they were thinking. They may have been in pain, of course, and that clouded your mind.

No. Hi8 didn't fit. Instead, a series of images could be used to create stop motion film. Hundreds had been taken, documenting the decline and decay. A Ray Harryhausen style animation was going to be mind-blowing. Quite the finale.

Until the next project.

For now, though, it was important to plan the last capture. It would need to be different. And it would need to be soon. The last doll might not be so easy to collect.

It would be all the more satisfying, though.

27

Lucas was in the paddock with Mabel and Zoe when the postman arrived. In reality he was tangled up in his sleeping bag on the wrought iron bed, but in dreamland he and his two lost friends were in the long grass, talking.

'You shouldn't have done it, Lucas,' Mabel was saying. 'You know you shouldn't have done it.'

She was holding Sid on his chain and the little glass stopper was marking out triangle shapes in the air, which seemed fitting. They had been a triangle, the three of them, all that summer. 'Three's a crowd,' said Zoe, from under her pile of rocks.

'I never meant this to happen,' Lucas said, splashing red and purple paint across the grass and coating ants and grasshoppers in it until they went stiff and still, entombed in acrylic.

'Too late for your apologies,' said Zoe and she began to push up through the rocks, sending them tumbling into the long grass. Lucas screwed his eyes shut to avoid seeing her blood-soaked hair and dead fish eyes, but he could still hear the rocks clunking and knocking…

He shot up in bed, sweaty and jangly, and realised the knocking was real. He staggered out into the hall and made out the shape of the postman through the opaque glass in the front door. His late aunt's old sunburst wall clock showed 7.13am.

'Bloody hell, you're keen,' said Lucas as he opened the door.

'Sorry mate,' said the postman, a middle-aged guy who handed him a padded envelope. 'We start early. Couldn't fit this through the letterbox.'

Lucas accepted the parcel, waved the guy off and went back inside. There was nothing on the envelope to spook him but hairs were prickling on the back of his neck as he took it into the kitchen and peered at the label. In the cool grey light which shafted through the window above the sink, the handwriting looked familiar but he couldn't quite place it. Some voice inside him said: *Don't.* He took a moment, drew breath, and then ripped the top end of the parcel open.

A face smiled vapidly up at him. A doll? He tipped the plastic figure out onto the draining board and stared at it. A naked Barbie.

Why the hell was someone sending him a naked Barbie?

He looked inside the envelope again and this time found a scrap of notepaper with a message on it. 'Oh Jeeezuz,' he groaned. 'What the hell?'

This was held by the RG. Do your thing, Lucas. K

He left the doll on the drainer and sat down at the table, feeling winded. And angry. Wasn't it enough that she had already dragged him into this thing and made him a prime suspect? What the hell else did she want from him?

Suppose he *did* try to pick something up from this doll. And suppose it led him somewhere. To another body probably. Then what?

A helpful call to Chief Supt Kapoor? 'Hi! It's me, again! You know, that suspect that you can't quite pin anything on yet..? Well, maybe this will help. I've just found another body!'

Fuck it. He just wasn't going to get any further into this. She could take this bloody thing back.

He went into his room, threw on his clothes and then grabbed his leathers and his helmet. He could get on the Triumph and deliver this right back to her within the next half hour. Catch her early, before she went to work, and tell her straight to leave him out of it.

He got the bike out of the garage and nearly took off before he realised he'd left the doll behind. And Sid. He'd left Sid. He felt another rush of anger as he returned to the kitchen and seized the doll. Now he had to get Sid out again. He knew where Kate lived; he'd followed her home as far as her road, discreetly, after that night in the woods when he'd nearly been discovered. He'd not ridden right up to her door but he was pretty sure he'd know it. Pretty sure wasn't quite enough, though - he needed Sid inside his shirt to be certain he wasn't about to have a wasted journey.

He found the backpack and emptied everything out of it, released Sid from his sock, put the chain around his neck and then strode back out to the bike, bag in one hand, a Jiffy bag of Barbie in the other. Astride the Triumph he pulled the doll out for a moment and looked into her depthless eyes. *Should he try?*

A memory of his swabs being taken yesterday came to him, making him grit his teeth. He shoved the doll back into the padded envelope and slung it the backpack, shrugging the bag onto his shoulders before pulling on his helmet. He throttled up and headed off towards the city, doing seventy on fossil fuel and fury.

A minute after he'd gone, the two plain clothes officers in the unmarked car parked along his lane radioed in to base.

'Henry's just taken off on his motorbike,' said one of them. 'And guess what he just shoved into a backpack?'

28

Kate hadn't slept well. She was haunted by her actions over the past few days. She'd always been such a keen follower of procedure; not because she was a slave to it but because she knew of too many occasions when not sticking to it meant an otherwise watertight case could just be thrown out in court. She didn't see the point of putting in days of detective work and getting a collar, only to see it all fall apart because someone failed to read the rights or fill in the forms or follow the simple rules that kept a copper - and a suspect - safe.

She guessed it didn't take a psychoanalyst to point out that working on a case where women had gone missing might just be chiming with her inner child. Memories of Mabel were never far from her mind.

They hadn't been especially close but only, she suspected, because of the age gap. There was a five year gulf between them - not quite enough for Mabel to feel maternal towards her and way too much for them ever to share the more grownup secrets Mabel spoke to Zoe about. Occasionally Mum would make Mabel take her little sister along with her on those long summer walks to the fields and streams and quarry. Mabel *hated* taking her. A ten-year-old tagging along seriously cramped her style.

Oddly, Mabel's friends were quite sweet to her and included her much more than her sister did. Zoe talked to her about school and teased her about a boy in her year she confessed to fancying. Zac and Eddie showed her how to use the slingshot. Lucas called her Titch and laughed at the things she said - in a nice way. She'd had a bit of a thing for Lucas. Unspoken, of course. Once he'd sort of rescued her when she tried to climb the quarry wall up to the cheese pie; an odd bit of rock overhang which did look vaguely like a slice of pie and lit up yellow in a bright sunset. He'd noticed her halfway up to it one day when the others weren't keeping an eye out. He'd run across the bottom of the quarry and climbed up after her, arriving just at the point when she'd got scared and frozen, dizzy with the height and realising she'd made a stupid mistake. He had talked her into giving him her hand and then, slowly and carefully, guided her back down to safety.

Mabel had laughed at him and told him he should be a Girl Guide leader.

It was the last outing Kate remembered with Mabel.

She'd never tried to bury what had happened. Indeed, her mother had done much to keep Mabel's memory alive and encouraged Kate and Francis to talk about her often.

She had also taken more practical steps, enrolling them both in martial arts classes about three months after the day when Zoe's body had been found and Mabel's had not. 'I can't spend the rest of my life wondering if one of you is going to be taken from me too,' she had said. 'I want you both to promise me you will do this properly. I want to know you can look after yourselves. I want you to get all the belts. All of them.'

There had been no argument from either of them, although six-year-old Francis was cut a little slack and didn't actually get beyond his brown belt. He let the practice slip when he got to secondary school. Kate had scored her black belt before she was twelve - and she continued to attend classes and even teach the younger kids until she left the area for university.

She often wondered if the outcome would have been different if her sister had been a black belt too. Lying in the soft light of dawn, half awake in the few minutes before her alarm would go off at 6am, Kate tried to picture Mabel's face. She was finding it harder and harder to do. She needed to look at the photos in the hallway again and try to recommit those pretty features to her memory. To lose sight of Mabel, even in her mind's eye, seemed like a betrayal.

She went around to collect Reggie at 6.15. She had decided to do this late last night and had let Sally know. She felt bad that she'd not taken the dog out yesterday morning, thanks to the arrival of Barbie. She knew Sally's sister hadn't helped out yet, either. A dog like Reggie really needed exercise. Besides, part of her needed to do something normal before she went off on the more significant of her runs that morning. And running with Reggie, irritating as it was, had become a normal thing over the past two weeks.

She got into her gear and pulled on her Asics before letting herself out into the cool of the morning. It was a little overcast and that autumnal chill was already in the air, but she knew after five minutes of running she would be warmed through.

Sally passed the dog and his lead through the front door, still in her dressing gown. 'You're a bloody angel,' she said, as Reggie launched himself at Kate's chest. 'Don't you go anywhere off the track, though!' She raised her eyebrows warningly.

'I won't,' said Kate, neglecting to mention that this was the very next thing on her plan for her working day, once she'd delivered Reggie back home.

The lead looped at an angle across her chest, she set off with her furry, four-footed satchel bag, trying to convince it to run neatly by her side and not pull ahead or suddenly dart sideways into a garden or across the road whenever it smelt a cat. Reggie, to be fair, was getting a little bit better at this with every trip they took, once he got past his ritual attempts to snog her. Perhaps biting his ear had helped.

They did a circuit of the park, reaching it along a leafy access lane at the end of the cul-de-sac, where Reggie tried repeatedly to first drag the pair of them into the bushes and then under a dark blue van in pursuit of a squirrel or a rat or something. But once past this point he settled into a fairly steady trot. Coming out this early meant there were blissfully few people around; just a woman carrying a lead on the edge of the trees at the far side, presumably waiting for her dog to emerge from the undergrowth.

Kate did three laps of the park with Reggie on the lead and then let him off so he could run around a bit and deposit some droppings on the grass. She collected them in one of the biodegradable sacks Sally had given her and responsibly deposited the bag in a bin. She checked her watch. OK. Time to take Reggie back and then get the proper run in.

She called him over. He ignored her. She got a gravy bone biscuit out and called again. He came running. She connected the lead to his collar.

'Have you seen a terrier?'

She jumped and looked around to see a short, middle-aged man walking past with his spaniel. 'Lady over there says she's lost her dog,' he said, glancing towards the far end of the park where Kate had noticed the woman standing alone earlier.

'No, I haven't - what does it look like?' Kate asked.

'Sandy and brown, apparently. Border terrier I think,' he said. 'Answers to Billy.'

'Oh - OK - I'll keep an eye out,' she said. 'Although we're off home now, so...' But the fellow dog walker had moved on with a wave.

LUCAS PARKED the Triumph a little way up the road, leaving it resting on its kick stand while he strode down the pavement towards Kate Sparrow's house. He reached her front door with a few prompts from Sid and then tried to shove the Barbie through the letter box. It wouldn't fit. It was too bulky. He pulled the doll out and weighed up just shoving it through without the envelope.

He came close to ringing the bell and handing it to her in person... but that would mean a discussion and he had decided, on his journey, that entering into a discussion with her was unwise. And anyway, she wasn't there. As soon as he allowed his dowsing mind to focus he could sense that. She wasn't far away, though, and he suspected she would be here soon. And he should get gone before then. Even without the peculiar and unwelcome circumstances of meeting her, he found DS Kate Sparrow unsettling. There was something both attractive and repellent about her which he couldn't fathom. He could certainly work out why he would be attracted - she was borderline beautiful and clearly intelligent and interesting. What bothered him was the goosebumps he felt whenever they had been close, like on that car journey to the woods.

Of course, she was a police officer - and his past experiences with Wiltshire Police had been pretty traumatic. But it was something more than that; he'd felt utterly discombobulated. Sid was positively thrumming with it. It was disconcerting and in truth, Lucas just didn't want to pursue it. He hadn't returned to Wiltshire intending to stay; he'd always meant to sell up the bungalow and get out again, fast. It was only meeting Mariam and getting talked into the exhibition which had slowed him down, really. Probably.

Why would he want to be here? Why return to the place where his teenage life had been wrecked?

Unfinished business, said Sid. Or some part of his inner psyche. But some unfinished business needed to stay unfinished. He came out of his reverie, realising he was standing on her step, in broad daylight, holding a naked Barbie doll. It was early but there were people up and about. Cars passing by. He needed to make a decision. He shoved the doll back into the envelope and rested it inside the alcove of the arched brick porch, where it would be seen by anyone who got up close to the door. He kept the note in his pocket, though. Just in case... of... something.

He walked three steps away and then stopped, gritted his teeth, turned back and picked up the envelope. Damn it. He couldn't leave it there. It might be significant. It might actually lead him to- NO. Just NO, he told himself. He wouldn't do it. But what if..?

He strode back up the road to his bike, clutching the envelope and feeling like an idiot. An idiot who couldn't make one simple decision. Already he could feel an almost static charge coming from the doll. Patterns were trying to form in his head; frequencies were ready to buzz. Sid was warm against his skin.

And then Sid was cold. Very, very cold.

A few steps from his bike, Lucas stopped dead.

REGGIE SEEMED agitated as they ran along the cut and into the access lane which led away from the park. It was 6.45am and Kate knew she needed to get him home and do a quick turnaround to start her regular route at seven. She mustn't keep potential stalkers waiting. Things to do, places to go, murderous kidnappers to snare.

Reggie whined and pulled against the lead, jolting her out of her pace. Then she realised Reggie wasn't the only one whining. She could hear another noise... something else... whimpering. She glanced around at the shadowy undergrowth, sighing. It would be just her luck to find that bloody runaway terrier and have to take it back to its owner. That would throw her timings out even further.

There was nothing to see though. Although she could definitely hear whimpering; high-pitched and keening, and Reggie was straining to get closer to the sound... which now seemed to be coming from the other side of that blue van they'd passed earlier. Or maybe under it.

'Bloody hell,' she muttered. She noticed one of the dented back doors was open slightly... the gap was wide enough for a dog to get through. 'Reggie, stay here,' she said, looping his lead around a tree trunk and clipping it securely. If the terrier was in there she didn't want boisterous Reggie to bash his way in and freak it out. It might bolt before she could catch it.

Freed from her furry charge, she moved quietly towards

the van. There was more whimpering and even a scratching noise. Kate eased the door open and peered into the gloom, ready to grab what was inside.

When the cool material covered her face she had just enough time to register how deeply stupid she had been before she lost consciousness.

Lucas's left hand found the note in his pocket while his right clutched at the pendulum, which felt like ice against his skin. He spun around and stared back up the road, gripped by a sudden and complete sense of dread.

Kate. It was about *Kate.*

He was about to break into a run when he realised his bike would be quicker. He turned around to get to it and then two dark figures stepped out of a car parked just the other side of it. They were upon him before he could draw breath.

'Lucas Henry,' said one of them, pulling his arms behind his back. 'I am arresting you on suspicion of the kidnap and murder of Caroline Reece, Tessa McManus and Melissa Hounsome. You do not have to say anything but-'

Lucas swung his elbows violently and pushed the two male officers off him before one of them could clip the handcuffs around his wrists. Dropping the padded envelope, he sprinted along the pavement, hotly pursued, in the direction of the trees at the far end of the cul-de-sac. *There.* That was where she was. *Kate.*

'STOP! POLICE!' bellowed his pursuers. They were only two seconds behind him; he had to be faster; he had to get there *now.* The icy glass juddering against his heart was taking no argument.

'It's not me!' he yelled back. 'We've got to get to Kate! NOW!' He should have saved his breath though, because he needed every lungful. He was reasonably fit. He'd run away from the authorities before, but that had been for by-law infringements - painting in continental tourist spots without a permit - not for kidnap and murder. Kidnap and murder tended to turbo-charge a copper's chase rate. They were close enough that he could feel the swipe of a baton. He also heard their feverish radio communications, calling in the location and requesting back up. Then... oh bollocks... a rising electrical whine.

A second later he felt his body go completely rigid. He tipped onto the pavement, his limbs dead, unable even to put out his hands to break his fall. His face hit the edge of the pavement with a clunk that sent his teeth through his tongue. He lay, spasming, dribbling blood, completely incapacitated as his eyes rolled up into his skull. It was probably for only five seconds, but it felt like five minutes. Five minutes in which he was unable to speak. Five minutes in which he lay with his right cheek squashed into the gutter, nose down in grit and oil, and watched the narrow line of light beneath the undercarriage of a parked car where a set of tyres rolled past, unhindered and unnoticed. If anyone was out on this road, all eyes would be riveted on him. Nobody would note what that vehicle looked like... not its colour... certainly not its number plate. Nobody would have a clue what had taken Kate Sparrow away, because nobody even knew it existed. A murder suspect lay groaning incoherently on the floor, very possibly pissing his pants as all bodily control deserted him. Who was going to be looking anywhere else?

Nobody would know and Lucas was quite unable to tell them.

29

She was very dimly aware of the journey; she knew they were travelling, but she had no idea how long it took. As well as the chloroform or whatever had hit her face, she'd felt the prick of a needle in her arm and now it was as if she was encased in something like the expanding foam they injected into wall cavities. She couldn't move or speak or see and her hearing was muffled, like she was underwater. The smell, though, was overwhelming... chemical and sickly sweet. It made her gag.

Her mind floated, veering from nothingness to panic and dread, back to nothingness and then to absolute fury with herself. How easy she'd been. She hadn't felt rage like it since her first term at uni when a fellow undergrad had talked her into bed with a sob story about his mum dying in the summer. When she'd spoken about it to another student, the girl had smothered her face, trying not to laugh, and explained that the same second year had shagged at least half a dozen girls across fresher's week using that very line. His mother was as alive and kicking as his sex drive. It had taken all Kate's self-control not to go and kick down the door of his grotty digs and incapacitate the little shit for the rest of the term.

Today she was incapacitating nobody. Today *she* was the one lying motionless, sliding helplessly on the greasy metal floor of an old van as it turned a corner and drove away from her home, away from her brother, her neighbour, the dog, and all hope of rescue.

Stay sharp! Her head voice said. *Notice things! Work out where you're being taken!*

But she couldn't do any of those things when she was barely conscious. She tried not to let her mind wander across the grim collage of photos she knew so well on the Marathon display back at base; photos that made up a storyboard for her short-term future. She knew what was planned for her. If Caroline, Tessa and Melissa had had any advantage over Kate Sparrow, it was that they, at least, had not known the full horror of what awaited them.

The van stopped. The back door opened. She was wrapped in a blanket or a sack, pathetically unable to resist. She was carried through a dim passageway, from outdoors to indoors, aware of the shifting of the light through the weave of the material over her face. Her vision was returning, grainy and grey.

She lost consciousness again for a while and then came to, aware that her captor was pulling her running tights off. She kicked feebly against it but the undressing continued with a solid, relentless purpose. Soon she lay naked and shivering on what felt like a thin, damp mattress.

A face loomed in front of her. She screwed up her eyelids, trying to focus. The face looked familiar.

'No...n-n-noooh,' she heard herself utter. She felt her hands move, scrabbling feebly in the air.

This was the Runner Grabber? Of all the people...

'DRINK THIS.'

Lucas took the cup of tea with a reasonably steady hand. Then a latent tremor caused it to splash hot liquid down his wrist. He put the cup down on the stained wooden table top and sat still, seething.

Once the taser had done its job he was in a patrol car, cuffed and subdued, within a couple of minutes. A small crowd had gathered to watch; residents alerted by the shouts and stepping outside to gawp at the scene. He wished they'd stepped outside a little sooner; they might have noticed the vehicle.

He had tried to alert them as soon as he could speak, on the way back in the car, but his furious and garbled delivery, not helped by his sore and bleeding tongue, did not endear him to his captors. Given that they clearly believed he *was* the Runner Grabber (you didn't need high level dowsing powers to work *that* out) he guessed he shouldn't be surprised.

'Call Kate,' he said, feeling extraordinarily wired and angry 'Call her now! I'm telling you, she's been taken. By the RG. I'm not making this up!'

'Yeah sure,' said the guy sitting next to him, taser at the ready.

'She went past in a van or a car... while you had me on the pavement.'

'Is that right?'

'Just... please... call her. Radio her. Do what you do. I'm telling you, she's not going to answer.'

The guy with the taser stared him down and said: 'And why would that be?'

'Because she's been taken!' he yelled. 'For god's sake! You're wasting time!'

'If you're so keen to help out, tell us what you've done with Melissa Hounsome,' said the guy in front.

Lucas shook his head, defeated. Sid burned like ice against his skin. There was only one way he was going to get help for Kate. On his own.

But the guy in the passenger seat was at least radioing into base. He was talking in codes, but he mentioned DS Sparrow and was clearly waiting for news.

By the time they'd got him in the interrogation room, uncuffed him and offered the tea, he knew they were worried. They couldn't track her down. She wasn't answering her mobile or her radio. She wasn't where they thought she would be.

They didn't know where she was.

The problem was, they were convinced *he* did.

Kapoor was back. He was the one who'd brought tea. There wasn't much sympathy in that gesture. Lucas suspected that rehydration was in the Manage Your Recently Tasered Suspect chapter of the police handbook.

Sitting next to him was DC Michaels, the guy who'd taken his statement back in the woods two days ago. Michaels looked just about ready to launch himself across the table and rip Lucas's face off.

Kapoor was carrying the padded envelope. Wearing sterile gloves, he extracted the Barbie from it and placed it on the table in front of Lucas.

'Can you tell me why you were trying to post this through DS Sparrow's front door an hour ago?'

Lucas sighed. 'Because she sent it to me. I got it in the post. She asked me to use it to help dowse for your Runner

Grabber... or his victims. Check with the Royal Mail - the postman will verify it.'

'The postman will know what was in the parcel?' asked Kapoor, raising an eyebrow. 'The things they can do in the 21st century!'

'No... I mean he will verify that he delivered a package,' said Lucas, struggling to hold on to his patience. 'And you can check the handwriting on it - I'm guessing you've got samples of Kate's writing. In fact... there's a note from her. It was in the parcel but then I had it in my pocket.'

'A note,' repeated Kapoor. 'From DS Sparrow. To you.'

'Yes. You emptied my pockets. You should have found it.'

The two men exchanged glances. The younger one shook his head. Then said, for the benefit of the tape: 'We have logged the contents of Mr Henry's pockets and I can confirm there was no note of any kind found in them.'

Lucas closed his eyes for a few seconds. It was entirely possible he'd dropped the note during the chase. His fingers had been wrapped around it when he'd been jumped by the police patrol; it could easily have been pulled from his pocket and lost when he withdrew his hand and turned to run.

'So... what's the Barbie about?' asked Kapoor in a light, conversational tone. 'Does it symbolise the women you've kidnapped and murdered? Or... is it connected to Zoe Taylor and Mabel Johanssen?'

Lucas felt as if he'd been tasered again. He gripped the table and breathed in and out, trying to fathom what on earth he could say to get his freedom. Because if he couldn't, then there was next to no hope for Kate.

Finally, it came to him. He flattened his palms on the table top and looked Kapoor in the eye.

'I can take you to them,' he said.

'Take us to whom?' asked Kapoor.

'The victims. I can take you to them today. Now. But only now. This next hour. If you can't make that happen, then I won't help you.' He looked at the utilitarian clock up on the grey panelled wall. 'I'm counting down from now, and I'm not going to say another word until you take me out of here and let me lead you to them. If you can't do that within an hour, my offer has ended.'

KATE WAS ON A WOODEN CHAIR. Her wrists were attached to the back of it with what felt like plastic ties. Each of her ankles were bound to the front legs of the chair in the same way.

There was something behind her. It wasn't a wall but some kind of vertical panel which crackled and rasped. It was close enough to make contact with her hair, which was no longer in the high ponytail she'd put it into for her morning run. When she turned her head, which she was still just about able to do, she wondered if she was hallucinating. Her sideways glance was met by myriad other sideways glances. Smiling faces. Rosebud lips. Shiny hair. Someone had hung heavy duty plastic sheeting across this basement. Suspended from brackets on the low, mould-spotted ceiling, the opaque curtain was studded with rings and wire ties. Held in the rings and ties was a vast collection of Barbies. The hair styles, skin colour and vintage were wildly varied, but every one of them was naked and each carefully posed in her bindings. The effect was like the frescos of people that had been found in the cursed tombs of Egyptian kings. Kate suspected she was in a tomb now, and similarly cursed.

In fact, as she peered dizzily around to her left and right she wasn't certain they were *all* Barbies. Some of them looked like Sindys; the UK equivalent of Barbie back in the 70s and 80s. There were others, too, less identifiable; cheaper plastic knock-off dolls which could wear the same outfits but never quite pull off the genuine Barbie style. Clearly the interior designer on this job had experienced some sourcing issues and cut corners.

'You're lucky,' her captor had said. 'You get to see it. You get to *understand* it; to appreciate it. None of the others have had that.'

There was a rustling sound ahead of her. Another curtain, hung from more ceiling brackets, was being pulled open. Pearly white light was dancing about as the vinyl moved in waves.

'You will be here soon. Taking her place when she's finished.'

Kate's head wasn't fixed in position... not yet. She could look away if she wanted to. And she did want to. The smell that wafted across once the curtains had parted was enough to make her gag. She recognised the shape that was revealed; the woman hanging there, head tipped to one side, mouth slack and dry. Crucifixion was the word that sprang to mind. Melissa Hounsome looked terrible; her pale skin mottled like marble. Kate could just about make out the faintest rise and fall below her starkly outlined rib cage.

But the exhibition had worse to display than poor, dying Melissa. Melissa was positioned on, and in front of, a large roll of suspended white paper. The kind of thing photographers use in their studios.

Behind the roll of paper, hung in the far corner of the room and only dimly lit, was the desiccated body of another woman, long dead. That had to be Tessa McManus, Kate realised, with a thud of horror and sorrow. Literally hung out to dry like a piece of biltong.

Noticing the direction of Kate's gaze, the creator of this horror show shrugged as if apologising for an untidy kitchen. 'I've got a bit behind with the plan. She should be buried by now. Still - making art isn't a perfect process, and meeting *you* threw everything out! Now I've got you here, though, everything will be fine. I will get all of this finished... and it'll be nice to have some company for the last part. You'll still be able to talk for a while...'

30

Five officers went along. Three travelling with him and two in another patrol car. It had taken Kapoor less than half an hour to arrange it, and he wasn't leaving this field trip to his subordinates. The chief superintendent was in the front passenger seat while DC Mulligan drove and another officer - the one who had tasered him in the street - sat to his left in the rear. Two more - one of them DC Michaels - followed in another unmarked car close behind.

He was cuffed and under no illusions that Taser Boy was more than happy to stun him again for the slightest reason. The rage inside the car was like a fog; he could virtually see it. There was also, threading through it, increasing anxiety about Kate as no reports of her whereabouts came in. They'd found something, though, he knew this. Nobody was telling *him* anything, obviously, but he sensed something had been discovered which perhaps gave some validity to his claims that she'd been taken. Maybe there were signs of a struggle at her home; a dropped ID badge, a puddle of blood.

Lucas gulped, his own fear for her now smogging up the space even further. He needed to contain it. Getting emotional was never helpful when you needed to dowse. Emotional *connection* - yes. That was very useful, when it was contained and channelled. But fear and panic were no good to anyone.

It was clearly not lost on Kapoor where they were going. The chief saw the significance and was already putting two and two together and coming up with thirty-seven. Good. Lucas had decided to put the man's ever hardening convictions about him to good use. They were travelling towards the summerlands of his youth; towards the woods, the heath, the quarry. Because if Lucas Henry *had* come back to repeat crimes of the past, why *wouldn't* he revisit the scene of Zoe's death and Mabel's disappearance? It was page two in the Sick Bastard Killer's Handbook.

But that wasn't the reason he'd chosen Critchley Down.

They stopped the car at a gravel parking spot which overlooked the sloping landscape. No other traffic was visible on the B-road. The day was flat and grey and the view lay before them like a dull tapestry. The woods, on the mid-point horizon, were entering the darkest phase of their greenery before giving in to the palette of autumn. The edge of the quarry was marked by a rise and fall of silver heather and yellow gorse to the west and the unnamed river marked a meandering grey scar through the heathland to the east.

He was helped roughly out of the back seat by Taser Boy. The other patrol car pulled up and the additional officers got out, one carrying a camera bag. Everybody stood, looking at Lucas, faces impassive.

'Are you leading us to bodies?' asked Kapoor. 'Or are they still alive?'

'I don't know,' said Lucas.

Kapoor was suddenly in his face; his features a mask of fraying restraint. 'What have you done with Kate Sparrow? Is she out here?'

Lucas held out his handcuffed wrists. 'These have to come off.'

'That's not going to happen.'

'You have the pendulum, yes?' Lucas asked. They had taken Sid, along with the contents of his pockets, back at the station. He'd made it clear he would not help them without it.

DC Michaels took the pendulum out of a plastic bag in his jacket pocket and held it up, his face colder than January.

'I can't dowse in handcuffs,' said Lucas.

'Why do you need to dowse?' asked Kapoor. 'Surely you remember where you left them? The women you kidnapped? And tortured. And murdered.'

'I literally cannot help you,' said Lucas, 'without free hands and my pendulum.'

There was a long moment. Lucas held his connected wrists higher. 'Look - there's five of you and one of me. And at least one of you has a taser. How far do you think I can get?'

Kapoor looked at Taser Boy and then at DC Michaels. Between them they communicated plenty and Lucas was getting the gist of it. They were on the clock and on the rack; genuinely scared about their colleague. Well good. They fucking needed to be.

Kapoor nodded and Taser Boy grabbed Lucas's wrists and unlocked the cuffs. Lucas rubbed the chafed skin and then held a hand out to Michaels, who upended the bag and dropped the contents into their prime suspect's palm.

'Thank you,' said Lucas. He snagged the chain into his

fingers and allowed the blue glass to swing for a few seconds. Then he angled himself south, towards the woods and the river, and began to walk. He moved like a visiting president, surrounded on all sides by a security detail. He wondered how long it would be before his escorts began to regret their footwear choices.

Most of Salisbury Plain was high and dry, a vast area of grasslands and chalk down, much of it used by the military for army manoeuvres. It was not an area that would be thought of as wetland. But here, at its southernmost point, the boundaries - blurred and much argued over on Google Maps and Wikipedia alike - were green. Very green. Water ran everywhere, over land, under land, in channels and tables and springs saturating vast sponges of chalky sediment just below the vegetation. The route he was leading them along went east of the visible river, but much of that river's journey was sunk below ground, fanning secretly through the absorbent earth, a bare finger's prod away from discovery but quite invisible to the naked eye. The bogs didn't run deep but they did run wide. Back in the last summer of his childhood they had made a game of it, using the high wiry tussocks as stepping stones across the suspiciously green parts of this shallow valley. Get it wrong and you were apt to lose a shoe. They were natives, though. They tended to lose a shoe only the once before they remembered where not to tread next time.

Lucas, always able to sense the exact depth and placement of the idling water course, had never stepped away from the solid ground. Well, only when he had to rescue Zoe that time and then only up to his ankles. Now, as he led the knot of coldly seething officers deeper into the green he could sense his path with complete certainty. Straight on for ten paces, then a kick to the right and then on again and then a curve to the left, then a flat out sprint and up over the semi-submerged log...

The question was, could he get far enough ahead to avoid another tasering? Maybe. If he kept his cool.

He heard the first one get a bit stuck. There was a grunt and a curse. He walked on, not reacting; not looking back, holding the pendulum out as if he was following it. He wasn't. He knew this place well enough without Sid, but he needed to give the impression that he was dowsing his way towards two or three serial killer victims. He wasn't.

Just four or five steps ahead was a wide tract of mire, up to half a metre in depth, with a single skinny ridge of chalk bedrock running through it just below the surface.

Someone else had sunk down now. There was more angry muttering and Kapoor called out: 'Watch where you're going! This is marsh. Lucas Henry - why the hell are you taking this path?'

'Because,' said Lucas, reaching the tract, 'I know where to tread.' He leapt forward and landed one foot on the ridge. Even as his boot struck the rock he heard the electrical charge of the stun gun and felt Taser Boy lunging towards him. But Taser Boy's boot sunk suddenly and deeply, throwing him off balance, and the metal talons of the device shot wide, anchoring themselves and their wire tails to a chunk of decaying log instead of their intended target.

Lucas fled along the ridge, amid shouts of warning and fury and the squelch, squelch, squelch of all his pursuers sinking to their knees. The urgent velocity of their chase doomed them to pile drive themselves down to the water table. Radio back up calls were being bellowed amid more shouts of rage and impotence, and he kept running, eyes straight ahead. If they'd been in America he'd probably be dead by now, shot in the back. Or at least in the leg, flailing and bleeding in the mud while they slowly caught up. They obviously hadn't felt this expedition warranted a chaperone from the firearms division. More likely Kapoor just hadn't wanted to waste the time organising it. Good for him. Good call. Good, Lucas hoped, for them all.

He didn't look back. He didn't need to see them; he could sense the space opening up between them. Ten metres, twenty metres, a kick to the right and then on again, thirty metres, and then a curve to the left, a forty-metre sprint and up over the semi-submerged log... into the woods.

Lucas ran hard and fast and took the animal trails wherever he could, the thick foliage shielding him from the sightline of the officers clambering around in the bog and attempting to give chase. Now that he'd done it - *he'd done it!* - great waves of panic and fear were rolling over him, threatening to drop him to his knees with palpitations. No. NO. There was no time for this. He marshalled his breathing and clenched his fists before putting the chain back around his neck and allowing the stopper to send its urgent chills through his skin. The marsh wasn't deep enough to hold his pursuers for long and he needed to get far enough away that they wouldn't hear him crashing across the woodland floor. He absolutely could not slow down.

He needed to get back to the outskirts of Salisbury. He needed to retrace his steps; find that route again that he'd found before.

Because that doll, that stupid, brainless Barbie doll, although she'd only reclined in his palm for a matter of moments, *had* told him something. Had told him quite a lot. He was still uncertain who the killer was but he was quite sure now about *where* the killer was. Sid had been right. Sid had tried to take him there even before Barbie showed up to corroborate the plan.

On Day One, Sid had taken him to within shouting distance of the Runner Grabber. On DAY ONE! And *he* had confused that with encouragement to get dating again. How stupid could you get? Outwitted by a lump of glass.

But he'd finally caught up and now he at least had some kind of a plan. As soon as he cleared these woods he would have to flag someone down and get a lift to East Sarum Lodge Nursing Home.

31

There was something about Graeme which made the hair prickle up on the back of Wendy's neck. Something about the way he was *looking* at her these days. That *knowing* expression. Maybe today she should just accept the inevitable. Admit to herself what she wanted to do with him. The thought had been in her mind before; she wasn't a machine, she couldn't resist forever. She sometimes wanted to do things that she absolutely shouldn't. People around here thought she was so strait-laced, but they were wrong. They'd be surprised if they knew.

He was hanging around the staff cottages a lot; too often for it to be coincidence, parking his old blue van round the back, in sight of her door, when he could just as easily have left it up near the house. OK, so there were some gardening supplies in the old barn and she knew he liked to go in there. Mostly for a smoke. And not just of cigarettes. She wondered how he'd got away with it for so long, without Margaret, the manager, noticing. But then he'd only been working at East Sarum Lodge since May. And he was the nephew of that trustee, so maybe Margaret turned a blind eye… or a blocked nostril.

Wendy was the only member of staff now living on the site; she'd been here for six years. There had been another woman - Gemma - who'd stayed next door in the row of three staff cottages, until March. She'd gone off to a new job, though, and her replacement lived in Salisbury and didn't need the digs. It suited Wendy fine. She liked the peace and quiet. She liked her place here. It was pretty basic - a two-up-two-down with a miniscule shower room on the ground floor - but the light in the back bedroom was good and she liked to work on her pictures in there on her days off; she'd even sold a couple of the wildlife watercolours to families of the residents. She'd recently accepted that painting was never going to make her rich or famous, but she still did it, when she had time.

There hadn't been much time recently. More important work took up a lot of her energy; dispensing drugs, hoisting those increasingly frail bodies around, making them look presentable for the days when they would be seen.

It took its toll, physically, though. She ached from it and sometimes she longed for a hot bath, rather than the feeble jet of shower water. Sometimes she imagined how it would feel for someone to lift *her.* To place her. To undress her. To transform her.

In the late afternoon she stepped out into the backyard area of the cottages, where the weathered flagstones were spattered with moss and lichen and an old well stood, over-grown with ivy, its wide circle of bricks topped with a thick wooden lid to prevent anything - or any one - falling into it. She eyed the well for a few moments and then went across to it to test the lid. It had been nailed in place many years ago and it was beginning to rot. It rattled up and down, the old iron pegs giving up their grip in the brick without much fight. That was pretty dangerous. Here was something for Graeme.

The blue van was parked there again. He was in the barn. Wendy felt her pulse quicken. Maybe now. She wasn't on shift for another hour. She could do Graeme in that time. It would be something to see the shock on his face as he realised the truth about her. She felt a quickening in her belly; between her thighs. Desire wasn't a regular visitor; she really didn't get much out of the violent thrust and the release of bodily fluids. She was a delayed gratification kind of girl. But today, she might be ready to go with the animal instinct.

She was in her work tunic, pockets already primed with what she needed. She'd been thinking of going in early and grabbing some food in the staff room before she clocked on... but now she needed to be satisfied in another way. She might tease him with a little naked flesh first. Why not? A glimpse, maybe; watch his face; get his reaction.

She drew a deep breath, glanced around to be certain there was nobody else about (no major worry; there never was) and stepped into the barn. The scent of damp timber, mildew and cannabis wrapped around her along with the gloom of the building. The space was lit only by three small skylights high up in the rafters. Shafts of dull grey seeped weakly through curtains of dust-laden cobwebs. The barn was cluttered with overspill junk from the house; pee-stained chairs and rusting bathroom hoists; bales of old plastic-topped mattresses, sagging cardboard boxes with faded marker pen scrawled across them, gaffer taped bin bags full of nameless shapes. In a gap between all this sat Graeme, in a fold-out wheelchair, inhaling deeply on a roughly rolled joint. An open can of Stella rested on a large wooden crate beside him, along with a glass ashtray. When he saw her he sat up straight, coughed, and waved the personal fug away from his face.

'Well, this *is* an honour,' he said. 'Welcome to my castle.'

'It's not yours,' she said.

He shrugged and looked around. 'Nobody else wants it. I'm the only one who comes in here; it might as well be mine.'

'You're not the only one,' she said. '*I've* just come in here.' She'd been in here before, too. She knew the outbuildings better than he did; in fact, she felt that *he* was the intruder, poking around, smoking and drinking and probably wanking over the stack of porn she'd seen on one of the dusty old shelves.

'Well... I'm just planning the clear out,' he said, taking another drag in a self-righteous way (if such a thing was possible). 'Why are *you* in here? Have you come for my body?' He winked and held out his arms, displaying his broad chest under a sweaty grey T-shirt. Weirdly, it made her want to grab him all the more. She could hear moaning and thought, for a moment, that she'd made the noise herself, involuntarily. How fucked up was *that?*

He blinked and glanced around, suddenly edgy. She guessed he was realising his bluff had been called. Here she finally was. A fine figure of a woman; what was he going to do about it?

A whimpering sound rose between them. Neither of them was making it.

'What's that?' she asked.

He looked mystified. 'What?'

'That noise... that... crying sound.'

He shrugged. 'I dunno... a rook? An owl?'

They looked at each other, silent, for several seconds,

and then it came again; a moaning cry. There was no denying where it was coming from.

'Move the crate, Graeme,' she said.

KATE WAS ROUSED from her drugged stupor by the sound of footsteps overhead. Across the room, Melissa didn't move. She might already be dead. Kate couldn't see any motion.

There were voices. *Voices.* It sounded like a man and a woman. Unless her captor was a ventriloquist, there were two people upstairs… and one of them might not know what was below their feet. This, surely, was the time. Kate threw her head back and screamed.

Except all that came out was a feeble moan. *Shit.* She was going to have to try harder. She had been given the privilege of consciousness so she could play the rapt audience for the artist. It seemed Caroline, Tessa and Melissa had never had the chance to meet each other but, for the sake of this psycho's ego, Kate was to be allowed to witness the grim finale of Melissa before she stepped into the role of Dying Doll herself.

She screamed again and found the noise jerked her leaden, cold body and allowed her hands to twitch in their ties. Her fingers brushed the foot of a doll, suspended behind her. She grabbed it… just because she could. Being able to move her fingers was something. Better than nothing.

There were more voices upstairs and then a scrape and the sound of something being shifted across the floorboards. Kate's heart, so sluggish for so many hours, began to pump a little harder. Could this be a police visit? Had they tracked her down? Ah but no, she remembered, she had been wearing the wrong shoes. In her defence, she *had* always intended to put on the Nikes with the tracker in the insole, but when she'd got ready to do her quick mercy trot with Reggie she had, through force of habit, put the Asics on. She'd noticed this as they set out together but she was tight for time and didn't want to retrace her steps and go back in and change. She had decided to change her footwear once she'd handed Reggie back. She would be safely trackable when she set out for the woods without the dog.

Only, of course, she'd never got back home. So no, her colleagues would not be coming to the rescue. Nor would Lucas. The idea that anyone could save her from this hell with a swinging pendant or some twitching metal rods was plainly ludicrous. Like Zoe, under her rocks, and like Mabel, lying somewhere cold and unknowable, Kate knew she was doomed.

But now there was a noise; people coming down steps, and suddenly two of them stood in the room; one staring around, gaping in shock and the other wearing a smile of pride and satisfaction. Another private viewing; clearly Kate's fixed attention wasn't quite enough.

'Jesus fucking *Christ!*' The visitor staggered back against the cellar wall, taking in the desiccating corpse in the corner, the dying woman on the frame and the white paper and the slightly livelier one trapped against a curtain of Barbies. 'Jesus! Jesus! What the hell have you done?'

Wendy turned to Graeme, her face livid and her eyes glittering. And then she stuck a scalpel blade through his neck.

32

Nobody wanted to stop and give a lift to a frantic-looking guy running along a B road in the middle of Wiltshire. Lucas only saw five cars go past anyway - and they all resolutely ignored his outstretched thumb. He couldn't blame them.

Stop. Calm down. Think.

The police search would be widening out by the second. There would be patrol cars and probably a drone on its way right now. He could keep running through the woods and fields but there was every chance his heat signature would give him away within the next hour.

Calm down. Think.

Lucas paused and then walked off-road to a tree with obligingly low boughs. He climbed up and rested his back against its trunk, allowing the vibrations of 200 years of untroubled arboreal growth to seep into him. After two minutes of steady breathing he plucked Sid out of his shirt and dangled him in a short drop between his fingers.

'Show me the way, Sid,' he murmured. The pendulum began to swing, pulling determinedly to the south. Lucas glanced south between the crisping dark green leaves and spotted a silver shimmer. The river. The unnamed river which was so flat and shallow and fused with the land up above the Critchley Down woods had deepened its course and found more resolute form in the farmlands further down the valley. Lucas climbed out of the tree and followed Sid's direction, crossing the road and pushing through some undergrowth to reach a recently harvested field on the far side. The unnamed river ran along the perimeter of the field, its course picked out by thicker vegetation; a lot of it was under tree cover. Lucas realised this was his route - but how? He wasn't into wild swimming.

He followed the fast-flowing water, clear and brown in some parts and filled with green streamers of weed in others, until he found the boat. Yes. A boat, tied up to a small wooden platform at the end of someone's big rolling green lawn, on the far bank. Through elegant specimen trees he spotted a yellow-stone mansion of some kind. He guessed the owners could probably scrape together enough to replace a boat and a pair of oars. He sighed, stepped into water and waded across; the rippling surface well above his knees.

The boat was wooden clinker built, with a flat plank seat across the middle and a smaller seat in the stern. He clambered up onto the wooden platform and then set his soggy boots carefully into the base of the boat before settling on the plank seat and checking for oars. He'd rowed before, during a spell of working at a holiday camp in Italy, so he didn't need to waste time working it out. He unhooked the rope from the jetty and sped away downstream, doing his best to ignore the fizzing on the nape of his neck which told him the distant buzzing he could hear was not a wasp, but a drone. He hoped the current was fast enough.

The current *was* fast. It was easy to row, and the action calmed him; allowing him to focus on the next stage of the plan as the banks streamed past. This river ran towards Salisbury but it couldn't be travelled by boat all the way; it became shallower and narrower and dropped below ground. He couldn't check this out on Google maps (he'd had his mobile confiscated back at the station) but in his dowsing state the twists and wrangles of the waterway were explained eloquently enough. He understood he would reach a point, within twenty minutes, where he would need to get out and get back to the road.

This point came at a bridge on the more industrial edge of the city where the unnamed river disappeared abruptly, flinging itself through a grille and down into a concrete culvert. The area around it was thick with undergrowth and trees, which he was thankful for as he grabbed at a lower branch of a rhododendron and pulled his craft to the bank. He managed to get out and tie the boat to the branch, saving it from endlessly butting the metal grille and eventually disintegrating. Under the branch and its canopy of waxy leaves his escape vessel was hard to see, and that was no bad thing.

After battling his way through many metres of rhododendron, buddleia and other overgrown weeds, he arrived on a back road which led past some industrial units. Five minutes later he reached a junction with a bus stop. *Wait,* said Sid. *It's coming.*

'Great idea, Sid,' he muttered, watching the bend of the road and expecting a patrol car to tear around it at any moment. 'But... no money!' The pendulum shivered and pushed his thinking to the far side of the stop where there was a pile of crushed cans, assorted fag butts and a plastic Sainsbury's carrier bag. Inside the bag was a dark blue woolly hat, half a dozen bottle tops... and some coins. Lucas laughed dryly, pocketed around £3.40 in change and checked the hat for obvious signs of dandruff or fox shit. Finding neither, he put it on, carefully tucking away his long shaggy hair. It wasn't much of a disguise but it was better than nothing. On a whim he also picked up the cans and shoved them in the bag, giving himself something to carry. He didn't know why but he felt it made him look less like a fugitive from justice. It might also hide the fact that his jeans were soaking wet from the mid-thigh down.

The bus arrived seconds later and he got on, discovering that the money Sid had found for him was just enough to get him into the city. It would take another twenty minutes. Twenty minutes during which the bus's security cameras might tip off the officers currently scouring the public transport live feeds.

And then what? Assuming he wasn't arrested as soon as he stepped off in Guildhall Square - then what? He needed to get out to the nursing home, and that wasn't on any regular bus route. His bike was, he assumed, still on Kate's road - but going back there would be idiotic. The police were certain to be watching the area.

Where could he go? Who could he call on?

Sid gave him a gentle nudge. A sarcastic nudge. He all but gave off a Homer Simpson 'D'oh!'.

Twenty minutes later Lucas stepped off the bus with his bag of empty cans, head down in someone's lost woolly hat, and made his way to The Henge Gallery.

33

The gardener guy didn't die well. He screamed and then gargled with his own blood supply as it came bubbling up through his split neck. He looked, pleadingly, across at Kate, as if she could do anything to help him. Wendy knelt over him and studied his contorted features for some time as he flailed and spluttered, then, perhaps growing bored with the spectacle, she went in again with the scalpel and cut deep enough to silence him permanently.

The blood travelled in a widening river across the cellar floor, pooling in a straight line along the edge of the white paper Melissa was suspended over. The nurse stood up and folded her arms, the scalpel still in her fingers, watching the scarlet stream of the man's spent life force with interest.

'It could almost work,' she said. 'But the red is too vivid.' She sighed. 'I'll have to mop that up before it seeps right into the main shot.'

Kate was to stunned to speak. For a whole three seconds she had thought maybe the creepy gardener was going to turn out to be a hero after all. He was still checking her out;

his dead eyes wide and fixed in her direction. She gripped the plastic doll's leg tightly, anchoring herself to it to keep her mind from backflipping with panic. Her thumb found its thigh, its knee, the curve of its calf, tapering to the slim ankle.

'Don't worry,' said Wendy. 'I'll tidy this all up.' She grabbed a white towel from somewhere behind her and threw it onto the blood. Red roses began to bloom through the white immediately. 'I'll have to leave him here for a while, because I'm due on shift in...' she checked the fob watch clipped to her tunic, '...half an hour. I'll need to wait until dark to get rid of him.' She sighed and shook her head. 'I'll get rid of Tessa too. She really smells.'

Kate widened her eyes, pitch dark humour prodding her. *Honestly! Bloody Tessa and her smelly deadness!*

'What does it mean?' she croaked. Not 'why are you doing this?' or 'please let me go'. Kate realised that this insane woman was probably only reachable on one level. Playing the part of a gallery goer, fascinated and impressed, might get Wendy talking. And the more Wendy talked, the better the odds were for Kate - and maybe even Melissa - to stay alive.

'Mean?' Wendy turned to look at her, the bloody scalpel flicking idly up and down between her fingers.

'Yes... why the runners? Why the dolls? What are you trying to say?'

Wendy sighed and looked up towards the ceiling. 'Art cannot be explained in a line. It's a composite. A melting pot.'

Kate nodded, waiting.

'Have you heard of the art of decay?' Wendy asked, at length.

Kate considered, remembering the discussion with

Conrad Temple last night. Plucking anything she could from her mind that might help the connection she was making with her probable killer she said: 'Um... yes. I think Damien Hirst is the most famous exponent, isn't he?'

'Yes!' Wendy's face was suddenly alight. 'He is. Although he's a bit obvious with his shark in formaldehyde. I mean, technically that's not decay - that's preservation. Mind you, the galleries don't allow actual rotting to occur in case it makes the visitors throw up.'

'I can understand that,' said Kate.

I prefer Dieter Roth,' Wendy went on, plucking a wipe from her tunic pocket and carefully cleaning the scalpel. 'He uses food and allows maggots to infest it. It's beautiful. I also liked the chocolate and seed bust he did of himself, allowing it to be eaten by birds.'

'That's... different.'

'I was meant to go to art college, you know,' said Wendy, with a sudden coldness in her voice. 'I was talented. Those watercolours in the lodge... I painted those.'

'Oh. Yes. I saw those,' said Kate. 'Distinctive.'

Wendy made a waving gesture with the scalpel and the wipe. 'They're nothing. They're just people-pleasers. I'd like to show my real work but I guess the art of decay might be a little too on the nose for a nursing home.' She laughed for a few seconds, impressed with her joke.

'What happened to the art college thing?' asked Kate, gripping the doll's leg like a talisman and commanding herself to stay calm and focused, despite swooping waves of dizziness clouding her thoughts.

Wendy's mirthful smile faded. 'My mother happened to it,' she said. 'She was old and ill. She didn't want me to go.'

'That must have been hard.'

Wendy stepped towards her, scalpel still unsheathed. 'You have no... fucking... idea,' she snarled.

Kate thought she might be wetting herself. She said, quickly: 'Family... they can really screw you up, right?'

Wendy stepped back, dropped the wipe, put the little plastic cover on the blade and returned it to her pocket. She stepped over the body of the gardener, careful to avoid the blood-soaked towel, and leant against the wall. 'She had me late, when she was forty-five. Dad died when I was six. He was ancient even before I was born. I was 18 and about to finally start my life when she threw her spanner in the works. Cervical cancer, the bitch. No art college for me. Oh no. I had to stay home and look after her. And she took her fucking time, dying. I watched her as she faded. I photographed her and painted her right up to the day she died. And for a little while afterwards. You don't actually have to notify anyone of a death for five days, so I made the most of that. A body changes quite a lot in five days; there's a lot to work with. I have a collection of images devoted to her. I call it *Hurry Along, Mother*.'

Kate could think of nothing to say to that.

'After the funeral I applied to the art college again,' said Wendy. 'I sent them some of the pictures - not the post-death ones, though. That would be pushing it, without, you know, context.' She sighed and gave a tight, angry smile. 'They sent a letter turning me down and suggesting counselling.'

Kate waited a beat and then said: 'Didn't you try other places?'

'No,' said Wendy. 'I decided to go my own way. Study for myself. That's when I started reading about the art of decay. I saw myself in Dieter Roth and Damien Hirst, in Matthew Barney and Elizabeth Peyton. I knew what my calling was then, but I had no money and creating art isn't cheap. I needed big canvases, photographic materials, a taxidermy course, things like that...'

Kate nodded as if this all made perfect sense.

'So I became a nurse,' Wendy went on. 'I was well qualified already, after caring for Mother for years, and I knew I'd be good at it. I wanted to work with the elderly, too, and they're always crying out for geriatric nurses. I just had to make my collections and exhibitions in my own time. I thought about creating a collection of images of the elderly as they fade and die. It would have been beautiful. But Margaret - that's the manager - wasn't keen. She thought it was intrusive and in poor taste. She doesn't see the beauty of it.'

'So... you had to come up with something else,' prompted Kate.

'I know what you're doing,' said Wendy, giving her a sly look. 'You're trying to get the whole story out of me.'

Kate shrugged with some difficulty in her bindings. 'If I'm going to end up like the others... I'd like to at least understand why,' she said.

Wendy regarded her a while longer. Then she nodded. 'Fair enough. I always intended to tell you. That's why you're able to talk; able to listen. The others, they didn't know anything about it. I drugged them all very carefully; I didn't want them to be in too much pain.'

You've got a heart of gold, thought Kate. 'They're fascinated,' she said, 'back at the station. Your work is mounted on a glass wall. The title is Marathon.

'Because they're runners?' asked Wendy, looking delighted. 'That's actually quite good. Because dying is a marathon too. Not twenty-six miles but maybe twenty-six days. I wanted fit women; women who weren't going to die too fast. And I wanted them to look good too; to be in excellent shape. You get so much more of a contrast that way. And I knew I was going to pose them, like dolls. That's when I started thinking about the Barbies. God, there's a dozen Barbies in every charity shop you go to. And the other dolls too. Do you know you can get pop star dolls? I think there's a Taylor Swift somewhere up there...' She eyed the curtain of plastic figures behind Kate.

'Really?' said Kate.

Wendy scanned the dolls, frowning. 'She's definitely there somewhere.'

'Wendy... could you get me some water, do you think?' asked Kate. 'Before you go on your shift? I'm so thirsty.'

Wendy folded her arms and considered. 'All right,' she said. She stood up and walked towards the cellar steps. 'I'll be right back. Don't go anywhere.' She laughed. Kate didn't join in.

34

'Oh dear god,' said Mariam, the moment she saw him. Lucas had an inkling it wasn't just the woolly hat.

He turned and flipped the OPEN sign over to CLOSED before locking the shop door. He could see nobody else inside.

'Lucas - what the hell is going on?' asked Mariam. 'You were all over the Radio Wiltshire news just now; your picture's on the website! They're saying *you're* the Runner Grabber!'

Lucas moved further into the gallery, anxious to stay away from the windows. 'That's bollocks - I didn't do it!'

'Of *course* it's bollocks!' said Mariam. 'I know that. I don't give exhibition space to murderers.'

'I need your car,' said Lucas. 'Right away. I have to get out of the city.'

'Lucas, listen to me,' said Mariam. 'Calm down. You're not thinking straight. You can't go on the run - you have to sort this out with the police.'

'It's not about that. It's about Kate - the detective who

came to ask me for help. She's been taken by the *real* Runner Grabber and I think I know where to find her.'

'So tell *them* that!' said Mariam. 'Take them to her.'

'It won't work!' said Lucas. 'They won't give me the space to dowse. I know the site... I think... but it's big and I'll need to work with Sid. I need a clear head and they'll be right in my face, ready to taser me at any moment. It kind of messes with my vibe, you know? The prospect of imminent electrocution.'

Mariam grabbed his arm and hauled him across to the narrow staircase at the back of the gallery. She led him up to the first floor. Off its tiny landing was a bathroom, a small office and a sitting room with a kitchenette. 'Sit down and have a hot drink,' she said, indicating a two-seater Chesterfield sofa. 'If what I've learned is right, he doesn't kill them quickly. You've got time.'

Lucas screwed up his face. 'I'm getting the sense that this whole thing is speeding up. I can't wait.'

'Lucas - you're not getting my car keys until you've told me all of it,' she said. 'And you're going to have a hot drink while you tell me. I need to see that you've calmed down enough to be able to drive. Right now you look like you'd crash into a traffic light. I might have to drive for you.'

She put the kettle on, deliberately filling it with slow, calm movements, designed to bring his panic level down a notch. She was a woman used to dealing with hysterical creatives; he had to give her her due.

He found a mug of hot sweet coffee between his palms as he talked through the events of the past two days. She listened with great concentration, perched on a chair by the kitchen counter, and then went to her handbag and pulled out a set of keys. 'I'll drive,' she said. 'You're too rattled.'

'You shouldn't get caught up in this,' said Lucas, taking a

gulp of the hot coffee and wincing at the sharp sting that shot through his wounded tongue. 'You should stay out of it.'

Mariam shrugged. 'I'm already caught up in it. So, in for a penny, in for a pound!'

'No - but - if the police-'

There was a sudden crash below and they both jumped violently as a voice outside the gallery yelled: 'OPEN UP! POLICE!'

'You were saying?' said Mariam.

'Shit! Shit, shit, *shit!*' breathed Lucas. He put down the mug and got to his feet. 'Don't answer!'

There was hammering on the glass out front and another, louder, shout: 'POLICE! OPEN UP!'

Mariam went to the window above the sink and draining board.

'Don't look out!' Lucas hissed. 'They mustn't see you!' He couldn't help sidling up to the window himself though and glancing around the frame. There was a flash of movement in the side alley below. The static buzz of a two-way radio could be heard quite clearly.

'I think they're surrounding us,' gulped Mariam. 'You might have to give yourself up, Lucas. I'll help you. I'll tell them everything you've told me.'

'No,' said Lucas, urgency surging through him. 'That's *not* happening. I've already done a bunk from them today; they're not going to let me off the leash again. Where else can I go? Is there a basement? An attic?'

'Yes, a basement, but no way out of it,' she whispered, as they both instinctively drew back against the wall, out of sight from any angle. She glanced up to the small hatch above the kitchen counter. 'There's an attic but I've never used it. I don't know if it'll help. They'll probably check it.'

'No - that's good,' said Lucas, focusing his dowsing mind and already feeling through the space above; tracing the water tank, the lagging, the rafters, the skylight *and* the unsound brick wall that separated it from the neighbouring property. 'I can get out that way. Just get me up there!'

He leapt onto the kitchen counter and reached the hatch without difficulty.

'Wait - take the key!' Mariam handed up a VW fob. 'My Beetle's in the Salt Lane car park. But don't jump in and race off. You don't want to be stopped for speeding. Remember - you need to drive like a granny.'

He pocketed the key and pushed up on the white painted board. It gave easily, with a light shower of dust, and folded into the darkness above, coming to rest on its hinges. He reached up, hoping his daily chin lift exercises had prepared him for this.

There was a crash and the sound of splintering down in the gallery. 'Hurry!' hissed Mariam, giving his flailing feet a boost with both hands. That and a burst of adrenalin carried him up and over the hatch threshold and he had it closed again two seconds later. He crouched, still and silent, and tried to listen past the panicky pulsing of blood in his ears.

He heard a toilet flushing below while heavy footsteps ascended the stairs and then Mariam's voice, indignant and haughty, addressing someone. 'I very much hope you have a warrant, young man. What the hell do you think you're doing?'

'Mariam Aziz? We have reason to believe you're harbouring a man by the name of Lucas Henry,' came the reply. 'He is wanted in connection with kidnap and murder. Where is he?'

'He isn't here,' she replied.

'So why couldn't you come out and tell us that?' asked a female officer; DC Sharon Mulligan, Lucas thought, catching her northern accent.

'I was in the *toilet!* And frankly, right now, I need to go right back in there!'

Lucas grinned to himself, in spite of the drastic situation he was in. Mariam was a class act. Now he needed to block out the noises below and focus. He held on to Sid and allowed his mind map to overlay the gloom of the attic. A thin grey shaft was filtering through the grimy skylight, but he could not make out the wall with his eyes alone. He crawled, painfully slowly to avoid any giveaway creaks, across the hardboard flooring which topped the rafters and loft insulation. The brick wall was only one skin thick and loosely built. He knew this was commonplace in old terraces; the builders of 150 years ago hadn't expected the attic to be used or visited too often. Some of them didn't even bother to divide the roof space across several houses. It was a free run for rats and mice. Here there were brick walls... but they were half-heartedly built.

He reached the edifice of bricks and found the draft flowing easily through it. There was a large hole up to his left. Big enough to fit through and into the next building along. Lucas moved through it like a cat burglar trying to avoid laser trip beams. He could hear much more commotion below. Mariam was being loud and theatrical. He knew she was doing it for him - making as much fuss and noise as she could, to disguise any creaks and bumps from above. Reaching the other side of the wall, Lucas was glad of it. His foot landed with a creak which made his heart stop. But after a few seconds the commotion downstairs went on much as before. Only slightly quieter; more distant. He was *very slowly escaping.*

There hadn't been much clutter in Mariam's attic but the next one was filled with boxes which he had to work around, dislodging dust and cobwebs and affronted spiders. He saw a thin rectangular frame of light and recognised the neighbours' hatch, but a quick consultation with Sid told him there were people below. There was also another easy walk through to the next attic and this felt more hopeful.

Lucas pushed on, quietly, carefully, hearing nothing now of the disturbance in The Henge Gallery. He felt bad for Mariam. He would have to pay for that door to be fixed. If he ever earned any money. He reached the next shoddily built brick screen and found another gap, high against the slanted underside of its old slate tiled roof. If the skylights had been bigger he might have considered climbing out, but there would be no way off the roof. No. He had to go down.

The next hatch offered up no light; he found it on his hands and knees. He paused, clutching at Sid beneath his shirt, and focused. The dwelling below was quiet and empty... except for a... cat. There was a cat. He felt around for a grip and pulled the wooden panel up into the void.

There was no handy built-in ladder to aid his descent, but he edged his legs down carefully, lowering himself as far as he could before dropping to the carpeted landing. He appeared to be in a flat above a ground floor shop unit. He could sense movement below in the shop, but also an exit out to the back which didn't connect with the shop.

He ran lightly down the narrow stairway to a small ground floor kitchen where the cat leapt up onto a counter, hissing. The kitchen, an 80s throwback of varnished pine, had a door which led to a small courtyard. Lucas turned the key in the door and stepped outside. There was a gate set into a brick wall at the far end, but it was heavily padlocked. Lucas thought the wall looked climbable and the other side of it appeared to be an access alley, leading to the road.

He cocked his head, listening for police communications or more loud arguing from Mariam two doors up, but could only hear the normal sounds of small town traffic. He pulled the woolly hat down firmly and then ran at the wall and scaled it, dropping to the far side without, apparently, drawing any attention. The cobbled lane was narrow and dark and led away from the gallery direction. Lucas gripped the VW key fob and allowed it to lead him to Mariam's Beetle. It took him along two back streets and around a corner to the open square of the Salt Lane car park. He could see the bright green car in a corner bay, close against a stone wall.

Just walk normally; be natural, he told himself. Then he ducked behind a big yellow skip as two police officers appeared on the far side of the car park, walking along with urgency, scanning left and right and using their radios. He plastered himself against the cold metal and marshalled his breathing. Calm. Stay calm. No panicky vibrations. His years of study and practice had taught him that everyone was capable of dowsing to some degree, whether they knew it or not. What people regarded as spooky intuition or that sense of 'being watched' was often simply an instinctive reading of vibrations. So even those coppers could do it if they were in the right state.

Happily, they were not. They marched on past, looking left and right, and then turned into The Pheasant Inn, clearly hoping their quarry might have nipped in for a pint.

Lucas knew this was his moment. He walked swiftly to the Beetle, bleeped it open and got inside. It started without fuss (Mariam loved her car and kept it well maintained) and he drove out of the car park and headed for the ring road.

As he slowly passed The Pheasant the two officers emerged from it and walked right past him without a second glance. This was an undeniable benefit of driving Mariam's girly car - complete with massive silk dahlia mounted next to the steering wheel.

He didn't push his luck, though. Resisting the urge to roar away he took a long, slow breath and pulled across the junction like a granny.

Driving like this all the way to East Sarum Lodge was going to be torture, but he would have to do it. If he was captured he would be in a cell and there would be no further outings.

As *matter of life and death* races went, this one would need to be entirely legal.

By the time he hit the B-road, though, he couldn't prevent himself hitting 60mph. The thrumming in his solar plexus was telling him time was running out.

35

'How did you do it?' asked Kate, when Wendy stood in front of her with the water bottle and straw. She took a sip from it while the nurse weighed up her reply.

'I dug pits in the woods they ran through,' she said. 'I'm really strong. You have to be to manage all these old people. We use hoists, like these.' She indicated the metal mechanism Melissa was attached to. 'But even so, there's a lot of heavy lifting. And old people can fight, you know? Especially the demented ones; they can really kick off. A six stone old lady gave me a black eye once and they all pinch like a bitch. So I know how hard it can be to subdue someone.'

She gave Kate another chance to suck in the water, which Kate did. She had no idea when she would get another drink. She wanted Wendy to go to her shift, though. She needed time alone.

'So I knew that if I wanted to collect young, fit, healthy women I would need to make a trap, get them down... prone... where I could take them by surprise. It was bloody hard work, all that digging in the dark. Should've got Graeme to do it for me.' She smirked at her deceased colleague, lying in his congealing bed of blood and towelling. 'I did take his spade, though. And his van. And now he's been down here it should be even easier to peg all this on him when the police come looking. And they will, won't they?'

'Eventually,' said Kate. She didn't want Wendy to think it would be any time soon; didn't want to push this psychopath's agenda forward.

'So, I'd bring them down, anaesthetise them and carry them back to the van. Once I tried using the wheelchair, but it's too awkward in the woods and I can do a fireman's lift easily enough. I wrapped them in blankets - the ones Graeme sat on in his little secret weed smoking den upstairs - and then got them back here.

She paused, put the drink down and then went to the dead man, plucking several hairs out of his scalp. She went over to Melissa and worked some of the hairs around her senseless fingers and under the nails. Kate realised the nurse was wearing surgical gloves and a plastic apron. Wendy noticed her eye line and waved her blue fingers in the air. 'Easy to get hold of these! And easy to put anything that worries me into the medical waste bin. It all gets incinerated.'

'Is she... is she still alive?' Kate asked.

Wendy reached up and took Melissa's pulse. 'She's good for another few hours, I think,' she said with a matter-of-factness that took Kate's breath away. 'I've had to hurry her along a bit with the injections. Shame. Always better to let nature take its course but meeting you made me pick up the pace - even made me change my... MO... is that what you call it?'

Kate nodded.

'Modus operandi,' said Wendy, with relish. 'Couldn't wait for days, working out your running route and digging a pit. Had to be inventive.' She made a whining noise just like the missing dog that had never existed and then chortled to herself.

'Clever,' said Kate. 'I totally fell for that.'

Wendy smirked and then looked at her watch. 'Got to go. I can tell you more when I see you after my shift. Don't worry if you lose bladder or bowel control. I'm used to that; I'll tidy you up. It's nothing to be ashamed of.'

So considerate, thought Kate.

As she watched Wendy skip over the dead man and up the cellar steps, all hope of creating a bond with her captor evaporated. If ever there was a textbook case of someone with zero empathy, Wendy was it. Women, Kate remembered, made the best psychopaths; they were good at mimicking other women's behaviour and shielding their true nature. Wendy had been chatting away to her like a best friend, not because she had an ounce of compassion for her latest collector's item but because she was loving the live audience. Sharing her genius plan and the resultant Art of Decay was clearly the best fun she'd had in years. Kate had no doubt that as soon as she'd sufficiently stroked her own ego Wendy would be keen to move to the next phase; drugging her final victim into silence and then withdrawing water and watching her dry up like an autumn leaf while slowly starving to death. Taking beautifully lit photos all the way.

Kate shuddered as she imagined Kapoor, Michaels and Mulligan all peering in horror at the photos of their dying colleague when the prints arrived in the post. Temple had been spot on in his assessment of the killer - it was all about the exhibition; the ego. The crime psych would see her death shots too. It made her flinch inside to think of it.

But she squeezed the doll's leg hard and felt the tiniest of scratches; something she'd been clinging to for the past hour, since she'd found it. The leg was old, rubbery and perishing; she could feel a graininess to it and already there was a wound in the back of its knee. She had been working that leg back and forth and making the wound deeper.

Because just inside it was a spike of metal wire. This was a poseable doll, like the one she and Francis had thrown out of the window for laughs in their childhood. The legs were designed to bend at the knee but they'd obviously been bent a little too often. The spike was breaking through.

Kate worked the leg back and forth, pushing the knee joint inside out until finally - with a small click - the spike burst through the perished vinyl. Kate gave a dry laugh of surprise and hope. The spike was sharp enough to jab the skin on her thumb like a badge pin. If she twisted one hand around with the spiked leg inside it, she could start work on her bonds.

She took deep breath, reminded herself that there should be time. Wendy would be gone for hours. She just needed to stay calm and keep at it. Then she set to work with a broken doll's leg and grim determination.

THE HELICOPTER overhead suggested to Lucas that they were on to him. He was maybe ten minutes away from the nursing home by road, but what was the betting they'd found out Mariam's car and registration number? It wouldn't be a stretch to work out how she'd helped him. When they asked where her Beetle was parked and she couldn't show it to them, they would know he was using it for his getaway. She could bluster like a pro but she couldn't magic a car out of nowhere.

He didn't *want* to believe this. He wanted to think the helicopter in the sky behind him was just an air ambulance or a private chopper, but there was a determination in the way it was hugging the contours of this road. It was searching. Very likely for him. Very likely following up some very recent camera evidence on ANPR. It would be overhead in a minute, maybe two.

He was entering a wooded stretch where the canopy of the trees met over the road, shielding him from aerial view - probably for no more than ten seconds of driving time before he was out the other side and in plain view again. Lucas saw what looked like a Forestry Commission track leading off to the left. With a curse he pulled abruptly onto it and followed the track as far as the deep, muddy ruts would allow. The Beetle's low profile tyres were not happy and he knew he couldn't get far like this. He spotted a tall triangle of logs, neatly stacked by some efficient foresters, and drove around it, pulling the car out of the eyeline of any idle passer-by. He considered trying to cover it in branches and bracken, but abandoned that idea. He'd make better use of that time fleeing through the woods and attempting to reach Kate cross-country.

Now he had to take a moment, block out the sound of the chopper overhead, which was getting louder all the time, get Sid out and focus on his best and quickest route.

Leaning against the side of the car, he took several long, deep breaths, closed his eyes and allowed his mind to cool. He drew his elbows in to his torso, steepled his hands and let the pendulum spin. Sid spiralled like a demon for twenty seconds before beginning to swing back and forth, offering a good direction.

Lucas opened his eyes and saw the route; a deer trail through the trees which didn't look too narrow or winding. He shoved Sid back inside his shirt and began to run.

And as he ran he heard something which scared him much more than the helicopter. Dogs.

36

Mrs Newton was kicking off again. She'd been getting worse and worse this week and Wendy wondered if this had anything to do with her. The woman kept drivelling on about her smell... looking at her almost as if she *knew*... (Also, Mrs Newton's dosage was little lower than it should be.)

Wendy was feeling wired. Killing Graeme had given her an almost sexual thrill; sitting astride him and driving the blade into his neck; watching the horror and astonishment in his eyes as he finally understood what this 'fine figure of a woman' really was... it was quite a kick. Even a turn on. When she had finished this work she might well move on to men. Something more visceral; more sexual. Wendy knew she wasn't good-looking in the conventional sense; someone had once commented that she looked like a Soviet shot-putter. But she also knew there were some men who were into that kind of thing. She could do the whole S&M thing with them; a sexual Mrs Trunchbull; put them in the choky. Set up cameras between the spikes.

'It's wrong,' said Mrs Newton, staring up at her with tightly pursed lips. 'I can smell it on you.'

'Just take your pill, Elsie,' said Wendy, in the calm, measured voice that would help her collect all those stupid men. She was curious, though. In her time working here she had often wondered if some of her charges had a little ESP. She suspected that as you neared the end of your time your senses were dulled in some ways but heightened in others. Maybe you began to recognise the smell of death. Or maybe it was just developer fluid. She had a dark room in that cellar too; her work wasn't suitable for dropping in to Boots for prints. She had considered digital but she really didn't like it. There was a beautiful alchemy to developing your own images; the dodging and burning, the scent of developer, stop bath and fixer. The way Caroline, Tessa and Melissa had bloomed from the paper, below the liquid, was like a water birth.

'Mum!' Mrs Newton's daughter suddenly stumbled into the room. 'I'm sorry - I can't stay long.'

She was clearly upset, and Wendy suspected she knew why. 'Are you OK?' she asked.

The woman - Sally, her name was - looked flushed and agitated. 'Not really… my neighbour's gone missing.'

'Oh no, really?' Wendy pasted her concerned face on.

'Yes,' said Sally. She glanced at her mother. 'You know, Mum… the policewoman. She took Reggie out this morning and she didn't come back. We found Reggie tied to a lamp post.' Her face crumpled. 'The police have been up and down the street and everything. I've been in such a state. I had to drive myself up, even with my bad ankle. I couldn't stay there on my own.'

'What do they think has happened to her?' asked

Wendy. She felt like she had a ringside seat to her own crime thriller; this was turning out to be quite the day!

'They don't know,' said Sally, sitting down on the armchair opposite her mother and pressing her bandaged ankle with a wince. 'But she's caught up in this whole Runner Grabber case. And she was out running.' She clapped a hand over her mouth. 'With *my* dog! I should never have let her go.'

'At least you got your dog back,' said Wendy. She saw Sally flick an odd look at her; this happened from time to time. She said things that made perfect sense to *her,* but which other people seemed to find odd or inappropriate. It was one of the reasons she didn't talk much to family members when they visited.

'Yes, well, I suppose,' said Sally. 'I've had to put him in the back of the car, Mum... I didn't want to leave him at home. He's really unsettled. God knows what he saw; someone grabbing Kate.' She smothered a sob. 'I can't stay long, Mum. It's not fair on Reggie, leaving him in the car. I've had to leave the window open a bit for him.'

Her mother reached out for her hand and said: 'She's all wrong, poppet. All wrong. You can smell it on her.'

And she turned to glare balefully at Wendy.

Sally sniffed and glanced up at her. 'Sorry,' she said. 'I don't know where she gets it from.'

Wendy smiled and said it didn't matter and got out of the room. The way mother and daughter had just looked at her made some deep level alarm kick off inside her. The fizz of excitement she'd been surfing suddenly soured into tension. She had learned about DS Sparrow from those two; the daughter blabbing away about her young neighbour for her mother's entertainment. Then she'd seen the woman in reception and recognised the type; slim, pretty - *and* a runner. Discovering she was working on the Runner Grabber case had made her irresistible.

So Elsie and Sally were actually responsible for Kate's death. She'd love to see the look on their faces if they knew that.

But maybe Mrs Newton *did* know it. Maybe she was going tell her daughter...

Wendy shook her head and laughed out loud at herself. What could an old lady with dementia say which anyone would believe? Even if she *did* know something... which she couldn't possibly.

The unease wouldn't go, though. She knew she had come a little off the rails with this project. With the first three she had been so methodical; so organised, so *artful.* Marking them with the dolls had been such a sweet part of it - giving them a little clue to what they would soon become. The plan was so elegant and it had worked. But the snap decision to collect the policewoman... the change of method... the rushed killing of Graeme... it was all getting a bit too ad hoc. Sloppy.

Graeme had needed to die, of course. She'd realised that as soon as he'd told her about clearing out the barn. He would uncover the hatch to the cellar and he would go down into it. The clock had started ticking for him the moment he'd spoken about it. So Margaret was actually responsible for *his* death. Wendy had had no choice. It was inconvenient too, because without Graeme's little sideline, she would no longer have the drugs money coming in to pay for her art supplies.

They would miss him eventually. Maybe not for a day or two. She could drive the van somewhere tonight and abandon it. That might help. Plant some more evidence of his connection to the dead women in the cellar. First, though, she needed to get rid of his body. The well would do nicely. She'd heard tell it was 50 metres deep and, really, it couldn't be more convenient. She could nail the lid back on afterwards. They'd never find him. The smell couldn't travel up that far.

And then... she must finish the work. But she no longer had the luxury of time. Melissa was just about done but there wouldn't be time for any post-death decay shots with her - and she could barely get started with Kate. It was a shame, Wendy reflected, but there was no point denying it; she needed to move Kate on to the death phase much sooner. Tonight.

She would remove Melissa's body from the studio paper set up and then put Kate in place for a new position; some new decorations. She had some stuffed birds and one of them, happily, was a sparrow. That would be fitting. She would place the sparrow on the detective's outstretched hand. She might make a police badge too. Maybe pin it directly to her last doll's naked breast. She needed Kate alive long enough to register all of this in her expression; to get the shots. Then she would kill her by trebling the dose of barbiturates which had kept the others unconscious for so long. Get a few more pictures post-mortem. Finish the collection.

And then? She pictured a scene with her manager in a couple of days from now. Margaret would be wondering where Graeme had got to. Wendy would say 'I don't know... but I think I saw the van driving out late the night before last. Also, Margaret, I don't want to bother you, but I was collecting a wheelchair from the barn... I saw Graeme take it in there to use for a seat... and I noticed this smell.'

She could be there when Margaret found it all, a couple

of days from now. She could witness her boss's reaction while she faked her own.

It was messy... but she kind of liked it that way. It was more exciting than the first phase. She checked her fob watch. It was a long shift but she had a break coming up soon. She could just nip to the drugs store now and get a couple of syringes.

She could kill Melissa, if Melissa still needed killing. And then she could rig up Kate and probably still have time for a cup of tea in the staff room.

37

The dogs were getting closer. Lucas pressed his panic low into his belly, held it rigid, and ran on. He'd splashed along the bed of a shallow stream for some time, but he knew that wouldn't be enough. Leaping out of it, his boots and socks full of squelching water, he took off his jacket, tying the arms tight around his waist, as he ran towards a clump of trees. Then he pulled off his sweatshirt, damp with the richly scented perspiration of one very stressful day. The late afternoon air cooled his skin immediately as he galloped on. The thicket of holly around a clump of oaks looked about right. Scanning the trunks he thought he could climb three or four metres up.

He pushed through the holly, too intent on his purpose to even register the grazes the prickles left on his shoulders, arms and belly. He found hand holds on the thickest oak trunk and pulled himself up, fast. Then he found a knot of branches and ivy where he could shove the sweatshirt. He thanked Mother Nature for the cover of the leaves and dropped back down to the woodland floor. His scent, high in that thicket of trees, ought to delay the dogs and the search party for a good few minutes. It would take a while to establish he wasn't hiding up there.

He rejoined the stream, retracing his earlier tracks, and sped along as fast as its uneven bed would allow. A few minutes on, he spotted a wider stretch of water with muddy banks. Reaching the mud he dropped down and grabbed handfuls of it, wiping it across his armpits, his belly, over his shoulders and around his back as far as he could reach. He'd done some survival stuff with some soldier mates in Spain and had learned that a nice mud coating could sometimes protect you from mosquitos and other biting insects. They couldn't pick up the smell of your sweat so easily. He really hoped this worked for police dogs too.

He ran on, looking like a creature from a B-movie horror flick, Sid bouncing wildly on his chest. A change in light spoke of a break in the woodland, up on a slanted rise of the land. That was where he needed to go. He would need to leave the water now, but he was a good half a kilometre on from the high rise pungent sweatshirt; he ought to be safe.

Emerging from the trees he saw he was on the slope of some recently harvested cornfields; a corrugated landscape of stubble which followed the contours of the land in a gentle swell. On the top end of it was another small copse and this one he recognised as the woodland he had stalked Kate through two nights ago.

He cursed himself now, understanding that he had almost wilfully misread the signs from his dowsing mind; the vibrations from Sid. He had found Kate in the wood - he still had no idea why - and he'd assumed Sid had set him up on some kind of mission to get a date, when in fact the pendulum had been guiding him towards the very thing he really did not want to get caught up in. The dark, cancerous heart of the Runner Grabber case began and ended here. He had no doubt of it. This feeling of absolute certainty had occurred in his life before, and he had never been wrong when he felt it.

Lucas leant against the dry stone wall that bordered the field, drawing in deep, sucking breaths. He really needed to get fitter. His heart was pounding and his thigh and calf muscles were complaining bitterly. He couldn't hear the dogs but he sensed an animal quickening back in the woods; they had found the tree - their excitement was so intense the energy patterns reached him even here. He sensed he had pulled ahead enough; they wouldn't catch him now before he reached the lodge. But he had another problem. The field was wide; the rise to the boundary of the lodge, which ran to the west, out of the wood he had visited two nights ago, was some sprint from here. Even running full pelt, he was going to be exposed to any eye in the sky for a good two minutes. And he could still hear the distant chopping of the helicopter, although he couldn't see it. He guessed it was hovering over the epicentre of the dogs' excited reaction, probably deploying thermal imaging to see what was crouched high in the tree. It would circle outwards soon. He probably had two minutes if he went now.

He took another lungful of air, tightened the sleeves of his jacket around his hips, and then ran for it, keeping low to the ground and hugging the scant cover of the dry stone wall. The light was fading towards dusk and becoming more overcast, which was a welcome sight. A bit of shadow was what he needed out here.

He reached the lodge's perimeter wall without a helicopter chase; without being brought to the ground by dogs, and as he reached it he slowed. He untied the sleeves and put his jacket back on over his bare back and shoulders. The sense that he was within reach of Kate - *and* the person who meant to kill her - was very strong. The frequencies of panic and despair and a dark seam of sick satisfaction all hung in the air like the strata of a broken cliff. Jagged and splintered in places; it was hard to pinpoint what was *now* and what was *then*. Whenever he had dowsed, Lucas had noticed that different strands of history had a way of seeping through the current moment. It took focus to get into the dowsing state... to separate the strands.

He climbed over the wall and sat down, cross-legged, on the grass which grew in high tufts against the stone. He drew Sid out to hang in his fingers. Ahead of him was a garden with a vegetable plot which grew up to the low wall of the staff and visitors car park; beyond that, the lodge, where lights were coming on and tea was being made; the first of the evening rituals. The energy patterns of the staff - busy, engaged, jaded - mingled with the energy patterns of the residents; a meandering river in which confusion, agitation and boredom swum alongside comfort, distraction and a kind of peace.

To the right, bordering one end of the car park, was the wood and to the left a long slope of well-tended grounds, ending in a few outbuildings. Sid was moving in awkward, jerking motions, reflecting the turmoil in Lucas's mind. He was being pulled in two directions - to the lodge and to the outbuildings. The panic, despair and dark sickness were hard to separate; one moment he felt driven to run to the lodge, the next to run down the hill to investigate those outbuildings.

Perhaps, given the state of him, the outbuildings were his best first option. Lucas stood up, making the decision. Now that he'd made it, the call of the dowse was positively howling at him. *COME! Come NOW!*

A vehicle was arriving in the car park. The time to go

was now. He turned left and took a step, hearing a screech of tyres and a spray of gravel.

'STOP RIGHT THERE!'

He spun around, heart leaping, to see a uniformed officer flinging open the door of a patrol car and running towards him. In the back seat he just caught the wretched face of Mariam.

The officer appeared to be operating solo. In the split second he had left, Lucas guessed Mariam was being taken back to the station for further questioning. The guilt emanating from Lucas's friend and mentor in the back seat persuaded him she had spilled the beans about the nursing home; almost certainly thought it was the best thing to do.

And it would have been if he didn't have to go... *right now.*

38

The doll's leg was snapped in two now, the knee bent forward like a heron's. The wire was fully exposed and the sharp end was gradually carving through the plastic ties around her wrists. Kate had stabbed herself several times and the blood was making the whole exercise a bit slippery, but she was making progress.

Across from her Melissa was still motionless, but occasionally made the faintest of moans.

'Hang in there, Melissa,' said Kate. 'Oh god... sorry... I mean, just hold on. I will get to you soon, I promise. Don't let go. Don't give up.'

Kate felt a bit of play in the plastic curtain behind her and gave a few sharp tugs. There was a sound of tearing and the doll came away from its backdrop, its torso, head and arms flopping backwards and nearly slipping from her wet fingers. She clenched them together and held tight, breathing hard, before slowly, slowly re-establishing her hold; getting the balance right. If she dropped the doll now she and Melissa would be done for.

It was cold in the basement. There was obviously some

background heating because it wasn't *freezing*, but sitting here, naked and sweating with fear, she was getting increasingly chilled and shivery. Whatever Wendy had drugged her with was wearing off, which was good news for her speed of thinking - but it also gave her less insulation from the horror of her situation, scrabbling away at her bonds with a broken doll, a dying woman in front of her, a long-dead woman in one corner, a recently murdered man in another. It was like some kind of demonic feng shui experiment. Would a dead man in a corner bring prosperity? Did a naked woman with a broken doll invite bad chi?

Snap. The bond around her left wrist had just broken. She gave a little whimper of hope. Then she had to pass the doll's leg across to her left hand to start work on the tie around her right wrist. Or should she see to her ankles first - get them free? Yes. Because if she had to, she *could* run with a chair hanging off one arm.

She brought the doll around to the front in her freed left hand. It was an old doll, as she'd suspected; a cheap Barbie knock off with matted golden hair and blue eyes; a faint smile lurking on its plastic lips. Its cheeks were grubby with age. So were its perky plastic breasts. Kate suspected it looked a lot like she did at the moment - apart from a leg snapped off at the knee. She bit the lower limb away completely, tearing the perished plastic calf and foot off between her teeth so she could more easily use the spike. She had to be careful with it; it was old metal and starting to bend, but the end was still sharp enough. She worked it into the plastic tie on her left ankle and a short while later felt another hope-giving snap.

Melissa gave a shuddering breath.

'Don't you dare die!' said Kate. 'Don't you dare, Melissa!

Your mum and dad and Isaac are all waiting for you to come home. You *stay alive!*'

Wendy had left the bottle of water, still half-full, on a ledge above Graeme's body. Kate decided, as soon as she was free, to try to get some of the water into Melissa before she did anything else. Dehydration must be shutting her down, organ by organ. *OK, Kate - focus. One more ankle and then your right wrist. Keep going!*

Her energy levels were rising on a tide of hope and adrenalin as she worked on. She could do this. She *could* do this.

And then there was a thud above her head. Someone walking across the barn floor. The hatch being opened. 'Hello, ladies,' called Wendy. The lower half of the nurse appeared on the wooden steps, artfully uplit, throwing a sharp shadow on the wall. Then, the unmistakeable silhouette of a syringe, poised and ready in her hand.

39

The copper was on him before he could run. This one, it seemed, didn't have a taser, but he was handy with the police issue baton.

Lucas was handy too, though. He'd been caught up in many a scuffle during his years wandering Europe as a street artist. Sometimes he'd been so low on cash he'd needed to sleep on a park bench and to do this he had to be able to look after himself and his bag of pencils and paper and collapsible easel; the tools of his trade.

Lucas swung out a leg and caught the guy in the back of the knee, toppling him. He heard a shout of alarm from Mariam. He also heard a dog barking close by, but it wasn't one of the police patrol dogs, he knew. This dog felt more like it was on *his* side.

All this he picked up in microseconds as the copper flipped over and then twisted and cracked Lucas across the jaw with the baton. It sent stars shooting across his vision but not so badly that he couldn't grab the baton and wrench it away, taking the copper's arm with it. He bent the guy's wrist back and grabbed for the cuffs, already open on the belt, primed, no doubt, to restrain one Lucas Henry, wanted for kidnap and murder. In a pulse of instinctive movement Lucas slid the cuff around one wrist and then rolled the guy and grabbed the other. It was by no means easy, but quick-fire patterns from Sid, like a supersonic *Fight Club* satnav, guided his movements.

Lucas stood up, panting, while the guy writhed, face down, shouting dire warnings.

'I'm sorry!' Mariam was yelling. 'I got arrested. And then I got worried. I had to say where you thought the killer was!'

'Forget it,' Lucas said - and to the copper. 'Shut up and listen! Kate's here - I think I know where, but I haven't got time to wait for your say-so. Tell Mariam how to call for back up!'

Then he ran towards the outbuildings; distant grey outlines in the dusk.

WENDY HAD SLIPPED out of the lodge around the back way to get to the barn. There was too much coming and going in the car park and someone had left a dog barking in their vehicle too. Must be that ugly mutt belonging to Elsie's daughter.

She had mentioned, as she passed Margaret in the office, that she thought she might have a migraine coming on and needed to get her prescription pills from the cottage. Once out of here she was considering phoning in to say she needed a lie down. That could get her off shift for the rest of the night - give her time to finish the work.

Before she returned to the cellar she took an old screw-driver from a shelf in the barn and went to the well behind the cottages. As she'd expected, it was easy to get the lid off.

It was a good metre in diameter and only hip height. Easy for body-tipping. She would put her personal protection gear on before she carried Graeme up and dropped him in. She reflected once again how extremely useful it was to have disposable plastic coveralls and gloves freely available to her. As was the medical waste system, neatly disposing of evidence with daily collections. Amid all the blood, bile, pus, vomit and diarrhoea which routinely left East Sarum Lodge, it wouldn't be easy to trace the leftovers of her activities. Especially as it all got incinerated within 24 hours.

Graeme's blood would have to be got up off the cellar floor, of course. She sighed. Stabbing him in the throat was a bit of a self-indulgence, really. As good as it had felt, murder with drugs was altogether much tidier. But she had a good system for cleaning up the other bodily fluids her subjects emitted and it should work just as well for blood.

She let the old wooden well cover drop to the ground on one side of the structure and spent a few moments peering down into the inky depths. She couldn't see the water, but it was nearly dark now and there wasn't any light to reflect in it. The scent of damp brick and mildew wafted up. She dropped a pebble in and listened. She counted to three before she heard a distant splash. Excellent. A long, long, drop.

She pulled her plastic coverall out of the hazardous medical waste sack and put it on. Then she hooked her hands through its vents to pull her gloves and the loaded syringes out of her tunic pockets. Gloved up, she held the syringes, still capped, one in each hand, and entered the barn. Life sometimes felt like a film; she was always at its epicentre. Right now felt like the crescendo moment; the moment when it all came together; triumphant, emotional music flooding the scene. There was so much *meaning* in the way she walked, rustling in her plastic, needles between her fingers. So much *art.* She wished there could have been a small film crew following her; lighting her; tracking her motion with a steady-cam, pulling focus in and out to emphasise the drama. *The Making of the Dying Dolls,* she might call it. Or *The Final Mile of Marathon.*

'Hello, ladies,' she called, as she descended the stairs, careful to step over Graeme and his blood.

Melissa still hung like a chrysalis; dry and unmoving, probably dead already. Kate was slumped in her chair, her chin on her chest and her long blonde hair, which Wendy had freed from its regulation ponytail, hanging in a curtain across her face.

Wendy felt for the words. Her imaginary film crew was focusing in closely. 'I think it's time for the finale,' she said, kneeling down in front of the last doll and feeling quite emotional. This whole thing had been such a journey!

She uncapped the syringe. 'I wish we'd had more time together,' she said. 'I had so much to tell you. But at least you know you're part of something big. Something amazing. Your photos will be in all the true crime books. You'll be famous forever. You're the last of my dying dolls.'

She pushed the curtain of hair aside, pleased to see that Kate was with it enough to lift her chin.

And then Kate stabbed her in the eye.

Above her own scream she heard her last doll spit out: 'BARBIE SAYS HI!"

40

A scream, muted but still filled with terror, rang out from the buildings ahead. Lucas knew he was sensing more than hearing it. He vaulted another wall and found himself on a narrow track, just wide enough for a car, which led to an overgrown yard of flagstones, next to a barn and a row of cottages. His heightened senses charted the deep shaft of water to his left and a dark miasma of wrongness to his right... in the barn... *below* the barn.

The dead were speaking here. Not literally - not ghosts. He wasn't a medium and he didn't know if he believed in that stuff, but the energy patterns of extreme emotions were absorbed in the structures all around him. People had died here; in misery; in fear. Very recently.

Brighter and sharper were the patterns of what was happening *now.* Sid was ice cold against his skin, as he ran into the barn. A single bulb, hanging from a long flex, threw a dim wash of light across the junk filled barn. A square of brighter light was on the floor in the far corner; overlaid with his dowsing mindmap, there was no argument about where he was going.

Lucas found the open hatch and the top of the steps just as there was another shriek; this one filled with rage, pain, murder.

'KATE!' he bellowed.

'IN HERE!' she screamed back.

He crashed down the steps and nearly landed on the corpse of a man with a cut throat, staring glassily sideways. Across the room he saw Kate, naked and crouched at the feet of another dead-looking woman on a frame, like the frame he'd seen in the police photos. Kate had a wooden chair hanging off one arm and the maimed body of a doll in one hand as a burly woman in a nurse's uniform bore down on her, bellowing and clutching one eye. The woman's free hand held a syringe, needle unsheathed.

'YOU'VE FUCKING BLINDED ME, YOU BITCH!' screamed the nurse, raising her needle and preparing to stab down on Kate's defensive forearm. 'AND I WAS MAKING IT EASY FOR YOU!' Kate tried to move but slumped sideways, groaning.

Lucas threw himself onto the nurse's back just as she began to bring down her fist. He expected to floor her instantly - but she took his assault with just a shocked grunt and no corresponding collapse. Instead she began whirling around, stabbing backwards at him with the syringe.

'DON'T LET IT STAB YOU, LUCAS!' yelled Kate, getting unsteadily to her feet. She lifted her right arm and swung the attached chair through the air; a four-legged wooden club, which connected with the side of the nurse's head. But still the woman didn't go down.

The nurse backed up with Lucas still on her shoulders, smashing him against the wall by the steps. He dropped onto the corpse, forcing a post-mortem gasp from its deceased lungs. Lucas struggled to get up, his heels skidding through a pool of blood. But the nurse was now staring down at him from her one working eye; the other was a well of blood in her enraged face. She raised the syringe and took aim.

There was a banshee shriek behind her as Kate swung the chair again; cracking it across the back of the nurse's skull. The woman staggered and hit the floor, the syringe spinning across the white paper. She sagged, made a guttural grunting sound, and then her eyeballs rolled up into her head; one a white crescent, the other invisible in its bleeding socket.

Lucas stood, panting, staring at the felled killer. Across the room, Kate did the same. After a few seconds she said: 'Pass me the water - just behind you. Melissa's still alive. We've got to help her.'

Lucas found the bottle and straw and handed it over, his senses reeling from everything that had just happened in the last thirty seconds. Kate, disregarding the chair hanging from her bloodied wrist, held the bottle to the suspended woman's lips with her free hand. 'Come on, Melissa. Come on - drink for me!' She put down the bottle, patted the woman's cheek and then removed the straw and tipped the water between her parched lips.

It seemed that Melissa took some moisture; she coughed a little and gulped once or twice. Her gaunt face looked like it was made of paper.

'Jesus,' murmured Lucas. 'Jesus Christ on a bike.'

'Help me get her down,' said Kate.

'Wait,' he said. 'You first.' He stepped over to her, glancing around for something sharp to cut through the plastic tie binding the chair to her wrist. 'Try this,' she said, picking up the doll with a bloodied spike coming out below its knee and offering it up to him. 'It's Long John Silver Barbie,' she said. 'Collector's item.'

He stabbed the spike repeatedly at the plastic until it was punctured enough to tear away and free her from the chair. Then they set to work unwiring what felt like a dead woman from the frame. 'Call 999,' Kate said, as Melissa sagged to the floor.

He shook his head. 'No mobile. Your work buddies took it off me. They think this all my work.'

'Ah... sorry about that,' she said, an exhausted smile briefly lighting her shocked face. And he suddenly wanted to wrap himself around her. Instead, he took off his jacket and wrapped that around her. It fell to her mid-thigh area when she zipped it up. 'Thanks,' she said. 'Nice body paint.'

He looked down at his mud-slicked chest and grinned. 'It's the Escape From Police Dogs range,' he said.

He crouched and lifted the barely alive woman, who sagged in his arms like something broken. She *was* still alive - he could feel the energy faintly pulsing - but she might not be for long if they didn't get help. 'Let's go,' he said.

'What about her?' said Kate, staring down at the nurse.

'Is she dead?' he asked. He should know but the jangling frequencies of death in this room were overwhelming and confusing.

'I don't know. I... I don't want to touch her. To get too close,' said Kate. 'It's not very professional but I just want to get the fuck out of here.'

'I get that,' he said. 'We'll drop the hatch and put something heavy on it. Wait for back up, yeah?'

'Yeah,' said Kate.

'After you,' he said. She climbed the stairs ahead of him. He gallantly didn't look.

41

They pulled a heavy crate over the hatch. Lucas deposited Melissa into a wheelchair which happened to be nearby, then the pair of them shunted the box into place. Nobody was getting out through that hatch.

They found some blankets by the wheelchair and wrapped them around Melissa before Lucas pushed her out into the fresh air.

Kate felt as if she wasn't quite inside her body. She guessed she was in shock. The cold, gritty flagstones under her bare feet were literally grounding her, though, when she focused on them. She was feeling very cold, despite the heavy leather jacket.

'How did you find us?' she asked, pausing by a large disc of wood on the ground as the shakes began to rattle through her. 'Did the doll help?'

'Yes and no,' he said, turning Melissa around in her wheelchair and watching Kate closely. 'It was a good idea, but your buddies in blue saw me trying to post it back to you while I was going through my denial phase. There was tasering.'

'Oh god,' said Kate through chattering teeth. 'I'm so sorry.' She had volunteered to be tasered on a training course a couple of years back. It was not something she would ever volunteer for again.

'Actually, I was being an all-round idiot, even before they fried my brains. Sid led me here two nights ago. He knew something I didn't.'

'Wait,' said Kate, suddenly remembering. 'When I was in the woods and I sensed someone watching me... was that *you*?'

'Erm... yeah. Sorry about that. I wasn't stalking you, I promise. I was just following the dowse. I'd picked up something from the site in the woods, the pit, I guess, but I didn't know for sure what it was. And when I saw you, I thought Sid was sending me to you instead. He can be a romantic little dickhead. This dowsing thing; it's not always clear cut, you know.'

'So you just went home?' she said.

'Yup. Leaving this poor woman to another 48 hours of hell. I'm not proud.'

Melissa made another moaning sound. Kate was glad to hear it. Glad there was enough energy left in her to make it. She could see the distant glow of the lodge car park lighting and hear a familiar noise.

'Good news,' said Lucas, glancing around as blue light began to flash at the brow of the hill. 'You mates are here.'

Melissa murmured something. It sounded like '*No. No no no...*'

42

Wendy's head and eye socket burned with pain and she could only half see, her face numb down one side. Perhaps her faked migraine was now manifesting itself for real: a lesson to her about lying. She rolled over on her side and saw that only two people remained in the cellar with her and they were both dead.

The empty frame and the scattered props filled her with a rage so white hot that not even being half blind and badly concussed could prevent her from standing. She scrabbled around on the floor for a few seconds and then got to her feet, staggered across to the steps and, avoiding Graeme, crawled up to the hatch. It was closed. And it would not open.

She sat still for a few moments and then descended the steps and made her way to the far end of her studio, lurching past the curtain of dolls, past the camera, the lenses, the tripod; steadying herself on the boxes of photographic paper and reels of Kodak 200; shouldering the glass display case and rattling her taxidermy exhibits. Her centre of gravity kept shifting and she zig-zagged left and right, past her makeshift darkroom tent and on to the second set of wooden steps behind it, narrower and rarely used, which led to a smaller hatch.

Happily, there was nothing on top of this hatch. It rose up in a corner of the barn, behind a pile of wooden pallets. She got through it, one hand raised, and began to work her way to the outside where she could hear that fucking bitch who had half blinded her talking to the guy who'd jumped her.

Fury made the eye socket pulse so hard there was a fresh spurt of blood down her face. How dare they? Her collection was not finished. And it was *not* going to be left undone. She squeezed the syringe, still loaded up, still ready, scavenged from under the hem of the doll curtain. The film crew were focused on her now; she could *feel* them. Her triumphant theme music was being piped into the barn somehow. She was bloody, broken, nearly beaten... but art would win. Art could not fail.

She broke out through the wide barn doorway and ran for the woman in the black jacket, the strong, sharp needle held out at shoulder height, unstoppable, aiming for her throat.

Time slowed down. Melissa - who knew? - opened her eyes and started moaning: *'No. No no no...'*

The other two, gawping at each other like Romeo and Juliet, hadn't even noticed. She increased her speed, holding her trajectory despite the two-dimensional vision and the wrecked proprioception. Too late, her last dying doll looked around, face splitting into shock. Too late the bare chested man behind Melissa turned to see her. All too late. The needle was destined to find its skin.

There was screaming and yelping and then, just an arm's

length and half a second away from her target, Wendy felt claws on her thighs and fur at her ankles, and the ground began to tip up. A wide round hole opened before her single eye and she gave a long, shrill scream of horror because she knew she was going to be swallowed, head first.

43

Kate and Lucas knew little of Wendy's final moments beyond the increasingly terrified murmuring of Melissa, a sudden hissing rush and the arrival of an over-excited Staffy-Labrador cross who just couldn't stop himself jumping at strangers.

Kate had two seconds to register that she was about to die by syringe after all - and Lucas had a similar time frame to realise being a dowser didn't make you a superhero and he was about to lose her despite everything.

And then Certain Death in a Tunic was tripped abruptly by Reggie and sent into an unstoppable nosedive directly into what turned out to be a very deep well.

Her last scream was sickening to hear. Even Reggie sat down.

For a few seconds there was nothing but a shocked silence.

And then Lucas was thrown to the ground and incapacitated by a taser.

44

'It's looking good, isn't it?' said Mariam.

Lucas leaned against the recently mended door, wincing a little at the sharp throb under his shoulder blades, and took in his work. Mounted all around the white walls of The Henge Gallery, the paintings had an energy about them that seemed to travel like electricity, leaping from canvas to canvas. It was a thought that made his insides clench a little. He'd had enough of leaping electricity.

'We've already sold four,' said Mariam, pouring him a glass of Merlot. 'After I quadrupled the prices, too. And I've had to ticket the launch to keep the numbers down. If I'd kept it fully public they'd be queuing twice around the square.'

'Well, I'm glad my marketing plan paid off,' said Lucas. 'The helicopter chase and the police dog patrols were a master stroke, don't you think? Forget *The Salisbury Journal*; we made it onto *BBC Breakfast*!'

She came over and touched her finger to the side of his face, where the puffy purple bruising had at last given way to a sallow yellow. The baton had connected with it pretty thoroughly during his tussle with the officer in the East Sarum Lodge car park. 'Will you be making an official complaint?' she asked. 'You know... wrongful arrest... police brutality?'

He shrugged. 'Nah. You can't blame the guy. He thought I was a psycho bastard woman killer. I'd've done the same, in his position.'

In fact, the angry, handcuffed officer *had* taken his advice and yelled Mariam through the process of using the car's radio system, to bring in back up. A dozen police, some armed, had descended on the lodge minutes later. They'd poured down the track in pursuit of Wiltshire's most wanted, just in time to witness one woman falling into a well while their half-naked female colleague screamed and another woman sagged in a wheelchair under Lucas Henry's control.

They didn't notice the dog until later. They were busy tasering that bastard Henry.

It turned out that Reggie had been getting more and more agitated in the back of his owner' car. Sally - Kate's neighbour he'd later learned - had just ended a visit with her mother and was hobbling back to her vehicle as the police arrived. Distracted, she'd opened the car door and Reggie had shot past her before she could grab him - tearing down the track ahead of the law. When he got to the court-yard and saw a tall lady racing across the flagstones, he did what he apparently always did. He jumped up.

He probably didn't intend to trip her into a nosedive down a well. It was a good thing dogs didn't have guilt issues.

'I'm sorry I gave you up,' Mariam said, not for the first

time. 'I should have given you a bit more time; I could have saved you that battered face and the second stun gun.'

'No,' he said. 'It's fine. You bought me enough time to get there; that's the main thing.'

She peered into the top of his shirt. 'No Sid? I would've thought he'd be going everywhere with you, little dangly hero!'

'Nope,' said Lucas. 'Sid is safely back in his sock. He can stay there for now. I'm all dowsed out.'

'Will you be OK?' asked Mariam, creasing her brow in concern. 'For the launch tomorrow? I mean, it's only been a week since they released you. It's not too late to put it off a bit. Give you some more recovery time. They'd all still come. You're the hottest artist in England right now.'

'It's fine,' he said. 'I'll be OK.' He knew Mariam was very excited. And still feeling horribly guilty. Selling all his paintings at a good price and handling all the publicity for him was her way of making it up to him. And, for putting his friend and mentor in an impossible position with the police, he felt her owed her just as much. The publicity *was* something else. If he hadn't been named as a wanted man in the first place, the police wouldn't have needed to go on the record so fast about how he'd in fact helped bring them to the *real* killer - and saved the life of one of their own. He'd been demonised and canonised in the space of one day. There had been no mention of dowsing, though. And that suited Lucas just fine.

'Well, in that case, if you're sure you're OK, I wanted to tell you,' said Mariam, refilling her glass, 'The Mail on Sunday wants your story and they've said they'll feature at least three of your works in the double page spread. The arts editor from the Guardian's been in touch too. And - oh -

so many others. Half of the guest list is press. But I will look after you, I promise!'

Lucas felt a shiver at the idea of all the press. How much digging would they do? Would this story be enough in itself to prevent them going further back; discovering that this wasn't the first murder and disappearance case he'd been arrested for?

Nobody's past is history.

45

Melissa Hounsome woke up on a drip and found a woman by her side that she might have dreamed. So much of the past few days had been dreamlike.

'You were there, weren't you?' she croaked. 'In the room with me... on the chair.'

'Yeah,' said the woman, smiling and taking her hand as it rested on the bed sheet. 'I'm Kate. Pleased to meet you.'

'Did you really spike her in the eye with a doll's leg?' Melissa wondered.

'You saw that?'

'I guess I did. So much of it seems like dreams but yeah, I saw that. I wanted to cheer.'

'I'm a detective,' said Kate. 'I was one of the team looking for you... but I was also on Wendy Morris's list of Dying Dolls. She found me before I found her. I was going to be her last set of pictures. I... I shouldn't be talking to you about it. You'll have another officer come in to interview you soon. But I asked to come and see you, just quickly; see how you're doing. The doctors say you're amazing... constitution of an ox!'

Melissa gave her a watery smile. 'Feel more like oxtail soup,' she said.

'I know what you mean,' said Kate. The look on her face left no doubt.

'We're going to get past this,' said Melissa.

'Bloody right we are,' grinned Kate.

'You're a runner too, right?' asked Melissa.

'Yep,' said Kate.

'So... what do you say? London Marathon next year?'

46

Kate didn't go to Lucas's launch event. She wanted to see his work but there was no way she could manage a crowd.

After Lucas had been stunned to the ground her police family had swooped in around her, wrapping her up in foil blankets, carrying her to a waiting ambulance, talking to her with a weird tenderness she'd never experienced and didn't want.

Throughout it she had been shouting. 'Don't taser him again! Don't cuff him! It's not him - he came to rescue me! It was *her!* The one in the well... she's the Runner Grabber!'

Someone had been taking notes, although it hadn't been obvious. Kate hadn't been tired and in shock at that point; she'd been furious and stoked with an energy bordering on mania. 'There are more bodies down there,' she informed Kapoor and Michaels while a paramedic had checked her over. Her boss and her DC both had a grey horror behind their professional calm; she guessed she must look like hell. 'One is Tessa McManus - long dead - and the other is the gardener here - Graeme, I think his name is. She killed him a few hours ago.'

They wouldn't let her stay. After a few minutes of debrief she was made to get into the ambulance with Sharon Mulligan. Having established that she wasn't badly injured or about to go into serious shock, she was taken to the station's victim suite where she was photographed and gently checked over for physical evidence of her ordeal. The police doctor took blood and swiftly confirmed that whatever she had been drugged with would have no lasting effect.

It was some hours later that she was allowed to sink into a hot bath and finally attempt to wash away the horror. Later Francis was brought in to collect her, serious and shaken at what he'd heard, and she at last got home to bed.

The next few days were filled with debriefings and continual attempts to make her go home and rest. She argued that staying home and resting were very bad for her mental health. 'I just sit and obsess about it all,' she told Kapoor. 'It's way better for me to be here.' Grudgingly, he let her stay, on light duties.

She felt bad for Lucas, for what she'd put him through. She was also impressed by him; the way he'd stranded her colleagues in a bog and escaped. She could only imagine their fury and she felt for them all, too, of course, but picturing them scrambling about in the mud was one of the few things about the past week which made her smile.

She learned that Lucas had got away, cross country, and then rowed along a tributary of the River Avon before catching a bus on the edge of town to get to his friend - Mariam Aziz, at the Henge Gallery - for help. Then Mariam had covered for him while he climbed through a terrace of attics and escaped from a neighbouring property, taking her car to get him to the nursing home.

Kate still hadn't worked out just how he'd known to go there. Her brief exchange with him before Wendy had tried to kill her with the syringe suggested it was all down to dowsing. Again.

She shivered when she thought of how things might have gone without Lucas's involvement. It was so unlike her to play the maverick and get someone like him involved. But if she hadn't there was every reason to think she would currently be hanging, dead and desiccating, in Wendy Morris's art studio.

They would have found her, in the end. There were enough threads to pull on; enough evidence gathering and, as Conrad Temple said, there was a self-destruct element to the killer's contact with the police. Wendy, on some level, had wanted to be caught. She had craved a reaction to her work; a live audience. If she'd finally been arrested for the murders she would most likely have revelled in the interrogation and the court case and all its coverage... recognition at last!

As it was, she would never get that gratification. Her body had been retrieved the next day, snagged halfway down the well, neck broken. They'd needed to bring a crane in to get her out.

At least the families of Tessa and Caroline would be spared the spectacle of the court case. They would learn enough from the testimony of Melissa, Lucas and herself. It would, of course, all find its way into the press, once the coroner's court was convened some weeks from now. The gruesome details would come to light in the inquest and there would be acres of print and clickbait devoted to it; endless picking over of every detail on true crime websites; probably a docudrama one day. Kate couldn't allow herself to think about that. Not if she wanted to - as Melissa said - get past it.

Temple had found her, on the way out from her second or third debriefing session, and given her a very unprofessional hug. Well, he was an American. She allowed the hug; liked it. 'Guess you're never going to agree to meet me for a run again, are you?' he asked, smiling ruefully.

'Don't be so sure of that,' she said. 'Me and Melissa... we're planning to go in for next year's London Marathon.' She really didn't know if she was joking or not. She would have to get back to running. She really needed it.

There was something else she really needed. To see Lucas. To thank him... and apologise to him. To settle something between them. Maybe to explain the strange, intense connection that he possibly felt too. *'I thought Sid was sending me to you instead. He can be a romantic little dickhead.'*

In fact, during her light duties she had finally set him up as a consultant on the station's payroll. She'd said she would help him to get the lights back on in that bungalow and she wanted to deliver on that, if nothing else. Nobody could argue that he hadn't been useful. She still needed his bank details, though, and that seemed like a good reason to see him.

She pushed open the door to The Henge Gallery and its old-fashioned bell tinkled above her. The exhibition was called LUCAS HENRY - WAITING. It was made up of a dozen paintings, most of them as tall as she was. Every one had a SOLD sign next to it. She recognised the work he'd been creating on the day she'd arrived at his place - arcs of red spattered across planes of golden brown and black. It was framed now and all the more powerful for it. The plaque under it read: LUCAS HENRY and the title - *See me.*

Others had a similar feel about them, crackling with an

energy she couldn't quite pin down. Not all of them featured spattered paint; there were other techniques used to create the images. She saw places in them... a seascape with what looked like real sand embedded in the paint (*Reach Me*), a green drifting realm that could have been a water meadow (*Submerge Me*).

Others were called *Twist me* and *Forget me* and *Trace me.* All abstract; all open to whatever interpretation the viewer might like.

And then there was the quarry.

She stood very still, dimly aware of Mariam emerging from the back room; Kate had called Lucas's friend to set up the meeting here.

'What do you think?' asked Mariam, arriving and touching her lightly on the arm.

'It's... revealing,' she murmured, a thud pulsing in her head as she took in the colours; the muted palette of pale stone and charcoal shadow. The ragged, rough-hewn lines; the pile of broken texture at the lowest edge. The sunset yellow wedge-shaped overhang, like a piece of cheese pie.

'Very powerful, don't you think?' Mariam went on. 'He really has something to say.'

Kate allowed her eyes to drop to the metal plaque below the frame.

LUCAS HENRY (*Absolve me)*

'He should be here any minute,' said Mariam. 'I know he's looking forward to seeing you. I'll get some coffee on... or would you like some wine?'

'Actually,' said Kate. 'I... have to be somewhere... else. Tell him I'll contact him soon.'

Mariam opened her mouth in surprise but didn't say

anything as Kate turned and was out of the door in a matter of seconds.

LUCAS ARRIVED to find Mariam looking worried. 'Kate just left... almost as soon as she got here. I think maybe she was having a panic attack or something.'

Lucas frowned. 'Really?'

'Well, you know, after everything she's been through,' said Mariam. 'Panic attacks wouldn't be a surprise, would they? I mean, she was held prisoner by an artist, wasn't she? Do you know, I think I *met* that woman. I think she was the one who brought in her horrible stuffed animal ballet pictures...'

Lucas stepped outside, hoping that Kate might be loitering nearby. He had been thinking about seeing her all day. Wanting to somehow earth himself next to her; to talk through what had happened. He hadn't been sleeping well.

Ah bullshit. He just wanted to see her.

'Sorry - I couldn't stop her,' said Mariam when he went back in. 'She said she had somewhere she needed to be. She seemed very impressed though.' She waved around the collection. 'Especially with that one.' She pointed to *Absolve me.*

Lucas sat down.

There was a third person... someone else she was looking for, even though she wouldn't say it.

He closed his eyes. Saw the kid clinging to the rock below the cheese pie.

Now he *knew* they would meet again.

Sid had been telling him all along. There was no way of avoiding it.

What had happened in that quarry was never going to leave him alone.

Sooner or later, the truth would climb out.

ACKNOWLEDGMENTS

Like every print media trained writer I hate to let facts get in the way of a good story - but being fully NCTJ qualified I, like most genuine journos, also want to get things right.

So I am hugely indebted to Sarah Bodell, formerly of Wiltshire Police, for excellent guidance on the sprinklings of police procedure included in this story. Also to Gavin and Pete, my PC buddies among the dog-walking clan who are obliged to handle all kinds of random queries while fending off a lively labradoodle. If I stretch reality a touch here and there, I know they mostly forgive me.

Also big thanks to my lovely editor Beverly Sanford and my steadfast first reader, Nicola Sparkes - both of whom gave me great steers in this story (especially on the nursing stuff, thanks, Nicki!). Warm appreciation also to Kim Roberta-Summers for insights on nursing homes.

Can't forget The Collective. You know who you are...

And glowing appreciation, finally, for Simon Tilley, who is totally behind Henry & Sparrow and crucial to getting them out in the world.

HENRY & SPARROW
return in

DEAD AIR

Available now on Amazon

And for a free read
of the Henry & Sparrow prequel novella

UNDERTOW

subscribe on **www.adfoxfiction.com**

ABOUT THE AUTHOR

AD Fox is an award winning author who lives in Hampshire, England, with a significant other, boomerang offspring and a large, highly porous labradoodle.

With a background in newspaper and broadcast journalism, AD also likes to go running from time to time. Although slightly less so in the woods since writing The Dying Dolls.

Younger readers will know the AD alter ego as Ali Sparkes, author of more than fifty titles for children and young adults including the Blue Peter Award winning Frozen In Time, the bestselling Shapeshifter series and Car-Jacked, finalist in the national UK Children's Book of the Year awards.

For more on AD Fox visit **www.adfoxfiction.com**